Once Upon a Time

Timeless Tales for Young Hearts

Curated by Chris Ball

Chanthology

No part of this publication may be copied, recorded, transmitted or reproduced in any way without the publisher's express written permission.

All rights reserved
Published by: Chanthology Limited

www.chanthology.com

Paperback Edition: ISBN 978-1-915449-61-0
Kindle Edition: ISBN 978-1-915449-62-7
Hardback Edition: ISBN 978-1-915449-63-4

Contents

Introduction

This book is more than a collection of stories; it's a gateway to bonding, growth, and inspiration for your family. Born from my own nightly ritual of reading to my children, despite the day's demands, these moments became our sanctuary of joy and connection. This routine wasn't just about reading; it was an essential thread in the fabric of our family life, offering us all a chance to escape, dream, and learn together.

The stories selected for this compilation are those that resonated deeply with us, marked by laughter, awe, and sometimes, the learning that comes from facing challenges. These are tales that not only entertain but also build a foundation for young minds to navigate their own journeys. These narratives underscore resilience, courage, and the indomitable human spirit, qualities that every parent wishes to instil in their child.

Historically, such tales have been instrumental in teaching children about bravery, kindness, and wisdom. They show that obstacles are not dead-ends but detours towards growth, and that true strength lies in character and perseverance. These lessons are vital for developing resilient, thoughtful individuals ready to face life's challenges.

This collection is a tribute to the enduring power of storytelling in creating connections and guiding young minds. It's crafted with the hope that it will not only bring joy and wonder to your family but also serve as a tool for your children's development. By inviting these stories into your home, you're not just entertaining your children; you're helping them build the resilience, empathy, and strength they need to thrive in an ever-changing world.

Let this book be a catalyst for your own family's adventures in storytelling, a means to inspire growth, understanding, and the shared joy of discovering life's possibilities together. In sharing these tales, you're laying down stepping stones for your children to become not just thoughtful readers but empowered individuals.

A Child's Dream of a Star

by Charles Dickens

There was once a child, and he strolled about a good deal and thought of a number of things. He had a sister, a child too, and his constant companion. These two used to wander all day long. They wondered at the beauty of the flowers; they wondered at the height and blueness of the sky; they wondered at a depth of the bright water; they wondered at the goodness and the power of God, who made the lovely world.

They used to say to one another that, suppose all the children upon earth were to die, would the flowers, water, and sky be sorry? They believed they would be sorry. For, said they, the buds are the children of the flowers. The little playful streams that gambol down the hillsides are the children of the water, and the smallest bright specks playing at hide-and-seek in the sky all night must surely be the children of the stars; and they would all be grieved to see their playmates, the children of men, no more.

One clear shining star came out in the sky before the rest, near the church spire, above the graves. It was larger and more beautiful, they thought than all the others, and every night they watched for it, standing hand in hand at a window. Whoever saw it first cried out, "I see the star!" And often cried out together, knowing well when it would rise and where. So they grew to be such friends with it that, before lying down in their beds, they always looked out once again to bid it a good night; when they were turning round to sleep, they used to say, "God bless the star!"

But while she was still very young, O, very, very young, the sister drooped and came to be so weak that she could no longer stand in the window at night; and then the child looked sadly out by himself, and when he saw the star, turned round and said to the patient pale face on the bed, "I see the star!" And then a smile would come upon the face, and a weak little voice used to say, "God bless my brother and the star!"

And so the time came, all too soon! When the child looked out alone, and when there was no face on the bed; and when there was a little grave among the graves, not there before; and when the star made long rays down towards him, as he saw it through his tears.

Now, these rays were so bright, and they seemed to make such a shining way from earth to heaven, that when the child went to his solitary bed, he dreamed about the star; and dreamed that, lying where he was, he saw a train of people taken up that sparkling road by angels. And the opening star showed him a great world of light, where many more such angels waited to receive them.

All these angels, who were waiting, turned their beaming eyes upon the people who were carried up into the star. Some came out from the long rows in which they stood, and fell upon the people's necks, kissed them tenderly, and went away with them down avenues of light, and were so happy in their company that, lying in his bed, he wept for joy.

But many angels did not go with them; among them, one he knew. The patient face that once had lain upon the bed was glorified and radiant, but his heart found his sister among all the hosts.

His sister's angel lingered near the star's entrance and said to the leader among those who had brought the people thither, "Has my brother come?"

And he said, "No."

She turned hopefully away when the child stretched out his arms and cried, "O sister, I am here! Take me!" And then she turned her beaming eyes upon him, and it was night; the star was shining into the room, making long rays down towards him as he saw it through his tears.

From that hour forth, the child looked out upon the star as on the home he was to go to when his time should come, and he thought that he did not belong to the earth alone but to the star too, because of his sister's angel gone before.

There was a baby born to be a brother to the child, and while he was so little that he never had spoken word, he stretched his tiny form out on his bed and died.

Again the child dreamed of the opened star, the company of angels, the train of people, and the rows of angels with their beaming eyes all turned upon those people's faces.

Said his sister's angel to the leader, "Is my brother coming?"

And he said, "Not that one, but another."

As the child beheld his brother's angel in her arms, he cried, "O sister, I am here! Take me!" And she turned and smiled upon him, and the star was shining.

He grew to be a young man and was busy at his books when an old servant came to him and said,

"Thy mother is no more. I bring her blessing on her darling son!"

Again at night, he saw the star and all that former company. Said his sister's angel to the leader, "Is my brother coming?"

And he said, "Thy mother!"

A mighty cry of joy went forth through all the stars because the mother was reunited with her two children. And he stretched out his arms and cried, "O mother, sister, and brother, I am here! Take me!"

And they answered him, "Not yet." And the star was shining.

He grew to be a man whose hair was turning gray, and he was sitting in his chair by the fireside, heavy with grief, and his face bedewed with tears when the star opened once again.

Said his sister's angel to the leader, "Is my brother coming?"

And he said, "Nay, but his maiden daughter."

And the man who had been the child saw his daughter, newly lost to him, a celestial creature among those three, and he said, "My daughter's head is on my sister's bosom, and her arm is round my mother's neck, and at her feet, there is the baby of old time, and I can bear the parting from her, God be praised!"

And the star was shining.

Thus the child came to be an old man whose

once smooth face was wrinkled, his steps were slow and feeble, and his back was bent. And one night, as he lay upon his bed, his children standing round, he cried, as he had cried so long ago, "I see the star!"

They whispered to one another, "He is dying."

And he said, "I am. My age is falling from me like a garment, and I move towards the star as a child. And, my Father, now I thank you that it has so often opened to receive those dear ones who await me!"

And the star was shining, and it shone upon his grave.

The Story of Cinderella

by Logan Marshall

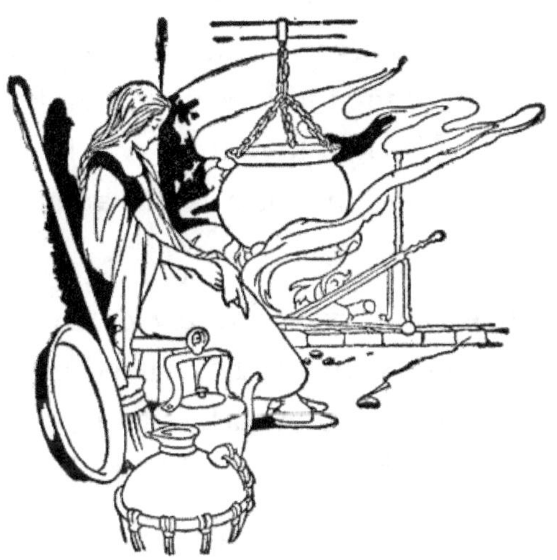

There was once a rich man whose wife died, leaving him with one little girl. After some years, hoping to give his child a mother's love and care, he married again, this time a widow with two grown-up daughters. But his second wife was arrogant and proud, her two daughters were even worse than their mother, and the poor little girl had a miserable time with her new relations. Her stepsisters were jealous of her, for she was charming, and they were plain and ugly. They did all they could to make her miserable, and, at length, through their wicked spite and envy, her life became a burden to her. The poor child was sent to live in the kitchen, where she had to do all the rough and dirty work, and because she was always dressed in rags and sat beside the cinders in the grate, they called her Cinderella.

It happened that the King of the country had an only son. He was very anxious that the Prince should be married, so he gave a great ball and invited all the grand ladies in the country to come to it. It was a splendid affair, lasting for three nights, and people were very eager to be invited to it, for it was known that the Prince would choose his bride from among the ladies present.

Cinderella's sisters received invitations, and from the day they arrived, they talked of nothing but what they should wear, for each of them secretly hoped that she would be chosen as the Prince's bride.

When the great day came, at last, they began to dress for the ball directly after breakfast. Cinderella had to help them, and they kept her busy all day doing their hair, running messages, and helping them to lace up their fine dresses.

When Cinderella saw their beautiful clothes, she wished she could go to the ball as well; but when she timidly asked if she might, they laughed in mocking scorn.

"You go to the ball!" they cried. "What would you do at the ball, with your rags and tatters and dirty face? No, no, Cinderella, go back to your seat amongst the ashes—that is the place for a little kitchen girl like you!"

So the two sisters and their mother drove away in a carriage and paired to the King's palace, and Cinderella was left behind. She sat down on the hearth before the kitchen fire and began to cry softly to herself because she felt so very lonely and miserable.

As she sat there in the dusk, with the firelight dancing over her and her face buried in her hands, she heard a voice calling:

"Cinderella, Cinderella!" With a start, she looked up to see who it could be.

An old woman leaning upon a stick on the hearth in front of her stood on the home. She was dressed in a long red cloak and wore high-heeled shoes and a tall black hat.

Where she had come from, Cinderella could not imagine. She certainly had not come in through the door nor the window, for both were shut.

Cinderella was so surprised to see her that she stopped crying and stared at her in astonishment.

"What are you crying for?" asked the old woman.

"Because my mother and sisters have gone to the ball, and I am left here all alone," said Cinderella.

"Do you want to go to the ball, too!" said the old lady.

"Yes, but it is no good; I have nothing but rags to wear," sobbed poor Cinderella.

"Well, well, be a good child, and don't cry anymore," said the old woman briskly. "I am your Fairy Godmother, and if you do what I tell you, perhaps you shall go after all. Run out into the garden and bring me in a pumpkin!"

Cinderella ran out into the garden and brought in the biggest pumpkin that she could find.

"Now go and fetch the mouse trap out of the cellar," said her Godmother, and Cinderella hurried to get it. There were six mice in the trap, and the old woman harnessed them to the pumpkin, put a rat on the top to drive them, and two lizards behind, and then waved her wand over them. Immediately the pumpkin turned into a gorgeous coach, the mice into six beautiful horses, the rat into a stately coachman, and the lizards into tall footmen with powdered hair and silk stockings. "There," said the old woman, "there's a carriage to take you to the ball."

"Alas," said Cinderella, "how can I go to the ball? I have nothing to wear but this!" She touched her ragged dress.

"Is that all?" said the Fairy Godmother. Once more, she waved her wand, and Cinderella's rags turned into the most beautiful dress in the world, all shining with gold and silver threads and covered with costly gems. In her hair was a circlet of pearls, and her feet were shod with the prettiest and daintiest pair of glass slippers that ever were seen.

"Now," said the Fairy Godmother, "you can go to the ball. But mind you come away before the clock strikes twelve, for should you linger beyond that hour, all your splendor will vanish, and your dress will turn into rags again."

Cinderella promised to obey her Godmother's instructions. Then she got into the beautiful coach. The footman shut the door, the coachman whipped up the horses, and away she went to the ball.

When she arrived, there was a great stir in the palace. So lovely a face and so costly and rich a dress had never before been seen, and everybody thought it must be some great Princess arrived from foreign lands.

All the courtiers and other guests stood back to let her pass, and when the Prince caught sight of her, he fell in love with her on the spot. He danced with her the whole evening, and people thought there was no doubt about whom he would choose for his bride.

At a quarter to twelve, Cinderella, remembering her Godmother's instructions, said goodbye to the Prince and came away.

She arrived home just as the clock struck twelve. At once, the coachman and footmen turned back into rats and mice and the coach into a pumpkin; and when the sisters came home a little later, there was Cinderella, dressed in her shabby old frock, sitting in her usual place amongst the cinders.

The two ugly sisters were full of the strange Princess who had come to the ball. They talked about her all the next day, little dreaming that all the while, the beautiful lady was their despised sister Cinderella.

In the evening, after they had gone again to the ball, the Fairy Godmother made her appearance. Once more, Cinderella drove to the palace in her coach and six, arrayed in a still more gorgeous and beautiful dress, and once more, the Prince danced with her all evening.

But when the third night came, Cinderella was enjoying herself so much that she forgot what her Fairy Godmother had said, until suddenly she heard the clock begin to strike twelve. She remembered that as soon as it finished striking, all her fine clothes would turn to rags again, and, jumping up in alarm, she ran out of the room. The Prince ran after her, trying to overtake her, and Cinderella, in her fright, ran so fast that she left one of her little glass slippers on the floor behind her.

The Prince stopped picking it up, giving Cinderella time to escape, but she was only in time. Just as she was crossing the Palace yard, the clock finished striking, and immediately all her finery vanished; and there she was, dressed in her old ragged frock again.

When the Prince came out upon the Palace steps, he could see no sign of the lovely Princess. The guards at the gate told him that nobody had passed that way except a little ragged kitchenmaid, and the Prince had to go back to the ball with only a little glass slipper to remind him of the beautiful lady with whom he was so desperately in love.

The next day the King sent out all his heralds and trumpeters with a Proclamation, saying that the Prince would marry the lady whose foot the slipper fitted. But though all the ladies in the land tried on the slipper, it would fit none of them—their feet were too big!

At last, the heralds came to the house where Cinderella lived. The eldest stepsister tried the slipper on first, but it was pretty impossible for her to get her foot into it, for her great toe was too big. Then her mother, who was watching eagerly, fetched a carving knife.

"Be quick, cut the toe off," she said; "what does it matter if you are lame—if you are the Prince's bride, you will always ride in a carriage!"

So the eldest sister cut off her big toe, but it was no use; the slipper would not fit, and she was obliged to hand it to her sister.

But the other sister had no better luck. She did get her toes inside, but her foot was much too long, and her heel stuck out behind. The mother urged her to cut it off.

"What does it matter?" she said. "If you are the Prince's bride, you will never need to walk anymore."

But although she cut her heel off, the slipper was still too small; at length, she also had to give up the attempt to force her foot into it.

Then Cinderella came shyly out from behind the door where she had been standing out of sight and asked if she might try on the slipper. Her stepmother and sisters were angry and about to drive her away with blows, but the herald stopped them.

"The Prince wishes every woman in the land to try on this slipper," he said; and asking Cinderella to sit on a chair, he knelt and tried the slipper on her foot.

And it fitted her exactly!

While everyone stood and stared in astonishment, Cinderella drew from her pocket the other slipper and put it on. No sooner had she done so than her ragged frock changed into the beautiful ball dress again, and she stood up before them—the lovely lady with whom the Prince had fallen in love at the ball.

The Prince was overjoyed to find her again, and they were married at once with much pomp amid great rejoicings.

As for the wicked sisters, they were so jealous that they both turned green with envy. They grew uglier and uglier every day until, at last, they grew so dreadfully ugly that nobody could bear to look at them any longer. But Cinderella became more and more beautiful and lived happily with the Prince forever afterward.

The Magicians' Gifts

by Juliana Horatia Ewing

There was once a king whose dominions lived no less than three magicians. When the king's eldest son was christened, the king invited the three magicians to the christening feast, and to make the compliment greater, he asked one of them to stand as godfather. But the other two, who were not asked to be godfathers, were so angry at what they held to be a slight that they only waited to see how they might best revenge themselves upon the infant prince.

When the moment came for presenting the

christening gifts, the godfather magician advanced to the cradle and said, "My gift is this: Whatever he wishes for, he shall have. And only I who give shall be able to recall this gift." For he perceived the jealousy of the other magicians and knew that, if possible, they would undo what he did. But the second magician muttered in his beard, "And yet I will change it to a curse." And coming up to the cradle, he said, "The wishes that he has thus obtained he shall not be able to revoke or change."

Then the third magician grumbled beneath his black robe, "If he were very wise and prudent, he might yet be happy. But I will secure his punishment." So he also drew near to the cradle and said, "For my part, I give him a hasty temper."

After which, the two dissatisfied magicians withdrew, saying, "Should we permit ourselves to be slighted for nothing?"

But the king and his courtiers were not at all disturbed.

"My son has only to be sure of what he wants," said the king, "and then, I suppose, he will not desire to recall his wishes."

And the courtiers added, "If a prince may not have a hasty temper, who may, we should like to know?"

And everybody laughed except the godfather magician, who went out sighing and shaking his head and was seen no more.

While the king's son was yet a child, the gift of the godfather magician began to take effect. There was nothing so rare and precious that he could not obtain it or so difficult that his mere wish could not accomplish it. But, on the other hand, no matter how inconsiderately he spoke or how often he changed his mind, what he had once wished must remain as he had wanted to it, in spite of himself. As he often wished for things that were bad for him and oftener still wished for a thing one day and regretted it the next, his power was the source of quite as much pain as a pleasure to him. Then his temper was so hot that he was apt to hastily wish ill to those who offended him and afterward bitterly regret the mischief he could not undo. Thus, one after another, the king appointed his trustiest counselors to the charge of his son, who, sooner or later, in the discharge of their duty, were sure to be obliged to thwart him; on which the impatient prince would cry, "I wish you were at the bottom of the sea with your rules and regulations;" and the counselors disappeared accordingly, and returned no more.

When there was not a wise man left at court, and the king himself lived in dread of being the next victim, he said, "Only one thing remains to be done: to find the godfather magician and persuade him to withdraw his gift."

So the king offered rewards and sent out

messengers in every direction, but the magician was not to be found. At last, one day, he met a blind beggar who said to him, "Three nights ago, I dreamed that I went by the narrowest of seven roads to seek what you were looking for and was successful."

When the king returned home, he asked his courtiers, "Where are there seven roads lying near each other, some broad and some narrow?" And one of them replied, "Twenty-one miles to the west of the palace is a four-cross road, where three field paths also diverge."

The king made his way to this place and, taking the narrowest field paths, went on and on till it led him straight into a cave, where an old woman sat over a fire.

"Does a magician live here?" asked the king.

"No one lives here but myself," said the old woman. "But as I am a wise woman, I may be able to help you if you need it."

The king then told her of his perplexities and how he was desirous of finding the magician to persuade him to recall his gift.

"He could not recall the other gifts," said the wise woman. "Therefore, it is better that the prince should be taught to use his power prudently and to control his temper. And since all the persons capable of guiding him have disappeared, I will return with you and take charge of him myself. Over me, he will have no power."

To this, the king consented, and they returned to the palace, where the wise woman became guardian to the prince, and she fulfilled her duties so well that he became much more discreet and self-controlled. Only at times did his violent temper get the better of him and lead him to wish for what he vainly regretted afterward.

Thus all went well till the prince became a man, when, though he had great affection for her, he felt ashamed of having an old woman for his counselor, and he said, "I certainly wish that I had a faithful and discreet adviser of my age and sex."

On that very day, a young nobleman offered himself as a companion to the prince. As he was a young man of great ability, he was accepted: whereupon the old woman took her departure and was never seen again.

The young nobleman performed his part so well that the prince became deeply attached to him and submitted in every way to his counsels. But at last, a day came when, being in a rage, the advice of his friend irritated him, and he cried hastily, "Will you drive me mad with your long sermons? I wish you would hold your tongue forever." On which the young nobleman became dumb and so remained. For he was not independent of the prince's power as the wise woman had been.

The prince's grief and remorse knew no bounds. "Am I not under a curse?" said he. "Truly, I ought to be cast out from human society and sent to live with wild beasts in a wilderness. I only bring evil upon those I love best—indeed, there is no hope for me unless I can find my godfather and make him recall this fatal gift."

So the prince mounted his horse and, accompanied by his dumb friend, who remained faithful to him, set forth to find the magician. They took no followers except the prince's dog, a noble hound, who was so quick of hearing that he understood all that was said to him and was, next to the young nobleman, the wisest person at court.

"Mark, well, my dog," said the prince to him, "we stay nowhere till we find my godfather, and when we find him, we go no further. I rely on your sagacity to help us."

The dog licked the prince's hand and then trotted so resolutely down a certain road that the two friends allowed him to lead them and followed close behind.

They traveled this way to the edge of the king's dominions, only halting for needful rest and refreshment. At last, the dog led them through a wood, and towards evening they found themselves in the forest's depths, with no sign of any shelter for the night. Presently they heard a little bell, such as is rung for prayer, and the dog ran down a side path and led them straight to a grotto, at the door of which stood an aged hermit.

"Does a magician live here?" asked the prince.

"No one lives here but myself," said the hermit, "but I am old and have meditated much. My advice is at your service if you need it."

The prince then related his history and how he was now seeking the magician godfather to rid himself of his gift.

"And yet that will not cure your temper," said the hermit. "It were better that you employed yourself in learning to control that and to use your power prudently."

"No, no," replied the prince; "I must find the magician."

And when the hermit pressed his advice, he cried, "Provoke me not, good father, or I may be base enough to wish you ill, and the evil I do I cannot undo."

And he departed, followed by his friend, and called his dog. But the dog seated himself at the hermit's feet and would not move. Again and again, the prince called him, but he only whined and wagged his tail and refused to move. Coaxing and scolding were both in vain, and when the prince finally tried to drag him off by force, the dog growled.

"Base brute!" cried the prince, flinging him from him in a transport of rage. "How have I been so deceived in you? I wish you were hanged!" And even as he spoke, the dog vanished, and as the prince turned his head, he saw the poor beast's body dangling from a tree above him. The sight overwhelmed him, and he began bitterly to lament his cruelty.

"Will no one hang me also," he cried, "and rid the world of such a monster?"

"It is easier to die repenting than to live amending," said the hermit, "yet is the latter course the better one? Wherefore abide with me, my son, and learn in solitude those lessons of self-government without which no man is fit to rule others."

"It is impossible," said the prince. "These fits of passion are as madness that comes upon me, and they are beyond cure. It only remains to find my godfather, that he may make me less baneful to others by taking away the power I abuse." And raising the dog's body tenderly in his arms, he laid it before him on his horse and rode away, the dumb nobleman following him.

They now entered the dominions of another king and arrived at the capital in due time. The prince presented himself to the king and asked if he had a magician in his kingdom.

"Not to my knowledge," replied the king. "But I have a remarkably wise daughter, and if you want counsel, she may be able to help you."

The princess accordingly was sent for, and she was so beautiful and witty that the prince fell in love with her and begged the king to give her to him as a wife. Of course, the king could not refuse what the prince wished, and the wedding was celebrated without delay. By the advice of his wife, the prince placed the body of his faithful dog in a glass coffin and kept it near him so that he might constantly be reminded of the evil results of giving way to his anger.

For a time, all went well. At first, the prince never said a harsh word to his wife; but by and by, familiarity made him less careful, and one day she said something that offended him, and he fell into a violent rage. As he went storming up and down, the princess wrung her hands and cried, "Ah, my dear husband, I beg you to be careful what you say to me. You say you loved your dog yet know where he lies."

"I know that I wish you were with him, with your prating!" cried the prince in fury; and the words were scarcely out of his mouth when the princess vanished from his side and when he ran to the glass coffin, there she lay, pale and lifeless, with her head upon the body of the hound.

The prince was now beside himself with remorse and misery, and when the dumb nobleman made signs that they should pursue their search for the magician, he only cried, "Too late! too late!"

But after a while, he said, "I will return to the hermit and pass the rest of my miserable life in solitude and penance. And you, dear friend, go back to my father."

But the dumb nobleman shook his head and

could not be persuaded to leave the prince. Then they took the glass coffin on their shoulders and foot, and weeping as they went, they retraced their steps to the forest.

The prince remained with the hermit for some time and submitted himself to his direction. Then the hermit bade him return to his father, and he obeyed.

Every day the prince stood by the glass coffin, beat his breast, and cried, "Behold, murderer, the fruits of anger!" And he tried hard to overcome the violence of his temper. When he lost heart, he remembered a saying of the hermit: "Patience had far to go, but she was crowned at last." And after a while, the prince became as violent as he had been. And the king and all the court rejoiced at the change, but the prince remained sad at heart, thinking of the princess.

One day he was sitting alone when a man approached him dressed in a long black robe.

"Good day, godson," said he.

"Who calls me godson?" said the prince.

"The magician you have so long sought," said the godfather. "I have come to reclaim my gift."

"What cruelty led you to bestow it upon me?" asked the prince.

"The king, your father, would have been dissatisfied with any ordinary present from me," said the magician, "forgetting that the responsibilities of common gifts, and very limited power, are more than enough for most men to deal with. But I have not neglected you. I was the wise woman who brought you up. Again, I was the hermit, as your dog was sage enough to discover. I am come now to reclaim what has caused you such suffering."

"Alas!" cried the prince, "why is your kindness so tardy? If you have not forgotten me, why have you withheld this benefit till it is too late for my happiness? My friend is dumb; my wife is dead, and my dog is hanged. When wishes cannot reach these, do you think what I may command matters to me?"

"Softly, prince," said the magician; "I had a reason for the delay. But for these bitter lessons, you would still be the slave of the violent temper you conquered and which, as it was no gift of mine, I could not remove. Moreover, when the spell which made all things bend to your wish is taken away, its effects also are undone. Godson! I recall my gift."

As the magician spoke, the glass sides of the coffin melted into the air, and the princess sprang up and threw herself into her husband's arms. The dog also rose, stretched himself, and wagged his tail. The dumb nobleman ran to tell the good news to the king, and all the counselors came back in a long train from the bottom of the sea and set about the affairs of the state as if nothing had happened.

The old king welcomed his children with open arms, and they all lived happily to the end of their days.

Princess of Canterbury

by Joseph Jacobs

There lived formerly in the County of Cumberland, a nobleman with three sons, two of whom were comely and clever youths. Still, the other, a natural fool named Jack, was generally engaged with the sheep: he was dressed in a parti-coloured coat and a steeple-crowned hat with a tassel, as became his condition. Now the King of Canterbury had a beautiful daughter, distinguished by her great ingenuity and wit. He issued a decree that whoever should answer three questions put to him by the princess should have her in marriage and be heir to the crown at his decease. Shortly after this decree was published, news of it reached the ears of the nobleman's sons, and the two clever ones determined to have a trial, but they were sadly at a loss to prevent their idiot brother from going with them. They could not, by any means, get rid of him and were compelled at length to let Jack accompany them. They had not gone far before Jack shrieked with laughter, saying, "I've found an egg." "Put it in your pocket," said the brothers. A little while afterwards, he burst out into another fit of laughter on finding a crooked hazel stick, which he also put in his pocket; and a third time, he again laughed extravagantly because he found a nut. That also was put with his other treasures.

When they arrived at the palace, they were immediately admitted to mentioning the nature of their business and were ushered into a room where the princess and her suite were sitting. Jack, who never stood on ceremony, bawled out, "What a troop of fair ladies we've got here!"

"Yes," said the princess, "we are fair ladies, for we carry fire in our bosoms."

"Do you?" said Jack, "then roast me an egg," pulling out the egg from his pocket.

"How will you get it out again?" said the princess.

"With a crooked stick," replied Jack, producing the hazel.

"Where did that come from?" said the princess.

"From a nut," answered Jack, pulling out the nut from his pocket. "I've answered the three questions, and now I'll have the lady." "No, no," said the king, "not so fast. You still have an ordeal to go through. You must come here in a week and watch for one whole night with the princess, my daughter. If you can stay awake the whole night, you shall marry her the next day."

"But if I can't?" said Jack.

"Then off goes your head," said the king. "But you need not try unless you like."

Well, Jack went back home for a week and thought over whether he should try and win the princess. At last, he made up his mind. "Well," said Jack, "I'll try my vorton; now for the king's daughter or a headless shepherd!"

And taking his bottle and bag, he shuffled to the court. In his way thither, he was obliged to cross a river, and pulling off his shoes and stockings, while he was passing over, he observed several pretty fish bobbing against his feet, so he caught some and put them into his pocket. When he reached the palace, he knocked at the gate loudly with his crook, and having mentioned the object of his visit; he was immediately conducted to the hall where the king's daughter sat ready and prepared to see her lovers. He was placed in a luxurious chair, and rich wines and spices were set before him as delicate meats. Unfused by such fare, Jack ate and drank plentifully so that he was nearly dozing before midnight.

"Oh, shepherd," said the lady, "I have caught you napping!"

"Noa, sweet ally, I was busy a-fishing."

"A fishing," said the princess in the utmost astonishment: "Nay, shepherd, there is no fish pond in the hall."

"No matter that, I have been fishing in my pocket and have just caught one."

"Oh me!" said she, "let me see it."

The shepherd slyly drew the fish out of his pocket and, pretending to have caught it, showed it to her, and she declared it was the finest she ever saw.

About half an hour afterwards, she said, "Shepherd, do you think you could get me one more?"

He replied, "Mayhap I may when I have baited my hook;" and after a little while, he brought out another, which was finer than the first, and the princess was so delighted that she gave him leave to go to sleep and promised to excuse him to her father.

In the morning, the princess told the king, to his great astonishment, that Jack must not be beheaded, for he had been fishing in the hall all night; but when he heard how Jack had caught such beautiful fish out of his pocket, he asked him to catch one in his own.

Jack readily undertook the task and bid the king lie down, and he pretended to fish in his pocket, having another fish concealed in his hand, and giving him a sly prick with a needle, he held up the fish and showed it to the king.

His majesty did not much relish the operation, but he assented to the marvel of it, and the princess and Jack were united the same day and lived for many years in happiness and prosperity.

The Golden Goose

by Brothers Grimm

There was a man with three sons, the youngest of whom was considered very silly, and everybody used to mock him and make fun of him. The eldest son wanted to go and cut wood in the forest, and before he left home, his mother prepared beautiful pancakes and a bottle of wine for him to take with him so that he might not suffer from hunger or thirst.

As he entered the forest, he met a gray old man, who bade him "Good morning" and said: "Give me a little piece of cake out of your basket and a drop of wine out of your bottle, for I am very hungry and thirsty."

But the clever son replied: "What, give me my cake and wine! Why, if I did, I should have none for myself. Not I, indeed, so take yourself off!" He left the man standing and went on.

The young man began cutting down a tree, but not long before, he made a false stroke: the axe slipped and cut his arm so badly that he was obliged to go home and have it bound up. Now, this false stroke was caused by the little gray old man.

The next day the second son went into the forest to cut wood, and his mother gave him a cake and a bottle of wine. As he entered the wood, the same little old man met him and begged for a piece of cake and a drop of wine. But the second son answered rudely: "What I might give to you I shall want myself, so be off."

Then he left the little old man standing in the road and walked on. His punishment soon came; he had scarcely given two strokes on a tree with his axe when he hit his leg with such a terrible blow that he was obliged to limp home in great pain.

Then the stupid son said to his father, "Let me go for once and cut wood in the forest."

But his father said: "No, your brothers have been hurt already, and it would be worse for you, who don't understand wood-cutting."

The boy, however, begged so hard to be

allowed to go that his father said: "There, get along with you; you will buy your experience very dearly, I expect."

His mother, however, gave him a cake that had been made with water and baked in the ashes and a bottle of sour beer.

When he reached the wood, the same little old man met him and, after greeting him kindly, said: "Give me a little of your cake and a drop from your bottle, for I am very hungry and thirsty."

"Oh," replied the simple youth, "I have only a cake, which has been baked in the ashes, and some sour beer, but you are welcome to share it. Let us sit down and eat and drink together."

So they seated themselves, and, lo and behold, when the youth opened his basket, the cake had been turned into a beautiful cake and the sour beer into wine. After they had eaten and drank enough, the little old man said: "Because you have been kind-hearted and shared your dinner with me, I will make you in future lucky in all you undertake. An old tree stands; cut it down, and you will find something good at the root."

Then the old man said "Farewell" and left him.

The youth set to work and very soon succeeded in felling the tree when he found a goose whose feathers were of pure gold sitting at the roots. He took it up and, instead of going home, carried it with him to an inn at a little distance, where he intended to pass the night.

The landlord had three daughters, who looked at the goose with envious eyes. They had never seen such a wonderful bird and longed to have at least one of its feathers. "Ah," thought the eldest, "I shall soon have an opportunity to pluck one of them," and so it happened, for not long after, the young man left the room. She instantly went up to the bird and took hold of its wing, but as she did so, the finger and thumb remained and stuck fast. In a short time after, the second sister came in with the full expectation of gaining a golden feather, but as she touched her sister to move her from the bird, her hand stuck to her sister's dress, and neither of them could free herself. At last, in came the third sister with the same intention. "Keep away, keep away!" screamed the other two; "in heaven's name, keep away!"

But she could not imagine why she should keep away. Why should she not be there if they were near the golden bird? So she made a spring forward and touched her second sister, and immediately she also was made a prisoner, and in this position, they were obliged to remain by the goose all night.

In the morning, the young man came in, took the goose on his arm, and went away without troubling himself about the three girls following close behind him. And as he walked quickly, they were obliged to run one behind the other, left or right of him, just as he was inclined to go.

In the middle of a field, they were met by the parson of the parish, who looked with wonder at the procession as it came near him. "Shame on you!" he cried out. "What are you about, you bold-faced hussies, running after a young man in that way through the fields? Go home, all of you."

He placed his hand on the youngest to pull her back, but the moment he touched her, he became fixed and was obliged to follow and run like the rest. In a few minutes, the clerk met them, and when he saw the parson running after the girls, he wondered greatly and cried out, "Halloa, master parson, where are you running in such haste? Have you forgotten that there is a christening today?" And as the procession did not stop, he ran after it and seized the parson's gown.

In a moment, he found that his hand was fixed and had to run like the rest. And now there were five trotting along, one behind the other. Presently two peasants came by with their sickles from the field. The parson called out to them and begged them to come and release him and the clerk. Hardly had they touched the clerk when they also stuck fast as the others, and the simpleton with his golden goose traveled with the seven.

After a while, they came to a city in which reigned a king who had a daughter of such a melancholy disposition that no one could make her laugh; therefore, he issued a decree that whoever would make the princess laugh should have her in marriage.

When the simple youth heard this, he ran before her, and the seven trotted after him. The sight was so ridiculous that the princess burst into a violent fit of laughter the moment the princess saw it, and they thought she would never leave off.

After this, the youth went to the king and demanded his daughter in marriage, according to the king's decree; but his majesty did not quite like to have the young man for a son-in-law, so he said that, before he could consent to the marriage, the youth must bring him a man who could drink all the wine in the king's cellar.

The simpleton went into the forest, for he thought, "If anyone can help me, it is the little gray man." When he arrived at the spot where he had cut down the tree, there stood a man with a very miserable face.

The youth asked him why he looked so sorrowful.

"Oh," he exclaimed, "I suffer such dreadful thirst that nothing seems able to quench it, and I cannot endure the cold water. I have emptied a cask of wine already, but it was just like a drop of water on a hot stone."

"I can help you," cried the young man; "come with me, and you shall have your fill, I promise you."

Upon this, he led the man into the king's cellar, where he opened the casks one after another and drank and drank till his back ached, and before the day closed, he had quite emptied the king's cellar.

Again the young man asked for his bride, but the king was annoyed at the thought of giving his daughter to such a common fellow, and to get rid of him, he made another condition. He said that no man should have his daughter who could not find someone able to eat up a whole mountain of bread.

Away went the simpleton to the forest as before, and there in the same place sat a man bound himself tightly with a belt and made the most horrible faces. As the youth approached, he cried, "I have eaten a whole oven full of rolls, but it has not satisfied me a bit; I am as hungry as ever, and my stomach feels so empty that I am obliged to bind it around tightly, or I should die of hunger."

The simpleton could hardly contain himself for joy when he heard this. "Get up," he exclaimed, "and come with me, and I will give you plenty to eat. I'll warrant."

So he led him to the king's court, where his majesty had ordered all the flour in the kingdom to be made into bread and piled up on a huge mountain. The hungry man placed himself before the bread and began to eat, and before evening the whole pile had disappeared.

Then the simpleton went a third time to the king and asked for his bride, but the king made several excuses and, at last, said that if he could bring him a ship that would travel as well by land as by water, then he should, without any further conditions, marry his daughter.

The youth went to the forest and saw the same old gray man to whom he had given his cake. "Ah," he said, as the youth approached, "it was I who sent the men to eat and drink, and I will also give you a ship that can travel by land or by sea because when you thought I was poor, you were kind-hearted, and gave me food and drink."

The youth took the ship, and when the king saw it, he was quite surprised; but he could no longer refuse to give him his daughter in marriage. The wedding was celebrated with great pomp, and after the king's death, the simple wood-cutter inherited the whole kingdom and lived happily with his wife.

Harry's Reward

by Mrs. Molesworth

I hate the sea and bathing, and I don't want to learn to swim. What's the use of learning to swim? I'm not going to be a sailor. I don't like ships, and I don't want ever to go in one, and I just wish, oh, I do wish papa hadn't come here!"

"Harry! how can you?" said his sister Dora. "Papa, who is so kind, and when we have all been looking forward to his coming."

"I know—that's the worst of it," said Harry. "I've been looking forward as much as anyone, and now it's all spoilt by his saying I must learn to swim."

"I only wish I could learn!" sighed Dora. She was two years older than Harry, but she had lately had a bad fever. The family had come to the seaside to give her a change of air, but not for some weeks yet, if at all this summer, was poor Dora to be allowed to bathe. And she loved the sea, bathing, boating, and everything to do with the sea. She was like her father, who, though not a sailor, had traveled much and far, both by land and water; whereas Harry "took after," as the country people say, his mother, who had lived in her youth in a warm climate, and shivered at every breath of cold or even fresh air. It did not matter so much for a delicate lady to be afraid of the wind and the sea, but it was a great pity for a healthy boy to be fanciful or timid, and Harry's mother herself was very anxious that he should become more manly. She was very disappointed that she could not get him to bathe when they came to the seaside, but it was no use, and she and nurse and Dora all agreed that the only thing to do was to "wait till Papa came."

Papa had come, and Harry had had his first "dip." It wasn't so very bad after all, but just when he was getting up his spirits again and thinking ten minutes or so every morning were quickly over, all his fears and dislike grew worse than ever when his father told him that in a day or two he should begin to teach him to swim.

"Everybody, especially every English man and boy, should know how to swim," papa had said. "There is never any knowing the use it may be off, both for oneself and others."

"Isn't it very hard to learn?" Harry asked, not venturing to say more.

"It takes some patience," his father said. "But by the time I have to go—in three weeks or so—you should be able to swim fairly well if you have a lesson every day."

And Harry came home to tell Dora his troubles, which he worked himself up to think were very great ones indeed.

There was no shirking it, however. Papa, though very kind, was very firm, and once he said a thing, it had to be done. So with a white face and looking very solemn, poor Harry set off every day for his swimming lesson.

His father knew he was a quick, clever, and strong boy. He would not have forced Harry to do anything for which he was unfit or that could have done him any harm. And after the first shivers of fear and trembling clinging to his father's hand were over, it went on better and faster than expected. Harry didn't mind it being difficult once he had left off being afraid, and a day or two before his father had to leave them, Harry had the pleasure of hearing him say to his mother, "He swims already very nearly as well as I do myself."

Now I shall tell you why I have called this little story "Harry's Reward."

Seacliff, where these children were spending the summer, was not a fashionable watering place, with terraces and donkey carriages and bathing machines, but a little village, where one or two cottages were to be had for the season. There were also a few gentlemen's houses in the neighborhood so that in fine weather, merry groups met at the little sheltered bay among the rocks, where the bathing was pleasantest.

One day, not very long before they were to leave Seacliff, Harry, having finished his own morning swim, set off to walk home at his ease, whistling as he went. He had chosen the high path, a footpath above the lane, which was the regular road from the village to the beach, but from which the lane could be seen all the way.

It was a lovely morning—bright and peaceful —and Harry, as he went, wished that poor Dora had got leave to bathe.

"Next year," he thought, "I hope we shall come again, and then what fun we shall have. Dolly will learn to swim in no time."

Suddenly a sound disturbed his pleasant thoughts. A horse and cart or carriage of some kind were rushing wildly along, coming nearer and nearer. Surely the horse, or pony, was running away as Harry now saw it. The boy, who had never been a coward except about "sea things," tumbled down the steep grassy slope in no time and stood in the middle of the road, eager to see what he could do. The flying vehicle was near enough for him to know it was the pony carriage of two girls, a little older than Dora, whose home was one of the pretty houses a little way from Seacliff. He had often seen them drive down in it to the shore to bathe.

But what a queer figure was driving now. The pony was not running away. On the contrary, it seemed as if it could not run fast enough to please the driver; a girl with hair streaming, dressed only in a blue flannel bathing gown, streaming too, who stood upright in the carriage, lashing the poor pony as if she were mad, while from time to time she screamed, in a shrill and yet choking voice, "Help, help—for God's sake, help!"

"What is it?" screamed Harry as she passed. She would not stop, but she threw back some words on the wind.

"My sister—Alice—drowning. Going to the village to fetch someone—can swim."

And then again came the terrible cry, as if she hardly knew what she was saying, "Help, help!"

"Oh," thought Harry, "if she could have stopped and taken me back, we'd have been at the shore in a moment. I can swim. I can swim."

And he could run too. It was not so very far from the bathing place. How he got there, Harry never could tell. On the rushed, tearing off his clothes as he went. Off flew hat, jacket, collar, and shirt, till there was nothing but trousers and tennis shoes to pitch away, as in his little clinging woven drawers only, brave Harry flung himself, fearless and dauntless, into the sea, and struck out for the round dark object, poor Alice's head, which it had taken. Still, it took an instant to point out to him.

"I can swim! I can swim!" were the magic words with which he was able at once to push off the friendly hands that would have drawn him back, whose owners now stood watching him with flushed faces and tearful eyes, murmuring many a fervent prayer for his success, or saying aloud with clasped hands, "The brave boy, the splendid little fellow! It is her only chance!"

It was her only chance. Long before poor Lilian, for all her headlong drive, was back with a sailor she had met just outside the village, Alice would have sunk to rise no more. She had been caught by the current and carried out far beyond her depth, and when Harry, panting, laboring, but swimming valiantly still, got near enough to see the long plait of hair, and so draw her gently after him to shore, she had all but lost consciousness. Better so, perhaps, for had she struggled or clung to him, both would have been lost.

As it was, there were plenty of hands to carry them to land once they were within a safe distance; but Harry was the hero, Harry, alone and unaided, had saved a human life, for of all the score or so of watchers on the beach, not one knew how to swim.

Was not this worthy of being called his "Reward?" even if the thanks of the two pretty sisters and their parents had been less sincere and heartfelt?

Harry and Dora often go to Seacliff now, even without the rest of the family; for there is a house near there where they are always most welcome visitors and where the only fear is that if Harry were not a very sensible boy, the attention of Alice and Lilian might spoil him.

The Blue Castle

by Abbie Phillips Walker

Once upon a time, in a far-off country, there lived a witch on top of a high mountain, and every year she came down into the country and appeared at the palace of the King and asked for a bag of gold.

One night when the King and his Queen were making merry and having a big feast in honor of the birth of their little daughter, Princess Lily, the old witch came to the palace and asked for her bag of gold.

"Tell her to begone," said the King to his servant. "I have used all the gold in the vaults for the feast; she will have to come next year."

Now the old witch was very angry when she heard this message, and she hid in the palace grounds until all were asleep that night, and then she entered the palace and carried off the baby Princess.

The Queen and the King were beside themselves with grief when they discovered their loss, and they offered big rewards for the return of their daughter, but she could not be found.

"Find the old witch who came here the night of the feast," said one of the King's wise men, "and you will find the Princess."

They hunted far and near, but the witch could not be found, for when anyone attempted to climb the mountain where the old witch lived, the insects would become as thick as mist and clouds, and they could not see where to go.

One after another gave up the attempt, and so after a while, the King and Queen mourned their daughter as dead, and the old witch never came to the palace again.

The Queen and King never had any more children, and every day they grieved because there would be no one to reign after they were gone.

One day one of the King's wise men said to him: "In a cave in the forest lives an ogre who has a wonderful horse; it is kept in a stable made of marble, and its stall is of gold, and it is fed on corn grown in a field of pearls.

"If we could get this horse, we might be able to climb the mountain where the old witch lives, and perhaps the Princess is still alive."

"But how can we get this horse?" asked the King.

"Ah! that is the hard part," answered the wise man. "The enchanted creature can only be caught and mounted by one who can feed him with the magic corn, and it is said that anyone who tries to gather the corn from the field of pearls finds himself sinking and has to run for his life, so that only the ogre, who knows the magic words that keep the pearls from drawing him down, can gather the corn."

When the King heard this, he sent for all the princes in the land to come to his palace, and when they came, he told them he would give to the one who could catch and mount the ogre's enchanted horse to his kingdom if he could find the lost Princess Lily, and she should become his wife.

But all the princes were rich enough and did not care to take such a risk, especially as they had never seen Princess Lily.

Then the King sent out word to all the poor young men in his kingdom to come to him, and he made them the same offer, but one by one, they turned away, and at last, there was only a poor peasant youth left.

"I will try, Your Majesty," he said, "but I will not marry the Princess unless I can love her, and if she does not wish to marry me, I will not hold you to that part of the bargain, either, but I will take the kingdom if I bring back your child."

So that night, the peasant boy went to a fairy that lived in the woods and asked her to help him.

"You can only enter the field of magic corn by wearing the magic shoes belonging to the ogre, and he sleeps with them under his bed. They are tied to the big toe of his right foot by a silken thread, and no one can cut it or break it without awakening the ogre.

"I will give you a feather, and if you are fortunate enough to enter his chamber without being caught, for he is guarded well by a dog with two heads, use this feather to tickle his left foot, and you can cut the silken thread without the ogre knowing it. This is all I can do to help you. The two-headed dog is not in my power to control."

So the peasant took the magic feather, and that night he went to the ogre's castle in the woods and waited until he heard his snore, and then he took from his pocket two big bones.

He opened the door to the castle, for the ogre was afraid of no one and did not lock his door at night.

The two-headed dog growled and sprang toward the peasant, but he quickly thrust the bones in each mouth, which quieted them.

The two heads began to eat, and while they were eating, the peasant crept softly into the room of the sleeping ogre and tickled his left foot, which was sticking out from under the bedclothes.

The old ogre began to laugh, and he laughed so hard and loud that no other sound could be heard, and the peasant had time to break the slender thread which was tied to the magic shoes with one hand while he kept tickling the ogre's left foot with the feather held in the other hand.

When he had the shoes under his arm, he crept softly away from the bed, leaving the ogre still laughing.

The two-headed dog was still eating the bones, and the peasant went out and sat on the castle's steps to put on the magic shoes.

He had just drawn the shoes on when the two-headed dog finished the bones and set up a bark that the peasant initially thought was thunder.

He ran to the field of pearls where grew the magic corn and was just pulling the ears when the ogre came dashing out of his castle, followed by the two-headed dog, with both mouths wide open and looking as though he would devour him.

Out of the field ran the peasant, but not before the ogre had entered, and down went the ogre out of sight, the pearls closing over his head, for, of course, he forgot all about his shoes when he heard the two-headed dog bark, and anyway he thought they were tied to the big toe of his right foot.

But though he was rid of the ogre, he was not of the two-headed dog, which ran after him, showing his two sets of big teeth and barking all the while. But the peasant was far ahead of the dog, so he reached the stable and fed the magic corn to the enchanted horse, who neighed in the most friendly manner and let the peasant mount him.

He wore a harness of gold and silver trimmed with rubies, and he was pure white, with a saddle of purple velvet, with gold and silver trimmings.

He was a horse fit for a king to ride, and the poor peasant looked strangely out of place on his back.

Just as the peasant rode into the castle's yard, the two-headed dog dashed at the hind feet of the enchanted horse to bite him, but the horse kicked at him, and over, he rolled.

The peasant looked back to see what had happened to the dog, but he was nowhere to be seen; where he had lain was a big black-looking rock with a ragged-looking top like a set of giant teeth.

The peasant was now rid of his pursuers, and he rode off toward the mountain where the King had told him the witch lived.

Up the mountain dashed the enchanted white horse as though he had wings instead of feet, and in a few minutes, he had carried the peasant to the top.

The peasant looked about him, expecting to see a cave, but to his surprise, he saw only a grove of trees with something glistening through their leaves which looked like a house.

When he rode nearer to the grove, he saw a deep-blue castle of glass without doors or windows, and inside he could see a girl spinning.

She looked up as the shadow of the horse and rider fell on the glass castle, and her eyes grew big with surprise, but before the peasant could jump from his horse, an old woman came up through the floor of the house and tapped the girl on the head with her cane, and she turned into a mouse.

The peasant was too astonished to move for a minute, but the old woman's laugh brought him to his senses, and he knew she must be the witch.

"Ha, ha! You caught the horse, but you cannot bring back the Princess until I will it!" she screamed and then disappeared through the floor.

The peasant walked around the blue castle, but no door or window could find or an opening of any kind.

He was leading the horse by his gold bridle when suddenly it lifted one of its front feet and struck the blue castle.

Crash! went the blue glass, and the peasant saw an opening large enough for him to enter.

He was about to leave the enchanted horse outside when he heard another crash—the enchanted horse was following him in; it had broken a place large enough for both of them to enter.

The mouse was crouching in one corner of the room, and the peasant picked it up carefully and put it in his pocket.

The horse went to the spot where the old witch had disappeared and tapped on the glass floor three times with one of his front feet, and up from the floor came the old witch. But this time, she was not laughing; she looked frightened and trembled, so she had to lean on her cane to keep from falling.

The enchanted horse took her by the dress and shook her three times, and out from her pocket fell a black bean with a white spot on it.

As it dropped, the old witch screamed and fell on the floor, and the horse picked up the bean and swallowed it.

The peasant, all this time, was standing watching all the strange happenings, not daring to move for fear of breaking the spell and wondering what would happen next.

As the horse swallowed the bean, he seemed to shrink from sight, and a blue mist filled the room. When it cleared, the peasant beheld a handsome young man where the horse had stood, and where the witch had been was a deep hole.

"Did she fall into it?" asked the peasant, not knowing what else to say.

"No; in that hole, we will find the magic charm that will restore the Princess to her form," said the young man. "The witch disappeared in the blue mist."

"Let us hurry and find the magic charm," he said, dropping into the hole, and the peasant followed him.

There was a ladder down which they climbed, and down they went until it seemed they would never reach the bottom.

But at last, their feet touched something firm and soft, and they stood in a beautiful room on a carpet of blue velvet.

The room was hung with velvet, the color of sapphire, and the chairs were burnished gold with velvet seats.

A gold fountain played in the middle of the room, and the water fell into a basin of sapphire.

"This is the magic fountain," said the youth. "You must throw the little mouse into it if you wish to bring back the Princess."

The peasant took from his pocket the trembling little mouse. "It is frightening," he said. "I hate to throw it into that deep water."

Without replying, the youth grabbed the mouse from the peasant and threw it with great force into the fountain, and it disappeared.

"Oh, you have killed it!" said the peasant, looking into the deep-blue water with frightened eyes.

Then he saw a head rise slowly from the bottom of the blue basin; it came above the water, and then a beautiful girl stepped from the fountain, her golden hair all wet and glistening.

A soft, warm breeze came through the windows, and soon her hair and clothes were dry, and the peasant thought he had never seen anyone so beautiful as the Princess.

"I am the Prince who was changed into the horse for the ogre," said the youth, addressing the Princess. "I was stolen at the same time you were, and the ogre who was the husband of the witch took the witch, and I took you, but this youth has rescued us, for it was here that the magic bean was kept that restored me to my form, and if it had not been for a fairy who came to me one night and told me the secret I should never have regained my form."

All the time the Prince spoke, the peasant saw the Princess looking at him with a loving glance, and he knew the Princess was not for him, and he knew he would never be happy in a palace.

They began to look about and found they were in a beautiful palace that the old witch had lived in, but now that she was gone for good, the peasant said he would take it as his reward and let the Prince and the Princess return to her father.

In the stables, they found beautiful white

horses, and on one of them, the Prince and Princess rode away after making the peasant promise to come to their wedding and to dance with the bride. "For we will never forget you," said the Princess, "and we must always be friends."

The father and mother of the Princess listened to the story the Prince told, and then the Queen said: "I can tell whether this is my lost child or not. Let me see your left shoulder; she bears her name on that shoulder if she is our child."

The Princess bared her shoulder, and the Queen saw a tiny lily that proved she was her child.

The King gave a great feast in honor of his daughter's return, and the Prince and Princess were married, and the peasant danced at the wedding as he promised.

Master Willie

by Mrs. W. K. Clifford

There was once a little boy called Willie. I never knew his other name, and as he lived far off behind the mountain, we could not go to inquire. He had fair hair and blue eyes, and there was something in his face that, when you had looked at him, made you feel quite happy and rested and thought of all the things you meant to do by and by when you were wiser, stronger. He lived all alone with his tall aunt, who was very rich, in the village's big house at the end. Every morning he went down the street with his little goat under his arm, and the village folk looked after him and said, "There goes Master Willie."

The tall aunt had a very long neck; on the top of it was her head, and on the top of her head, she wore a white cap. Willie often used to look up at her and think that the cap was like snow upon the mountain. She was very fond of Willie, but she had lived many years and was always sitting still to think them over. She had forgotten all the games she used to know, all the stories she had read when she was little, and when Willie asked her about them, she would say, "No, dear, no, I can't remember; go to the woods and play." Sometimes she would take his face between her two hands and look at him well while Willie felt quite sure that she was not thinking of him but of someone else he did not know, and then she would kiss him and turn away quickly, saying, "Go to the woods, dear; it is no good staying with an old woman." Then he, knowing she wanted to be alone, would pick up his goat and hurry away.

He had a dear little sister, Apple-blossom, but a strange thing had happened to her. One day she over-wound her very big doll that talked and walked, and the consequence was terrible. No sooner was the winding-up key out of the doll's side than it blinked its eyes, spoke very fast, made faces, took Apple-blossom by the hand, saying, "I am not your doll any longer, but you are my little girl," and led her right away no one could tell whither, and no one was able to follow. The tall aunt and Willie only knew she had gone to be the doll's little girl in some strange place where dolls were stronger and more important than human beings.

After Apple-blossom left him, Willie had only his goat to play with; it was a poor little thing with no horns, no tail, and hardly any hair, but still, he loved it dearly and put it under his arm every morning while he went along the street.

"It is only made of painted wood and a little hair, Master Willie," said the blacksmith's wife one day. "Why should you care for it; it is not even alive."

"But if it were alive, anyone could love it."

"And living hands made it," the miller's wife said. "I wonder what strange hands they were;—take care of it for their sake, little master."

"Yes, dame, I will," he answered gratefully, and he went on his way thinking of the hands, wondering what tasks had been set for since they fashioned the little goat. He stayed all day in the woods helping the children gather nuts and blackberries. In the afternoon, he watched them go home with their aprons full; he looked after them longingly as they went on their way singing. If he had had a father and mother, or brothers and sisters, to whom he could have carried home nuts and blackberries, how merry he would have been. Sometimes he told the children how happy they were to live in a cottage with the door open all day, the sweet breeze blowing in, the cocks and hens strutting about outside, and the pigs grunting in the styes at the end of the garden; to see the mother scrubbing and washing, to know that the father was working in the fields, and to run about and help and play, and be cuffed and kissed, just as it happened. Then they would answer, "But you have the tall lady for your aunt, and the big house to live in, and the grand carriage to drive in, while we are poor and sometimes have little to eat and drink; mother often tells us how fine it must be to be you."

"But the food that you eat is sweet because you are very hungry," he answered them, "and no one sorrows in your house. As for the grand carriage, it is better to have a carriage if your heart is heavy, but when it is light, you can run swiftly on your two legs." Ah, poor Willie, how lonely he was, yet the tall aunt loved him dearly. On hot drowsy days, he had many a good sleep with his head resting against her high thin shoulders and her arms about him.

One afternoon, clasping his goat, he sat by the pond as usual. All the children had gone home, so he was quite alone, but he was glad to look at the pond and think. There were so many strange things in the world. It seemed as if he would never have thought about them, not if he lived to be a hundred.

He rested his elbows on his knees and sat staring at the pond. Overhead the trees were whispering; behind him, in and out of their holes, the rabbits whisked; far off, he could hear the twitter of a swallow; the foxglove was dead, the bracken was turning brown, the cones from the fir trees were lying on the ground. As he watched, a strange thing happened. Slowly and slowly, the pond lengthened out and out, stretching away and away until it became a river—a long river that went on and on, right down the woods, past the great black firs, past the little cottage that was a ruin and only lived in now and then by a stray gypsy or a tired tramp, past the setting sun, till it dipped into space beyond. Then many little boats came sailing towards Willie, and one stopped quite close to where he sat, just as if it were waiting for him. He looked at it well; it had a snow-white sail and a little man with a drawn sword for a figurehead. A voice that seemed to come from nowhere asked—

"Are you ready, Willie?" Just as if he understood, he answered back—

"Not yet,—not quite, dear Queen, but I shall be soon. I should like to wait a little longer."

"No, come now, dear child; they are all waiting for you." So he got up and stepped into the boat, and it put out before he had even time to sit down. He looked at the rushes as the boat cut its way through them; he saw the hearts of the lilies as they lay spread open on their great wide leaves; he went on and on beneath the crimson sky towards the setting sun until he slipped into space with the river.

He saw land at last far on ahead, and as he drew near it, he understood whither the boat was bound. All along the shore, there were hundreds and hundreds of dolls crowding down to the water's edge, looking as if they had expected him. They stared at him with shining round eyes, but he just clasped his little goat tighter and closer and sailed on nearer and nearer to the land. The dolls did not move; they stood still, smiling at him with their painted lips, then suddenly they opened their painted mouths and put out their painted tongues at him; but still, he was not afraid. He clasped the goat a little closer and called out, "Apple blossom, I am waiting; are you here?" Just as he had expected, he heard Apple-blossom's voice answering from the back of the toy town—

"Yes, dear brother, I am coming." So he drew close to the shore and waited for her. He saw her a long way off and waved his hand.

"I have come to fetch you," he said.

"But I cannot go with you unless I am bought," she answered sadly, "for now there is a wire spring inside me; and look at my arms, dear brother;" pulling up her pink muslin sleeves, she showed him that they were stuffed with sawdust. "Go home and bring the money to pay for me," she cried, "and then I can come home again." But the dolls had crowded up behind so that he might not turn his boat round. "Straight on," cried Apple-blossom, in despair; "what does it matter whether you go backward or forwards if you only keep straight when you live in a world that is round?"

So he sailed on once more beneath the sky that was getting grey, through all the shadows that gathered round, beneath the pale moon, and the little stars that came out one by one and watched him from the sky.

I saw him coming towards the land of

storybooks. That was how I knew about him, dear children. He was very tired and fell asleep, but the boat stopped naturally as if it knew I had been waiting for him. I stooped, kissed his eyes, looked at his little pale face, and, lifting him softly in my arms, put him into this book to rest. That is how he came to be here for you to know. But in the toy-land Apple-blossom waits with the wire spring in her breast and the sawdust in her limbs; and at home, in the big house at the end of the village, the tall aunt weeps and wails and wonders if she will ever see again the children she loves so well.

She will not wait very long, dear children. I know how it will all be. When it is quite dark tonight, and she is sitting in the leather chair with the high back, her head on one side, and her poor long neck aching, quite suddenly, she will hear two voices shouting for joy. She will start up and listen, wondering how long she has been sleeping, and then she will call out—

"Oh, my darlings, is it you?" And they will answer back—

"Yes, it is us. We have come, we have come!" Willie and Apple-blossom will stand before her. The big doll will run down, the wire spring and the sawdust will have vanished, and Apple-blossom will be the doll's little girl no more. Then the tall aunt will look at them both and kiss them, and she will kiss the poor little goat, too, wondering if it is possible to buy him a new tail. But though she will say little, her heart will sing for joy. Ah, children, no song is sung by bird or bee or that ever burst from the happiest lips that is half so sweet as the song we sometimes sing in our hearts—a song that is learned by love and sung only to those who love us.

The Plate of Pancakes

by Maud Lindsay

Once upon a time, a woman was frying some pancakes, and as she turned the last cake in the pan, she said to her little boy:

"If you were a little older, I should send you some of these fine cakes for your father's dinner, but as it is, he must wait till supper for them."

"Oh, do let me take them," said the little boy named Karl. "Just see how tall I am. And only yesterday, my grandmother said I was old enough to learn my letters. Do let me go!"

And he begged and begged till at last she selected the brownest and crispest cakes, and putting them on a plate with a white napkin over them, she bade him take them.

Now the path from Karl's home to the saw-mill where his father worked was straight enough and plain enough, but it ran through the wood called Enchanted. Fairies lived there, so some people thought, and goblins liked to work mischief, and never before had the little boy been allowed to go there alone.

As he hurried along with the plate of pancakes in his hand, he glanced into every green thicket he passed, half hopeful and half fearful that he might find a tiny creature hidden in the leaves. Not a glimpse of fairy or goblin did he see, but when he came to the blackberry bushes where the sweetest berries grow, something seemed to whisper to him: "Stop, Karl, and eat."

"But I am taking a plate of pancakes for my father's dinner," Karl said aloud.

"A moment or two will make no difference. You can run fast," came the whisper again.

"Oh, yes, I can run fast," said Karl, and he put the plate down under the bushes and began to pick the berries. They were as ripe and sweet as they had looked, and everyone that the little boy put into his mouth made him wish for another, and if he turned away from the bushes, the whisper was sure to come: "One more and then go."

The pancakes grew cold on the plate, and the sun, which had been high in the sky when Karl started from home, slipped farther and farther into the west; but still, he lingered till suddenly the evening whistle of the mill sounded sharp and shrill in his ears.

"Why it is time for my father to come home," he cried. "Dear me, dear me, what shall I do?"

There was nothing for him to do but to go home, so home he went with the plate of cold pancakes in his hand and the tears rolling down his cheeks.

When he told his mother and grandmother what had happened, they looked at each other wisely as if they thought more about it than they would say; but they bade him dry his tears.

"You will be more careful another time," they said; and so the matter ended.

But Karl did not forget it. It was many a month before his mother fried pancakes again, but no sooner did he see her turning the cakes in the pan than he said:

"I wish my father had some of these fine cakes for his dinner, don't you, mother?"

"Indeed I do," said she, smiling at his grandmother as she spoke, and as soon as the cakes were made, she selected the brownest and crispest, putting them on a plate with a white napkin over them, and she bade him take them.

"I'll get there in time for my father's dinner today," he said as he started; but after a concise while, he was back with an empty plate in his hand, and the tears rolled down his cheeks.

"I only put the plate down for a minute while I chased a rabbit that said, 'If you catch me, you may have me,' and when I came back, every pancake was gone," he sobbed.

His mother and grandmother looked at each other wisely when they heard this.

"It is just as I thought the first time," said his mother. "The goblins are at work in the wood. He must never go there again."

But to this, the grandmother would not agree.

"Leave it to me," she said, and the very next day, she fried pancakes, and selecting the brownest and crispest, she put them on a plate with a white napkin over them and bade Karl take them to his father.

"And if any bid you stop or stay, or turn your feet from out your way, say but the word that is spelled with the fourteenth and fifteenth letters of the alphabet three times in a loud voice, and all will go well with you," she said.

"All right," said Karl, nodding his head proudly, for he knew all his letters by this time and could spell hard words like c-a-t, cat, m-a-t, and mat.

"All right," but he did not stop to count the letters, for he was in a great hurry to be off.

"I guess my father will be glad to get such fine pancakes for his dinner," he said; and he ran so fast that he was halfway to the mill before he knew it.

There was no whispering voice in the wood that day and no talking rabbit to tempt him to a chase; but as he came to a place where another path crossed his own, a bird called out from the heart of the wood:

"Quick, quick, come here, here, here——"

"Where, where?" cried Karl; and he was just about to start in search of the bird when he remembered what his grandmother had said:

"If any bid you stop or stay, or turn your feet from out your way, say but the word that is spelled with the fourteenth and fifteenth letters of the alphabet three times in a loud voice, and all will go well with you."

"A, B, C, D, E, F, G," he chanted, counting the letters on his fingers as he said them, "H, I, J, K, L, M, N, O:" N was the fourteenth letter and O was the fifteenth. N-O; that was easy.

"No! No! No!" he shouted, and—do you believe it?—in less time than it takes to tell it, he was at the mill door with every pancake safe and hot.

And the story goes that though he came and went through the Enchanted Wood all the days of his life, he was never hindered by anything; he never saw a goblin though he lived as old as his grandmother had been when he was a little boy.

The King of the Polar Bears

by L. Frank Baum

The King of the Polar Bears lived among the icebergs in the far north country. He was old and monstrous big; he was wise and friendly to all who knew him. His body was thickly covered with long, white hair that glistened like silver under the midnight sun's rays. His claws were strong and sharp that he might walk safely over the smooth ice or grasp and tear the fishes and seals upon which he fed.

The seals were afraid when he drew near and tried to avoid him, but the white and gray gulls loved him because he left the remnants of his feasts for them to devour.

Often his subjects, the polar bears, came to him for advice when ill or in trouble; but they wisely kept away from his hunting grounds lest they might interfere with his sport and arouse his anger.

The wolves, who sometimes came as far north as the icebergs, whispered among themselves that the king of the Polar Bears was either a magician or under the protection of a powerful fairy. No earthly thing seemed able to harm him; he never failed to secure plenty of food, and he grew bigger and stronger daily and yearly.

Yet the time came when this monarch of the north met man, and his wisdom failed him.

One day, he came out of his cave among the icebergs and saw a boat moving through the strip of water uncovered by the shifting of the summer ice. In the boat were men.

The great bear had never seen such creatures before and therefore advanced toward the boat, sniffing the strange scent with aroused curiosity and wondering whether he might take them for friends or foes, food or carrion.

When the king came near the water's edge, a

man stood up in the boat and, with a queer instrument, made a loud "bang!" The polar bear felt a shock; his brain became numb; his thoughts deserted him; his great limbs shook and gave way beneath him, and his body fell heavily upon the hard ice.

That was all he remembered for a time.

When he awoke, he was smarting with pain on every inch of his huge bulk, for the men had cut away his hide with its glorious white hair and carried it with them to a distant ship.

Above him circled thousands of his friends, the gulls, wondering if their benefactor were really dead and if it was proper to eat him. But when they saw him raise his head and groan and tremble, they knew he still lived, and one of them said to his comrades:

"The wolves were right. The king is a great magician, for even men cannot kill him. But he suffers from a lack of coverage. Let us repay his kindness to us by giving him as many feathers as we can spare."

This idea pleased the gulls. One after another, they plucked with their beaks the softest feathers from under their wings and, flying down, dropped them gently upon the body of the king of the Polar Bears.

Then they called to him in a chorus:

"Courage, friend! Our feathers are as soft and beautiful as your shaggy hair. They will guard you against the cold winds and warm you while you sleep. Have courage, then, and live!"

And the king of the Polar Bears dared to bear his pain and lived and was strong again.

The feathers grew as they had grown upon the bodies of the birds and covered him as his own hair had. Mostly they were pure white in color, but some from the gray gulls gave his majesty a slightly mottled appearance.

The rest of that summer and all through the six months of the night, the king left his icy cavern only to fish or catch seals for food. He felt no shame at his feathery covering, but it was still strange, and he avoided meeting any of his brother bears.

During this retirement period, he thought much of the men who had harmed him and remembered how they had made the great "bang!" And he decided it was best to keep away from such fierce creatures. Thus he added to his store of wisdom.

When the moon fell away from the sky, and the sun came to make the icebergs glitter with the gorgeous tintings of the rainbow, two of the polar bears arrived at the king's cavern to ask his advice about the hunting season. But when they saw his great body covered with feathers instead of hair, they began to laugh, and one said:

"Our mighty king has become a bird! Who ever before heard of a feathered polar bear?"

Then the king gave way to wrath. He advanced upon them with deep growls and stately tread and, with one blow of his monstrous paw, stretched the mocker lifeless at his feet.

The other ran away to his fellows and carried the news of the king's strange appearance. The result was a meeting of all the polar bears upon a broad ice field, where they talked gravely of the remarkable change that had come upon their monarch.

"He is, in reality, no longer a bear," said one; "nor can he justly be called a bird. But he is half bird and half bear and so unfitted to remain our king."

"Then who shall take his place?" asked another.

"He who can fight the bird-bear and overcome him," answered an aged member of the group. "Only the strongest is fit to rule our race."

There was silence for a time, but at length, a great bear moved to the front and said:

"I will fight him; I—Woof—the strongest of our race! And I will be King of the Polar Bears."

The others nodded assent and dispatched a messenger to the king to say he must fight the great Woof and master him or resign his sovereignty.

"For a bear with feathers," added the messenger, "is no bear at all, and the king we obey must resemble the rest of us."

"I wear feathers because it pleases me," growled the king. "Am I not a great magician? But I will fight, nevertheless, and if Woof masters me, he shall be king in my stead."

Then he visited his friends, the gulls, who were feasting upon the dead bear, and told them of the coming battle.

"I shall conquer," he said proudly. "Yet my people are in the right, for only a hairy one like themselves can hope to command their obedience."

The queen gull said:

"I met an eagle yesterday, which had made its escape from a big city of men. And the eagle told me he had seen a monstrous polar bear skin thrown over the back of a carriage that rolled along the street. That skin must have been yours, oh king, and if you wish, I will send a hundred of my gulls to the city to bring it back to you."

"Let them go!" said the king gruffly. And a hundred gulls were soon flying rapidly southward.

For three days, they flew straight as an arrow until they came to scattered houses, villages, and cities. Then their search began.

The gulls were brave, cunning, and wise. Upon the fourth day, they reached the great metropolis and hovered over the streets until a carriage rolled along with a great white bear robe thrown over the back seat. Then the birds swooped down—the whole hundred— and, seizing the skin in their beaks, flew quickly away.

They were late. The king's great battle was on the seventh day, and they must fly swiftly to reach the Polar regions by that time.

Meanwhile, the bird bear was preparing for his fight. He sharpened his claws in the small crevasses of the ice. He caught a seal and tested his big yellow teeth by crunching its bones between them. And the queen gull set her band to plumbing the king bear's feathers until they lay smoothly upon his body.

But every day, they cast anxious glances into the southern sky, watching for the hundred gulls to bring back the king's own skin.

The seventh day came, and all the Polar bears in that region gathered around the king's cavern. Among them was Woof, strong and confident of his success.

"The bird bears feathers will fly fast enough when I get my claws upon him!" he boasted, and the others laughed and encouraged him.

The king was disappointed at not having recovered his skin, but he resolved to fight bravely without it. He advanced from the opening of his cavern with a proud and kingly bearing, and when he faced his enemy, he gave so terrible a growl that Woof's heart stopped beating for a moment, and he began to realize that a fight with the wise and mighty king of his race was no laughing matter.

After exchanging one or two heavy blows with his foe Woof's courage returned, and he determined to dishearten his adversary by bluster.

"Come nearer, bird-bear!" he cried. "Come nearer, that I may pluck your plumage!"

The defiance filled the king with rage. He ruffled his feathers as a bird does till he appeared to be twice his actual size, and then he strode forward and struck Woof so powerful a blow that his skull crackled like an eggshell, and he fell prone upon the ground.

While the assembled bears stood looking with fear and wonder at their fallen champion, the sky darkened.

A hundred gulls flew down from above and dripped upon the king's body a skin covered with pure white hair that glittered in the sun like silver.

And behold! the bears saw before them the well-known form of their wise and respected master, and with one accord, they bowed their shaggy heads in homage to the mighty king of the Polar Bears.

The Frog-Prince

by Grimm Brothers

One fine evening a young princess put on her bonnet and clogs and went out to take a walk in a wood; when she came to a cool spring of water that rose in the midst of it, she sat herself down to rest a while. Now she had a golden ball in her hand, which was her favorite plaything, and she was constantly tossing it up into the air and catching it again as it fell. After a time, she threw it up so high that she missed catching it as it fell; and the ball bounded away and rolled along upon the ground till, at last, it fell into the spring. The princess looked into the spring after her ball, but it was so deep that she could not see the bottom of it. Then she began to mourn her loss and said, 'Alas! If I could only get my ball again, I would give all my fine clothes, jewels, and everything I have in the world.'

While she was speaking, a frog put its head out of the water and said, 'Princess, why do you weep so bitterly?' 'Alas!' said she, 'what can you do for me, you nasty frog? My golden ball has fallen into the spring.' The frog said, 'I want not your pearls, jewels, and fine clothes; but if you will love me, and let me live with you and eat from off your golden plate, and sleep upon your bed, I will bring you your ball again.' 'What nonsense,' thought the princess, 'this silly frog is talking! He can never even get out of the spring to visit me, though he may be able to get my ball for me, and therefore I will tell him he shall have what he asks.' So she said to the frog, 'Well if you will bring me my ball, I will do all you ask.' Then the frog put his head down and dived deep under the water, and after a little while, he came up again with the ball in his mouth and threw it on the edge of the spring. As soon as the young princess saw her ball, she ran to pick it up; and she was so overjoyed to have it in her hand again that she never thought of the frog but ran home with it as fast as she could. The frog called after her, 'Stay, princess, and take me with you as you said,' But she did not stop to hear a word.

The next day, just as the princess had sat down

to dinner, she heard a strange noise—tap, tap—plash, plash—as if something was coming up the marble staircase: and soon afterward, there was a gentle knock at the door, and a little voice cried out and said:

'Open the door, my princess dear,

Open the door to thy true love here!

And mind the words that thou and I said

By the fountain cool, in the greenwood shade.'

Then the princess ran to the door and opened it, and there she saw the frog, whom she had quite forgotten. She was sadly frightened at this sight and, shutting the door as fast as she could, returned to her seat. The king, her father, seeing that something had frightened her, asked her what the matter was. 'There is a nasty frog,' said she, at the door, that lifted my ball for me out of the spring this morning: I told him that he should live with me here, thinking that he could never get out of the spring; but there he is at the door, and he wants to come in.'

While she was speaking, the frog knocked again at the door and said:

'Open the door, my princess dear,

Open the door to thy true love here!

And mind the words that thou and I said

By the fountain cool, in the greenwood shade.'

Then the king said to the young princess, 'As you have given your word, you must keep it, so go and let him in.' She did so, and the frog hopped into the room and then straight on—tap, tap—plash, plash—from the bottom of the room to the top till he came up close to the table where the princess sat. 'Pray to lift me up on a chair,' said he to the princess, 'and let me sit next to you.' As soon as she had done this, the frog said, 'Put your plate nearer to me, that I may eat out of it.' This she did, and when he had eaten as much as he could, he said, 'Now I am tired; carry me upstairs and put me into your bed.' And the princess, though very unwilling, took him up in her hand and put him upon the pillow of her own bed, where he slept all night long. As soon as it was light, he jumped up, hopped downstairs, and went out of the house. 'Now, then,' thought the princess, at last, he is gone, and I shall be troubled with him no more.'

But she was mistaken; for when night came again, she heard the same tapping at the door, and the frog came once more and said:

'Open the door, my princess dear,

Open the door to thy true love here!

And mind the words that thou and I said

By the fountain cool, in the greenwood shade.'

And when the princess opened the door, the frog came in and slept upon her pillow as before till the morning broke. And the third night, he did the same. But when the princess awoke the following morning, she was astonished to see, instead of the frog, a handsome prince gazing at her with the most beautiful eyes she had ever seen and standing at the head of her bed.

He told her that he had been enchanted by a spiteful fairy, who had changed him into a frog; and that he had been fated so to abide till some princess should take him out of the spring and let him eat from her plate and sleep upon her bed for three nights. 'You,' said the prince, 'have broken his cruel charm, and now I have nothing to wish for but that you should go with me into my father's kingdom, where I will marry you and love you as long as you live.'

The young princess, you may be sure, was not long in saying 'Yes' to all this; and as they spoke, a gay coach drove up with eight beautiful horses, decked with plumes of feathers and a golden harness; and behind the coach rode the prince's servant, faithful Heinrich, who had lamented the misfortunes of his dear master during his enchantment so long and so bitterly, that his heart had nearly burst.

They then took leave of the king and got into the coach with eight horses, and all set out, full of joy and merriment, for the prince's kingdom, which they reached safely; there they lived happily for many years.

My Own Self

by Joseph Jacobs

In a tiny house in the North Country, far away from any town or village, there lived not long ago, a poor widow all alone with her little son, a six-year-old boy.

The house door opened straight onto the hillside, and all around about were moorlands and huge stones, and swampy hollows; never a house nor a sign of life wherever you might look, for their nearest neighbors were the "ferlies" in the glen below, and the "will-o'-the-wisps" in the long grass along the path side.

And many a tale she could tell of the "good folk" calling to each other in the oak trees and the twinkling lights hopping onto the very window sill on dark nights. Still, despite the loneliness, she lived from year to year in the little house, perhaps because she was never asked to pay any rent for it.

But she did not care to sit up late when the fire burnt low, and no one knew what might be about; so, when they had had their supper, she would make up a good fire and go off to bed so that if anything terrible did happen, she could always hide her head under the bed-clothes.

This, however, was far too early to please her little son; so when she called him to bed, he would go on playing beside the fire as if he did not hear her.

He had always been bad to do with since the day he was born, and his mother did not often care to cross him; indeed, the more she tried to make him obey her, the less heed he paid to anything she said, so it usually ended by his taking his own way.

But one night, just at the fore-end of winter, the widow could not make up her mind to go off to bed and leave him playing by the fireside; for the wind was tugging at the door and rattling the window panes and, well, she knew that on such a night, fairies and such like were bound to be out and about, and bent on mischief. So she tried to coax the boy into going at once to bed:

"The safest bed to bide in, such a night as this!"

she said: but no, he wouldn't.

Then she threatened to "give him the stick," but it was no use.

The more she begged and scolded, the more he shook his head, and when at last she lost patience and cried that the fairies would surely come and fetch him away, he only laughed and said he wished they would, for he would like one to play with.

At that, his mother burst into tears and went off to bed in despair, certain that after such words, something dreadful would happen, while her naughty little son sat on his stool by the fire, not at all put out by her crying.

But he had not long been sitting there alone when he heard a fluttering sound near him in the chimney, and presently down by his side dropped the tiniest wee girl you could think of; she was not a span high and had hair like spun silver, eyes as green as grass, and cheeks red as June roses. The little boy looked at her with surprise.

"...the tiniest wee girl you could think of..."

"Oh!" said he; "what do they call ye?"

"My own self," she said in a shrill but sweet little voice, and she looked at him too. "And what do they call ye?"

"Just my own self, too!" he answered cautiously, and they began to play together.

She certainly showed him some fine games. She made animals out of the ashes that looked and moved like life, and trees with green leaves waving over tiny houses, with men and women an inch high in them, who, when she breathed on them, fell to walking and talking quite properly.

But the fire was getting low, and the light dim, and presently the little boy stirred the coals with a stick to make them blaze; when out jumped a red-hot cinder, and where should it fall, but on the fairy child's tiny foot.

Thereupon she set up such a squeal that the boy dropped the stick and clapped his hands to his ears, but it grew to so shrill a screech that it was like all the wind in the world whistling through one tiny keyhole.

There was a sound in the chimney again, but this time the little boy did not wait to see what it was but bolted off to bed, where he hid under the blankets and listened in fear and trembling to what went on.

"...caught the creature by its ear..."

A voice came from the chimney, speaking sharply:

"Who's there, and what's wrong?" it said.

"It's my own self," sobbed the fairy child, "and my foot's burnt sore. O-o-h!"

"Who did it?" said the voice angrily; this time, it sounded nearer, and the boy, peeping from under the clothes, could see a white face looking out from the chimney opening.

"Just my own self, too!" repeated the fairy child.

"Then if ye did it your own self," cried the elf-mother shrilly, "what's the use of making all this fash about it?"—and with that, she stretched out a long thin arm and caught the creature by its ear, and, shaking it roughly, pulled it after her, out of sight up the chimney.

The little boy lay awake a long time, listening, in case the fairy mother should come back after all, and the next evening, after supper, his mother was surprised to find that he was willing to go to bed whenever she liked.

"He's taking a turn for the better at last!" she said to herself, but he was thinking just then that when next a fairy came to play with him, he might not get off quite so easily as he had done this time.

Little Red Riding Hood

by Charles Perrault
Edited by Capt. Edric Vredenburg

Many years ago, a dear little girl was beloved by everyone who knew her, but her grandmother was so very fond of her that she never felt that she could think and do enough for her. On her granddaughter's birthday, she presented her with a red silk hood; as it suited her very well, she would never wear anything else; and so she was called Little Red Riding Hood. One day her mother said to her, "Come, Red Riding Hood, here is a nice piece of meat and a bottle of wine: take these to your grandmother; she is weak and ailing, and they will do her good. Be there before she gets up; go quietly and carefully; and do not run, or you may fall and break the bottle, and then your grandmother will have nothing. When you enter her room, do not forget to say 'Good morning; do not pry into all the corners." "I will do just as you say," answered Red Riding Hood, bidding goodbye to her mother.

The grandmother lived far away in the wood, a long walk from the village, and as Little Red Riding Hood came among the trees, she met a wolf; but she did not know what a wicked animal it was, so she was not at all frightened. "Good morning, Little Red Riding Hood," he said.

"Thank you, Mr. Wolf," she said.

"Where are you going so early, Little Red Riding Hood?"

"To my grandmother's," she answered.

"And what are you carrying under your apron?"

"Some wine and meat," she replied. "We baked the meat yesterday so that grandmother, who is very weak, might have a nice strengthening meal."

"And where does your grandmother live?" asked the Wolf.

"Oh, quite twenty minutes' walk further in the forest. The cottage stands under three great oak trees, and close by are some nut bushes, by which you will at once know it."

The Wolf was thinking, "She is a nice tender thing and will taste better than the old woman; I must act cleverly that I may make a meal of both."

Presently he came up again to Little Red Riding Hood and said. "Just look at the beautiful flowers which grow near you; why do you not look about you? I believe you don't hear how sweetly the birds are singing. You walk as if you were going to school; see how cheerful everything is around you in the forest."

And Little Red Riding Hood opened her eyes. When she saw how the sunbeams glanced and danced through the trees and what bright flowers were blooming in her path, she thought, "If I take my grandmother a fresh nosegay, she will be much pleased; and it is so very early that I can, even then, get there in good time:" and running into the forest she looked about for flowers. But when she had once begun, she did not know how to leave off and kept going deeper and deeper among the trees looking for some still more beautiful flowers. The Wolf, however, ran straight to the old grandmother's house and knocked at the door.

"Who's that?" asked the old lady.

"Only a little Red Riding Hood, bringing you some meat and wine; please open the door," answered the Wolf.

"Lift up the latch," cried the grandmother; "I am much too ill to get up myself."

So the Wolf lifted the latch, and the door flew open, and without a word, he jumped onto the bed and gobbled up the poor old lady. Then he put on her clothes, tied her nightcap over his head, got into the bed, and drew the blankets over him.

All this time, Red Riding Hood was gathering flowers; when she had picked as many as she could carry, she thought of her grandmother and hurried to the cottage. She wondered very much to find the door open, and when she entered the room, she began to feel very ill and exclaimed, "How sad I feel! I wish I had not come today." Then she said, "Good morning," but received no reply, so she went up to the bed and drew back the curtains, and there lay her grandmother as she imagined, with the cap drawn half over her eyes and looking very fierce.

"Oh, grandmother, what great ears you have!"

"All the better to hear you with," was the reply.

"And what great eyes you have!"

"All the better to see you with."

"And what great hands you have!"

"All the better to touch you with."

"But, grandmother, what very great teeth you have!"

"All the better to eat you with," and hardly were the words spoken when the Wolf made a jump out of bed and swallowed down poor Little Red Riding Hood also.

As soon as he had thus satisfied his hunger, he laid himself down again on the bed, went to sleep, and snored very loudly. A huntsman passing by overheard him and said, "How loudly that old woman snores! I must see if anything is the matter."

So he went into the cottage; when he came to the bed, he saw the Wolf sleeping in it.

"What! are you here, you old rascal? I have been looking for you," he exclaimed, and taking up his gun, he shot the old Wolf.

But it is also said that the story ends in a different manner; for that one day, when Red Riding Hood was taking some presents to her grandmother, a Wolf met her and wanted to mislead her; but she went straight on and told her grandmother that she had met a Wolf, who said good-day; but he looked so hungrily out of his great eyes, as if he would have eaten her up had she not been on the high road.

So her grandmother said, "We will shut the door, and then he cannot get in."

Soon after, up came the Wolf, who tapped and exclaimed, "I am Little Red Riding Hood, grandmother;

I have some roast meat for you." But they kept quite quiet and did not open the door; so the Wolf, after looking several times round the house, at last, jumped onto the roof, thinking to wait till Red Riding Hood went home in the evening and then to creep after her and eat her in the darkness.

The old woman, however, saw what the villain intended. A large stone trough stood before the door, and she said to Little Red Riding Hood, "Take this bucket, dear: yesterday I boiled some meat in this water, now pour it into the stone trough." Then the Wolf sniffed the smell of the meat, and his mouth watered, and he wished very much to taste.

At last, he stretched his neck too far over so that he lost his balance and fell down from the roof, right into the great trough below, and there he was drowned.

Rapunzel

by Brothers Grimm

Once, a man and a woman had long, in vain, wished for a child. At length, the woman hoped that God was about to grant her desire. These people had a little window at the back of their house from which a splendid garden could be seen, which was full of the most beautiful flowers and herbs. It was, however, surrounded by a high wall, and no one dared to go into it because it belonged to an enchantress who had great power and was dreaded by all the world. One day the woman was standing by this window and looking down into the garden when she saw a bed which was planted with the most beautiful rampion (rapunzel), and it seemed so fresh and green that she longed for it, she quite pined away and began to look pale and miserable. Then her husband was alarmed and asked: 'What ails you, dear wife?' 'Ah,' she replied, 'if I can't eat some of the rampions in the garden behind our house, I shall die.' The man, who loved her, thought: 'Sooner than let your wife die, bring her some of the rampions yourself, let it cost what it will.' At twilight, he clambered down over the wall into the enchantress's garden, hastily clutched a handful of rampion, and took it to his wife. She at once made herself a salad of it and ate it greedily. It tasted so good to her—so very good that the next day she longed for it three times as much as before. If he was to have any rest, her husband must descend into the garden once more. In the evening gloom, therefore, he let himself down again; but when he clambered down the wall, he was terribly afraid, for he saw the enchantress standing before him. 'How can you dare,' said she with an angry look, 'descend into my garden and steal my rampion like a thief? You shall suffer for it!' 'Ah,' answered he, 'let mercy take the place of justice. I only made up my mind to do it out of necessity. My wife saw your rampion from the window and felt such a longing for it that she would have died if she had not got some to eat.' Then the enchantress allowed her anger to be softened and said to him: 'If the case is as you say, I will allow you to take away with you as much rampion as you will, only I make one condition, you must give me the child which your wife will bring into the world; it shall be well treated, and I will care for it like a mother.' The man, in his terror, consented to everything, and when the woman was brought to bed, the enchantress appeared at once, gave the child the name of Rapunzel, and took it away with her.

Rapunzel grew into the most beautiful child under the sun. When she was twelve years old, the enchantress shut her into a tower that lay in a forest and had neither stairs nor a door, but quite at the top was a little window. When the enchantress wanted to go in, she placed herself beneath it and cried:

'Rapunzel, Rapunzel,

Let down your hair to me.'

Rapunzel had magnificent long hair, fine as spun gold, and when she heard the voice of the enchantress, she unfastened her braided tresses, wound them around one of the hooks of the window above, and then the hair fell twenty ells down, and the enchantress climbed up by it.

After a year or two, it came to pass that the king's son rode through the forest and passed by the tower. Then he heard a song, which was so charming that he stood still and listened. This was Rapunzel, who, in her solitude, passed her time by letting her sweet voice resound. The king's son wanted to climb up to her and looked for the tower door, but none was to be found. He rode home, but the singing had so deeply touched his heart that he went out into the forest every day and listened to it. Once when he was thus standing behind a tree, he saw that an enchantress came there, and he heard how she cried:

'Rapunzel, Rapunzel,

Let down your hair to me.'

Then Rapunzel let down the braids of her hair, and the enchantress climbed up to her. 'If that is the ladder by which one mounts, I too will try my fortune,' said he, and the next day when it began to grow dark, he went to the tower and cried:

'Rapunzel, Rapunzel,

Let down your hair to me.'

Immediately the hair fell down, and the king's son climbed up.

At first, Rapunzel was terribly frightened when a man, such as her eyes had never yet beheld, came to her, but the king's son began to talk to her quite like a friend and told her that his heart had been so stirred that it had let him have no rest, and he had been forced to see her. Then Rapunzel loses her fear, and when he asks her if she would take him for her husband, and she sees that he is young and handsome, she thinks: 'He will love me more than old Dame Gothel does, and she says yes, and laid her hand in his. She said: 'I will willingly go away with you, but I do not know how to get down. Bring with you a skein of silk every time that you come, and I will weave a ladder with it, and when that is ready, I will descend, and you will take me on your horse.' They agreed that until that time, he should come to her every evening, for the old woman came by day. The enchantress remarked nothing of this until once Rapunzel said to her: 'Tell me, Dame Gothel, how it happens that you are so much heavier for me to draw up than the young king's son—he is with me in a moment.' 'Ah! You wicked child,' cried the enchantress. 'What do I hear you say! I thought I had separated you from all the world, yet you have deceived me!' In her anger, she clutched Rapunzel's beautiful tresses, wrapped them twice around her left hand, seized a pair of scissors with the right, and snip, snap, they were cut off, and the lovely braids lay on the ground. And she was so pitiless that she took poor Rapunzel into a desert where she had to live in great grief and misery.

On the same day that she cast out Rapunzel, however, the enchantress fastened the braids of hair, which she had cut off, to the hook of the window, and when the king's son came and cried:

'Rapunzel, Rapunzel,

Let down your hair to me.'

She let the hair down. The king's son ascended, but instead of finding his dearest Rapunzel, he found the enchantress, who gazed at him with wicked and venomous looks. 'Aha!' she cried mockingly, 'you would fetch your dearest, but the beautiful bird sits no longer singing in the nest; the cat has it and will scratch out your eyes as well. Rapunzel is lost to you; you will never see her again.' The king's son was beside himself with pain, and in his despair, he leaped down from the tower. He escaped with his life, but the thorns into which he fell pierced his eyes. Then he wandered quite blind about the forest, ate nothing but roots and berries, and did naught but lament and weep over the loss of his dearest wife. Thus he roamed about in misery for some years and at length came to the desert where Rapunzel, with the twins to which she had given birth, a boy and a girl, lived in wretchedness. He heard a voice that seemed so familiar to him that he went towards it, and when he approached, Rapunzel knew him and fell on his neck and wept. Two of her tears wetted his eyes, and they grew clear again, and he could see with them as before. He led her to his kingdom, where he was joyfully received, and they lived happily and contented for a long time afterward.

The King's Servant

by Maud Lindsay

There was once upon a time a faithful servant whose name was Hans. He served the king his master so long and so well that one day the king said to him: "Speak, Hans, and tell me what three things you most desire that I may give them to you as a reward for your faithfulness."

Adapted with a free hand from Grimm's "White Snake."

It did not take Hans long to answer the king.

"If you please, your majesty," he said, "I should

like best in all the world to go to see my mother; to have a horse on which to ride upon my journey, and to taste the food that lies hidden in the silver dish that comes each day to your majesty's table."

And when the king heard this, he made haste to send for the silver dish and, lifting the lid with his own hand, he bade Hans taste the food inside. What this food was, neither I nor anybody else can tell you, but no sooner had Hans tasted it than he understood what everything in the world was saying, from the birds in the tree-tops to the hens in the king's poultry yard.

"Goodbye, Hans," they called as Hans mounted the horse the king gave him and rode away through the gate.

"Goodbye," said Hans, and he cantered off in fine style down the king's highway.

Before he had ridden far, however, he heard such a moaning and complaining by the roadside that he stopped his horse from seeing what the matter was; and—do you believe it?—it was the ant people whose ant hill stood in the way, right where Hans was about to ride.

"See, see!" they cried, running to and fro in great alarm. "This giant of a man on his terrible horse will ride over our new house and crush us to death."

"Not I," said Hans. "If so much as one of you gets under my horse's hoofs, it will be your fault and not mine;" getting down from his horse, he led him around the ant hill and into the road on the other side.

"One good turn deserves another," cried the ant people running to and fro in great joy. "You have helped us, and we will help you someday," and they were still saying this when Hans mounted his horse and rode away.

Before long, Hans came to a great forest, and as he rode under the spreading branches of the trees, he heard a cry for help in the woods.

"What can this be?" said Hans; but the very next minute, he saw two young birds lying beneath a tree, beating their wings upon the ground and crying aloud:

"Alas! Alas! Who will put us into the nest again?"

"I, the king's servant and my mother's son, will put you into the nest again," said Hans, and he was as good as his word.

"One good turn deserves another," called the birds when they were safe in their nest. "You have helped us, and we will help you someday."

Hans laughed to hear them, for though it was easy for him to help them, he could not think what they might do for him.

Trot, trot, and gallop gallop he rode through the forest till he came to a stream of water beside which lay three panting fishes.

"We shall surely die unless we can get into the

water," they cried.

Their breath was almost gone, and their voices were no louder than the faintest whisper, but Hans understood every word they said, and he jumped from his horse and threw them into the stream.

"One good turn deserves another," they cried as they swam merrily away. "You have helped us, and we will help you someday."

Now it so happened that Hans came by and by to the land of a wicked king who broke his promises as easily as if they were made of spun glass and never thought of anybody but himself.

No sooner had Hans come into the land than the king stopped him and would not let him go on.

"No one shall pass through my kingdom," he said, "till he has done one piece of work for me."

Hans was not afraid of work. "Show it to me that I may do it at once," he said, "for I am hastening to see my mother."

Then the king took Hans into a room as large as a meadow where some of all the seeds in the world were stored. There were lettuce seeds, and radish-seeds, flax seeds and grains of rice, fine seeds of flowers, and small seeds of grass, all mixed and mingled till no two alike lay together.

Hans had never seen so many seeds in all his life before, and when he had looked at them, the king bade him sort them, each kind to itself.

"The lettuce seed must be here, and the radish seed there; the flax seed in this corner and the grains of rice in another; the fine seeds of flowers must be in their place, and the small seeds of grass all ready for planting before you can pass through my kingdom and go on your way," he said. When he had spoken, he went out of the room and locked the door behind him.

Poor Hans! He sat down on the floor and cried —the tears rolled down his cheeks, I do assure you—for he said to himself:

"If I live to be a hundred years old, I can never do this thing that the king requires. I shall never again see my mother or the good king, my master."

How long he sat there, neither I nor anybody else can tell you, but by and by, he saw a little black ant creeping in through a crack in the floor. Behind it came another and another, like soldiers marching; one by one, they came till the whole floor was black with hundreds and hundreds of the ant people.

"You helped us, and we have come to help you," they said; and they set to work at once to sort the seed as the king required.

The next day when the king came in to inquire how Hans was getting on, the work was done. The lettuce seed was here, the radish seed was there, the flax seed in one corner, and the grains of rice in another; the fine seeds of flowers were in their place, and the small seeds of grass were all ready for planting.

The king was astonished. He could scarcely

believe his eyes, but he would not let Hans go.

"Such a fine workman must do one other piece of work before he passes through my kingdom," he said; and he took Hans out in the open country and pointed to an orchard far away.

"Bring me one golden apple that grows in that orchard, and you shall go free," he said.

"Ah, what an easy task is this," said Hans, and he set off at once to the orchard.

But, alack, when he had come to the orchard gate, it was guarded by a fiery dragon, the like of which he had never seen in all his life! "Come and be devoured!" it cried as Hans came into sight.

Poor Hans! He sat down by the roadside and held his head between his hands and cried—the tears rolled down his cheeks, I do assure you—for he said to himself:

"If I go into the orchard, I shall be eaten alive by the dragon, and if I do not go, I shall never see my mother or the good king, my master, again."

How long he sat there, neither I nor anybody else can tell you, but by and by, he saw two birds flying through the air. Nearer and nearer they came till, at last, they reached the spot where Hans sat and lighted at his feet. And they were the very birds that Hans had helped. Their wings had grown strong enough by this time to carry them wherever they wanted to go, and they flapped them joyfully as they cried:

"One good turn deserves another. You helped us, and we have come to help you."

It was no trouble for them to fly into the orchard high above the dragon's head, and almost before Hans knew they were gone, they were back again, bringing the golden apple that the king desired.

He was astonished when Hans took it to him. He could scarcely believe his eyes, but he would not let Hans go.

Instead, he took a ring from his finger and threw it to the very bottom of the sea.

"Go and fetch me that ring," he said, "and you shall be free as the birds and the bees, but until it is upon my finger again, you shall not pass through my kingdom."

Poor Hans! He sat down on the seashore and cried—the tears rolled down his cheeks, I do assure you—for he said to himself:

"Who can do a task like this? I must either drown or stay here all the days of my life. I shall never again see my mother or the good king, my master."

How long he sat there, neither I nor anybody else can tell you, but by and by, three little fishes came swimming to the shore.

"One good turn deserves another," they called, for they were the very fish that Hans had thrown into the stream. "You helped us, and we have come to help you."

Then down they went to the very bottom of the sea where the king's ring lay. One of them took it in his mouth and brought it safely to Hans, who ran with it to the king.

And when the king saw the ring, he knew that he must let Hans go; he did not dare to keep him any longer.

So Hans mounted his horse and rode joyfully to his mother's home, where he stayed till the time came when he must return to the good king, his master, which he did by another road.

He worked well and was happy serving his master faithfully and making friends with birds and beasts all the days of his life, but never again did he go to the wicked king's country. And I, for one, think he showed his good sense by that.

Little Snow-White

by Brothers Grimm

Once upon a time, in the middle of winter, when the flakes of snow were falling like feathers from the clouds, a Queen sat at her palace window, which had an ebony black frame, stitching her husband's shirts. While she was thus engaged and looking out at the snow, she pricked her finger, and three drops of blood fell upon the snow. Now the red looked so well upon the white that she thought, "Oh, that I had a child as white as this snow, as red as this blood, and as black as the wood of this frame!" Soon afterward a little daughter came to her, who was as white as snow, with cheeks as a red as blood, and with hair as black as ebony, and from this, she was named "Snow-White." And at the same time, her mother died.

About a year afterward, the King married another wife, who was very beautiful but so proud and arrogant that she could not bear anyone to be better-looking than herself. She owned a wonderful mirror, and when she stepped before it and said:

"Mirror, mirror on the wall,

Who is the fairest of us all?"

It replied:

"The Queen is the fairest of the day."

Then she was pleased, for she knew that the mirror spoke truly.

Little Snow-White, however, grew up and became prettier and prettier, and when she was seven years old, she was as fair as the noonday and more beautiful than the Queen herself. When the Queen now asked her mirror:

"Mirror, mirror on the wall,

Who is the fairest of us all?"

It replied:

"The Queen was the fairest yesterday;

Snow White is the fairest, now, they say."

This answer so angered the Queen that she became quite yellow with envy. From that hour, whenever she saw Snow White, her heart hardened against her, and she hated the little girl. Her envy and jealousy increased so that she had no rest day or night, and she said to a Huntsman, "Take the child away into the forest. I will never look upon her again. You must kill her and bring me her heart and tongue for a token."

The Huntsman listened and took the maiden away, but when he drew out his knife to kill her, she began to cry, saying, "Ah, dear Huntsman, give me my life! I will run into the wild forest and never come home again."

This speech softened Hunter's heart, and her beauty touched him so that he had pity on her and said, "Well, run away then, poor child." But he thought, "The wild beasts will soon devour you." Still, he felt as if a stone had been lifted from his heart because her death was not by his hand. Just at that moment, a young boar came roaring along to the spot, and as soon as he clapped eyes upon it, the Huntsman caught it and, killing it, took its tongue and heart and carried them to the Queen for a token of his deed.

But now poor little Snow-White was left motherless and alone, and overcome with grief, she was bewildered at the sight of so many trees and knew not which way to turn. She ran till her feet refused to go farther, and as it was getting dark and she saw a little house near, she entered to rest. In this cottage, everything was very small but very neat and elegant. In the middle stood a little table with a white cloth over it, with seven little plates upon it, each plate having a spoon, a knife, and a fork, and there were also seven little mugs. Against the wall were seven little beds arranged in a row, each covered with snow-white sheets.

Little Snow-White, being both hungry and thirsty, ate a little morsel of porridge out of each plate and drank a drop or two of wine out of each mug, for she did not wish to take away the whole share of anyone. After that, because she was so tired, she laid herself down on one bed, but it did not suit her; she tried another, but that was too long; a fourth was too short, a fifth too hard. But the seventh was just the thing, and tucking herself up in it, she went to sleep, first saying her prayers as usual.

When it became quite dark, the owners of the cottage came home, seven Dwarfs, who dug for gold and silver in the mountains. They first lighted seven little lamps and saw at once—for they lit up the whole room—that somebody had been in, for everything was not in the order they had left.

Who has been eating off my plate?

The first asked, "Who has been sitting on my chair?" The second, "Who has been eating off my plate?" The third said, "Who has been nibbling at my bread?" The fourth, "Who has been at my porridge?" The fifth, "Who has been meddling with my fork?" The sixth grumbled, "Who has been cutting with my knife?" The seventh said, "Who has been drinking out of my mug?"

Then the first, looking round, began again,

"Who has been lying on my bed?" he asked, for he saw that the sheets were tumbled. At these words, the others came and, looking at their beds, cried out, too, "Someone has been lying in our beds!" But the seventh little man, running up to his, saw Snow White sleeping in it, so he called his companions, who shouted with wonder and held up their seven lamps so that the light fell upon the little girl.

"Oh, heavens! Oh, heavens!" said they; "what a beauty she is!" and they were so much delighted that they would not awaken her but left her to sleep, and the seventh Dwarf, in whose bed she was, slept with each of his fellows one hour, and so passed the night.

As soon as morning dawned, Snow-White awoke and was quite frightened when she saw the seven little men, but they were very friendly and asked her what she was called.

"My name is Snow-White," was her reply.

"Why have you come into our cottage?" they asked.

Then she told them how her stepmother would have had her killed, but the Huntsman had spared her life and how she had wandered about the Whole day until she had finally found their house.

When her tale was finished, the Dwarfs said, "Will you look after our household—be our cook, make the beds, wash, sew, and knit for us, and keep everything in neat order? We will keep you here if so, and you shall want for nothing."

And Snow-White answered, "Yes, with all my heart and will." And so she remained with them and kept their house in order.

In the morning, the Dwarfs went into the mountains and searched for silver and gold, and in the evening, they came home and found their meals ready. During the day, the maiden was left alone, and therefore the good Dwarfs warned her and said, "Be careful of your stepmother, who will soon know of your being here. So let nobody enter the cottage."

The Queen, supposing that she had eaten the heart and tongue of her stepdaughter, believed that she was now, above all, the most beautiful woman in the world. One day she stepped before her mirror and said:

"Mirror, mirror on the wall,

Who is the fairest of us all?"

and it replied:

"The Queen was the fairest yesterday;

Snow-White is fairest now, they say.

The Dwarfs protect her from thy sway

Amid the forest, far away."

This reply surprised her, but she knew that the mirror spoke the truth. She knew, therefore, that the Huntsman had deceived her and that Snow White was still alive. So she dyed her face and clothed herself as a peddler woman so that no one could recognize her, and in this disguise, she went over the seven hills to the house of the seven Dwarfs. She knocked at the hut's door and called, "Fine goods for sale! Beautiful goods for sale!"

Snow-White peeped out the window and said, "Good day, my good woman; what have you to sell?"

"Fine goods, beautiful goods!" she replied. "Stays of all colors." And she held up a pair which were made of many-colored silks.

"I may let in this honest woman," thought Snow White, and she unbolted the door and bargained for one pair of stays.

"You can't think, my dear, how they become you!" exclaimed the old woman. "Come, let me lace them up for you."

Snow-White suspected nothing and let her do as she wished, but the old woman laced her up so quickly and so tightly that all her breath went, and she fell down like one dead. "Now," thought the old woman to herself, hastening away, "am I once more the most beautiful of all!"

The Dwarfs were frightened at seeing their dear little maid lying on the ground. The Dwarfs were much frightened at seeing their dear little maid lying on the ground.

At eventide, not long after she had left, the seven Dwarfs came home and were much frightened at seeing their dear little maid lying on the ground, neither moving nor breathing, as if she were dead. They raised her up, and when they saw that she was laced too tight, they cut the stays to pieces, and presently she began to breathe again, and little by little, she revived. When the Dwarfs heard what had happened, they said, "The old pedlar woman was no other than your wicked stepmother. Take care of yourself, and let no one enter when we are not with you."

Meanwhile, the Queen had reached home, and, going before her mirror, she repeated her usual words:

"Mirror, mirror on the wall,

Who is the fairest of us all?"

And it replied as before:

"The Queen was the fairest yesterday;

Snow-White is fairest now, they say.

The Dwarfs protect her from thy sway

Amid the forest, far away."

As soon as it finished, all her blood rushed to her heart, for she was so angry to hear that Snow-White was still living. "But now," she thought, "will I make something which shall destroy her completely." Thus saying, she made a poisoned comb by arts which she understood, and then, disguising herself, she took the form of an old widow. She went over the seven hills to the house of the seven Dwarfs, and, knocking at the door, called out, "Good wares to sell today!"

Snow-White peeped out and said, "You must go farther, for I dare not let you in."

But still, you may look, said the old woman, drawing out her poisoned comb.

"But still, you may look," said the old woman, drawing out her poisoned comb and holding it up. The sight of this pleased the maiden so much that she allowed herself to be persuaded and opened the door. As soon as she had bought something, the old woman said, "Now let me for once comb your hair properly," and Snow White consented. But the comb was barely drawn through the hair when the poison began to work, and the maiden fell senseless.

"Your pattern of beauty" cried the wicked Queen, "is now all over with you." And so saying, she departed.

Fortunately, the evening soon came, and the seven Dwarfs returned, and as soon as they saw Snow-White lying, like dead, on the ground, they suspected the Queen, and discovering the poisoned comb, they immediately drew it out. Then the maiden very soon revived and told them all that had happened. So again, they warned her against the wicked stepmother and bade her open the door to nobody.

Meanwhile, the Queen, on her arrival home, had again consulted her mirror and received the same answer as twice before. This made her tremble and foam with rage and jealousy, and she swore Snow-White should die if it cost her her own life. She went into a secret inner chamber where no one could enter and made an apple of the most deep and subtle poison.

Outwardly it looked nice enough and had rosy cheeks, which would make the mouth of everyone who looked at its water, but whoever ate the smallest piece of it would surely die. As soon as the apple was ready, the Queen again dyed her face, clothed herself like a peasant's wife, and then over the seven mountains to the house of the seven Dwarfs, she made her way.

She knocked at the door, and Snow-White stretched out her head and said, "I dare not let anyone enter; the seven Dwarfs have forbidden me."

"That is hard on me," said the old woman, "for I must take back my apples, but there is one which I will give you."

"No," answered Snow White; "no, I dare not take it."

"What! are you afraid of it?" cried the old woman. "There, see—I will cut the apple in halves; do you eat the red cheeks, and I will eat the core." (The apple was so artfully made that the red cheeks alone were poisoned.) Snow White very much wished for the beautiful apple, and when she saw the woman eating the core, she could no longer resist but, stretching out her hand, took the poisoned part. Scarcely had she placed a piece in her mouth when she fell down dead on the ground. Then the Queen, looking at her with glittering eyes, and laughing bitterly, exclaimed, "White as snow, red as blood, black as ebony! This time the Dwarfs cannot reawaken you.

When she reached home and consulted her

mirror—

"Mirror, mirror on the wall,

Who is the fairest of us all?"

It answered:

"The Queen is fairest of the day."

The Queen is the fairest of the day.

Then her envious heart was at rest, as peacefully as an envious heart can rest.

When the little Dwarfs returned home in the evening, they found Snow-White lying on the ground, and there appeared to be no life in her body; she seemed quite dead. They raised her up and tried they could find anything poisonous. They unlaced her, even uncombed her hair, and washed her with water and wine. But nothing availed: the dear child was really and truly dead.

Then they laid her upon a bier, and all seven placed themselves around it and wept for three days without ceasing. Then they prepared to bury her. But she looked still fresh and life-like, and even her red cheeks had not deserted her, so they said to one another, "We cannot bury her in the black ground." Then they ordered a case to be made of glass. In this, they could see the body on all sides, and the Dwarfs wrote her name with golden letters on the glass, saying that she was a King's daughter. Now they placed the glass case upon the ledge on a rock, and one of them always remained by it watching. Even the birds lamented about the loss of Snow White; first came an owl, then a raven, and last of all, a dove.

For a long time, Snow White lay peacefully in her case and changed not but looked as if she were only asleep, for she was still white as snow, red as blood, and black-haired as ebony. It happened that a King's son was traveling in the forest and came to the Dwarfs' house to pass the night. He soon saw the glass case upon the rock and the beautiful maiden lying within, and he also read the golden inscription.

When he had examined it, he said to the Dwarfs, "Let me have this case, and I will pay what you like for it."

But the Dwarfs replied, "We will not sell it for all the gold in the world."

"Then give it to me," said the Prince, "for I cannot live without Snow White. I will honor and protect her as long as I live."

When the Dwarfs saw that he was so much in earnest, they pitied him and, at last, gave him the case, and the Prince ordered it to be carried away on the shoulders of his attendants. Presently, happened that they stumbled over a rut, and with the shock, the piece of poisoned apple which lay in Snow-White's mouth fell out. Very soon, she opened her eyes, and raising the lid of the glass case, she rose up and asked, "Where am I?"

Full of joy, the Prince answered, "You are safe with me." And he told her what she had suffered and how he would rather have her than any other for his wife, and he asked her to accompany him home to the castle of the King, his father. Snow-White consented, and they were married with great splendor and magnificence when they arrived there.

Snow-White's stepmother was also invited to the wedding, and when she is dressed in all her finery to go, she first steps in front of her mirror and asks:

"Mirror, mirror on the wall,

Who is the fairest of us all?"

And it replied:

"The Queen was the fairest yesterday;

The Prince's bride is now, they say."

At these words, the Queen was in a fury and was so terribly mortified that she knew not what to do with herself. At first, she resolved not to go to the wedding, but she could not resist the wish to see the Princess. So she went, but as soon as she saw the bride, she recognized Snow White and was so terrified with rage and astonishment that she rushed out of the castle and was never heard from again.

Hansel and Gretel

by Brothers Grimm

Hard by a great forest dwelt a poor wood-cutter with his wife and his two children. The boy was called Hansel, and the girl was Gretel. He had little to bite and break, and once great dearth fell on the land, he could no longer procure even daily bread. Now when he thought over this by night in his bed and tossed about in his anxiety, he groaned and said to his wife: 'What is to become of us? How can we feed our poor children when we no longer have anything for ourselves?' 'I'll tell you what, husband,' answered the woman, 'early tomorrow morning, we will take the children out into the forest to where it is the thickest; there, we will light a fire for them and give each of them one more piece of bread, and then we will go to our work and leave them alone. They will not find the way home again, and we shall be rid of them.' 'No, wife,' said the man, 'I will not do that; how can I bear to leave my children alone in the forest?—the wild animals would soon come and tear them to pieces.' 'O, you fool!' said she, 'then we must all four die of hunger. You may as well plane the planks for our coffins,' and she left him no peace until he consented. 'But I feel very sorry for the poor children, all the same,' said the man.

The two children had also been unable to sleep for hunger and heard what their stepmother said to their father. Gretel wept bitter tears and said to Hansel: 'Now all is over with us.' 'Be quiet, Gretel,' said Hansel, 'do not distress yourself. I will soon find a way to help us.' And when the old folks had fallen asleep, he got up, put on his little coat, opened the door below, and crept outside. The moon shone brightly, and the white pebbles in front of the house glittered like real silver pennies. Hansel stooped and stuffed the little pocket of his coat with as many as he could. Then he returned and said to Gretel: 'Be comforted, dear little sister, and sleep in peace. God will not forsake us,' He lay down again in his bed. When day dawned, but before the sun had risen, the woman came and awoke the two children, saying: 'Get up, you sluggards! we are going into the forest to fetch wood.' She gave each a little piece of bread and said: 'There is something for your dinner, but do not eat it up before then, for you will get nothing else.' Gretel took the bread under her apron as Hansel had the pebbles in his pocket. Then they all set out together on the way to the forest. When they had walked a short time, Hansel stood still, peeped back at the house, and did so again and again. His father said: 'Hansel, what are you looking at there and staying behind for? Pay attention, and do not forget how to use your legs.' 'Ah, father,' said Hansel, 'I am looking at my little white cat, which is sitting on the roof and wants to say goodbye to me.' The wife said: 'Fool, that is not your little cat. That is the morning sun which is shining on the chimneys.' Hansel, however, had not been looking back at the cat but had constantly been throwing one of the white pebble stones out of his pocket on the road.

When they reached the middle of the forest, the father said: 'Now, children, pile up some wood, and I will light a fire that you may not be cold.' Hansel and Gretel gathered brushwood together as high as a little hill. The brushwood was lighted, and when the flames burned very high, the woman said: 'Now, children, lay yourselves down by the fire and rest. We will go into the forest and cut some wood. We will come back and fetch you away when we have done.'

Hansel and Gretel sat by the fire, and when noon came, each ate a little piece of bread, and as they heard the strokes of the wood axe, they believed that their father was near.

It was not the axe but a branch that he had fastened to a withered tree which the wind was blowing backward and forwards. And as they had been sitting such a long time, their eyes closed with fatigue, and they fell fast asleep. When at last they awoke, it was already a dark night. Gretel began to cry and said: 'How are we to get out of the forest now?' But Hansel comforted her and said: 'Just wait for a little until the moon has risen, and then we will soon find the way.' And when the full moon had risen, Hansel took his little sister by the hand and followed the pebbles, which shone like newly-coined silver pieces, and showed them the way.

They walked the whole night long and, by break of day, came once more to their father's house. They knocked at the door, and when the woman opened it and saw that it was Hansel and Gretel, she said: 'You naughty children, why have you slept so long in the forest?—we thought you were never coming back at all!' The father rejoiced, for it had cut him to the heart to leave them behind alone.

Not long afterward, there was more great dearth throughout the land, and the children heard their mother saying at night to their father: 'Everything is eaten again, we have one-half loaf left, and that is the end. The children must go. We will take them farther into the wood so they will not find their way out again; there are no other means of saving ourselves!' The man's heart was heavy, and he thought: 'It would be better for you to share the last mouthful with your children.' The woman would listen to nothing he had to say but scolded and reproached him. He who says A must say B, likewise, and as he had yielded the first time, he had to do so a second time.

The children, however, were still awake and had heard the conversation. When the old folks were asleep, Hansel again got up and wanted to go out and pick up pebbles as before, but the woman had locked the door, and Hansel could not get out. Nevertheless, he comforted his little sister and said: 'Do not cry, Gretel. Go to sleep quietly. The good God will help us.'

The woman took the children out of their beds early in the morning. Their piece of bread was given to them, but it was still smaller than before. On the way into the forest, Hansel crumbled in his pocket and often stood still and threw a morsel on the ground. 'Hansel, why do you stop and look round?' said the father, 'go on.' 'I am looking back at my little pigeon, sitting on the roof, and wants to say goodbye to me,' answered Hansel. 'Fool!' said the woman, 'that is not your little pigeon. That is the morning sun that is shining on the chimney.' Hansel, however, little by little, threw all the crumbs on the path.

The woman led the children still deeper into the forest, where they never had in their lives before. Then a great fire was again made, and the mother said: 'Just sit there, you children, and when you are tired, you may sleep a little; we are going into the forest to cut wood, and in the evening, when we are done, we will come and fetch you away.' At noon, Gretel shared her piece of bread with Hansel, who had scattered his. Then they fell asleep, and evening passed, but no one came to the poor children. They did not awake until it was a dark night, and Hansel comforted his little sister and said: 'Just wait, Gretel, until the moon rises, and then we shall see the crumbs of bread which I have strewn about. They will show us our way home again.' When the moon came, they set out, but they found no crumbs, for the many thousands of birds that fly about in the woods and fields had picked them all up. Hansel said to Gretel: 'We shall soon find the way,' but they did not find it. They walked the whole night and all the next day, too, from morning till evening, but they did not get out of the forest and were very hungry, for they had nothing to eat but two or three berries, which grew on the ground. And as they were so weary that their legs would carry them no longer, they lay down beneath a tree and fell asleep.

It was now three mornings since they had left their father's house. They began to walk again, but they always came deeper into the forest, and if help did not come soon, they must die of hunger and weariness. When it was midday, they saw a beautiful snow-white bird sitting on a bough, which sang so delightfully that they stood still and listened to it. And when its song was over, it spread its wings and flew away before them, and they followed it until they reached a little house, on the roof of which it alighted; and when they approached the little house, they saw that it was built of bread and covered with cakes, but that the windows were of clear sugar. 'We will work on that,' said Hansel, 'and have a good meal. I will eat a bit of the roof, and you, Gretel, can eat some of the windows. It will taste sweet.' Hansel reached above and broke off a little of the roof to try how it tasted, and Gretel leaned against the window and nibbled at the panes. Then a soft voice cried from the parlor:

'Nibble, nibble, gnaw,

Who is nibbling at my little house?'

The children answered:

'The wind, the wind,

The heaven-born wind,'

and went on eating without disturbing themselves. Hansel, who liked the taste of the roof, tore down a great piece of it, and Gretel pushed out the whole of one round window pane, sat down, and enjoyed herself with it. Suddenly the door opened, and a woman as old as the hills, who supported herself on crutches, came creeping out. Hansel and Gretel were so terribly frightened that they let fall what they had in their hands. However, the old woman nodded and said: 'Oh, you dear children, who have brought you here? Do come in, and stay with me. No harm shall happen to you.' She took them both by the hand and led them into her little house. Then good food was set before them, milk and pancakes with sugar, apples, and nuts. Afterward, two pretty little beds were covered with clean white linen, and Hansel and Gretel lay down in them and thought they were in heaven.

The old woman had only pretended to be so kind; she was, in reality, a wicked witch, who lay in wait for children, and had only built the little house of bread to entice them there. When a child fell into her power, she killed it, cooked, and ate it; that was a feast day with her. Witches have red eyes and cannot see far, but they have a keen scent like the beasts and are aware of when human beings draw near. When Hansel and Gretel came into her neighborhood, she laughed with malice and said mockingly: 'I have them. They shall not escape me again!' Early in the morning, before the children were awake, she was already up, and when she saw both of them sleeping and looking so pretty, with their plump and rosy cheeks, she muttered to herself: 'That will be a dainty mouthful!' Then she seized Hansel with her shriveled hand, carried him into a little stable, and locked him in behind a grated door. Scream as he might, it would not help him. Then she went to Gretel, shook her till she awoke, and cried: 'Get up, lazy thing, fetch some water and cook something good for your brother. He is in the stable outside and is to be made fat. I will eat him when he is fat.' Gretel began to weep bitterly, but it was all in vain, for she was forced to do what the wicked witch commanded.

And now the best food was cooked for poor Hansel, but Gretel got nothing but crab shells. Every morning the woman crept to the little stable and cried: 'Hansel, stretch out your finger that I may feel if you will soon be fat.' Hansel, however, stretched out a little bone to her, and the old woman, who had dim eyes, could not see it and thought it was Hansel's finger and was astonished that there was no way of fattening him. When four weeks had gone by, and Hansel remained thin, she was seized with impatience and would not wait any longer. 'Now, then, Gretel,' she cried to the girl, 'stir yourself and bring some water. Let Hansel be fat or lean. Tomorrow I will kill him and cook him.' Ah, how the poor little sister did lament when she had to fetch the water and how her tears did flow down her cheeks! 'Dear God, do help us,' she cried. 'If the wild beasts in the forest had but devoured us, we should, at any rate, have died together.' 'Just keep your noise to yourself,' said the old woman, 'it won't help you at all.'

Early in the morning, Gretel had to go out, hang up the cauldron with the water, and light the fire. 'We will bake first,' said the old woman, 'I have already heated the oven and kneaded the dough.' She pushed poor Gretel out to the oven, from which flames of fire were already darting. 'Creep in,' said the witch, 'and see if it is properly heated so we can put the bread in.' And once Gretel was inside, she intended to shut the oven and let her bake in it, and then she would eat her, too. But Gretel saw what she had in mind and said: 'I do not know how I am to do it; how do I get in?' 'Silly goose,' said the old woman. 'The door is big enough; just look, I can get in myself!' She crept up and thrust her head into the oven. Then Gretel gave her a push that drove her far into it, shut the iron door, and fastened the bolt. Oh! Then she began to howl quite horribly, but Gretel ran away, and the godless witch was miserably burnt to death.

Gretel, however, ran like lightning to Hansel, opened his little stable, and cried: 'Hansel, we are saved! The old witch is dead!' Then Hansel sprang like a bird from its cage when the door was opened. How they rejoice, embrace, dance, and kiss each other! And as they no longer needed to fear her, they went into the witch's house, and in every corner stood chests full of pearls and jewels. 'These are far better than pebbles!' said Hansel, and thrust into his pockets whatever could be got in, and Gretel said: 'I, too, will take something home with me,' and filled her pinafore full. 'But now we must be off,' said Hansel, 'that we may get out of the witch's forest.'

When they had walked for two hours, they came to a great stretch of water. 'We cannot cross,' said Hansel, 'I see no foot-plank and no bridge.' 'And there is also no ferry,' answered Gretel, 'but a white duck is swimming there: if I ask her, she will help us over.' Then she cried:

'Little duck, little duck, dost thou see,

Hansel and Gretel are waiting for thee?

There's never a plank or bridge in sight,

Take us across on thy back so white.'

The duck came to them, and Hansel seated himself on its back and told his sister to sit by him. 'No,' replied Gretel, 'that will be too heavy for the little duck; she shall take us across, one after the other.' The good little duck did so, and when they were once safely across and had walked for a short time, the forest seemed to be more and more familiar to them, and at length, they saw from afar their father's house. Then they began to run, rushed into the parlor, and threw themselves around their father's neck. The man had not known one happy hour since he had left the children in the forest; the woman, however, was dead. Gretel emptied her pinafore until pearls and precious stones ran about the room, and Hansel threw one handful after another out of his pocket to add to them. Then all anxiety ended, and they lived together in perfect happiness. My tale is done. There runs a mouse; whosoever catches it may make himself a big fur cap out of it.

The Magician Turned Mischief-Maker

by Juliana Horatia Ewing

Once, a wicked magician prospered and did much evil for many years. But there came a day when Vengeance, disguised as a blind beggar, overtook him, outwitted him, and stole his magic wand. With this, he had been accustomed to turning those who offended him into any shape he pleased; and now that he had lost it, he could only transform himself.

As Vengeance returned to his place, he passed through a village, the inhabitants of which had formerly lived in great terror of the magician, and told them of the downfall of his power. But they only said, "Blind beggars have long tongues. One must not believe all one hears," and shrugged their shoulders and left him.

Then Vengeance waved the wand and said, "As you have doubted me, distress each other," and departed.

By and by, he came to another village and told the news. But here the villagers were full of delight, and made a feast, and put the blind beggar in the place of honor; who, when he departed, said, "As you have done by me, deal with each other always!" and went on to the next village.

In this place, he was received with an even warmer welcome; when the feast was over, the people brought him to the bridge which led out of the village and gave him a guide dog to help him on his way.

Then the blind beggar waved the wand once more and said;

"Those who are so good to strangers must be good to each other. But that nothing may be wanting to the peace of this place. I grant the beasts and birds in it that they may understand the language of men."

Then he broke the wand into pieces and threw

it into the stream. And when the people turned their heads again from watching the bits as they floated away, the blind beggar was gone.

Meanwhile, the magician was wild with rage at losing his wand, for all his pleasure was to do harm and hurt. But when he came to himself, he said: "One can do a good deal of harm with his tongue. I will turn mischief-maker, and I can escape in what form I please when the place is too hot to hold me."

Then he came to the first village, where Vengeance had gone before, and here he lived for a year and a day in various disguises, and he made more misery with his tongue than he had ever accomplished in any other year with his magic wand. Everyone distrusted his neighbor and was ready to believe ill of him. So parents disowned their children, husband and wives parted, lovers broke faith, and servants and masters disagreed. Old friends became bitter enemies till, at last, the place was intolerable even to the magician, and he changed himself into a cockchafer and flew to the next village, where, Vengeance had gone before.

He also dwelt for a year and a day, leaving it because he could do no harm. Those who loved each other trusted each other, and the magician made mischief in vain. In one of his disguises, he was detected and only escaped with his life from the enraged villagers by changing himself into a cockchafer and flying on to the next place, where Vengeance had gone before.

He made less mischief in this village than in the first and more in the second. And he exercised all his art and changed his disguises constantly, but the dogs knew him.

One dog—the oldest dog in the place—was keeping watch over the miller's house when he saw the magician approaching in the disguise of an old woman.

"Do you see that old witch?" said he to the sparrows, who were picking up stray bits of grain in the yard. "With her evil tongue, she is parting my master's daughter and the finest young fellow in the countryside. She puts lies and truth together with more skill than you patch moss and feathers to build nests. And when she is asked where she heard this or that, she says, 'A little bird told me so.'"

"We never told her," said the sparrows indignantly, "and if we had your strength, Master Keeper, she should not malign us long!"

"I believe you are right!" said Master Keeper. "Of what avail is it that we have learned the language of men if we do not help them to the utmost of our powers? She shall torment my young mistress no more."

Saying which, he flew upon the disguised magician as he entered the gate and would have torn him limb from limb, but the mischief-maker changed himself as before into a cockchafer and flew hastily from the village.

And thus, he might doubtless have escaped

doing yet further harm had not three cock-sparrows overtaken him just before he crossed the bridge.

From three sides, they hemmed him in, crying, "Which of us told you?" "Which of us told you?" "Which of us told you?"—and pecked him to pieces before he could transform himself again.

After which peace and prosperity befell all the neighborhood.

Jack and the Beanstalk

by Joseph Jacobs

There was once upon a time a poor widow with an only son named Jack and a cow named Milky-white. And all they had to live on was the cow's milk every morning, which they carried to the market and sold. But one morning, Milky-white gave no milk, and they didn't know what to do.

"What shall we do, what shall we do?" said the

widow, wringing her hands.

"Cheer up, mother. I'll go and get work somewhere," said Jack.

"We've tried that before, and nobody would take you," said his mother; "we must sell Milky-white and, with the money, do something, start shop or something."

"All right, mother," says Jack, "it's the market day today, and I'll soon sell Milky white, and then we'll see what we can do."

So he took the cow's halter in his hand and started off. He hadn't gone far when he met a funny-looking old man who said to him: "Good morning, Jack."

"Good morning to you," said Jack, and he wondered how he knew his name.

"Well, Jack, where are you off to?" said the man.

"I'm going to market to sell our cow here."

"Oh, you look the proper sort of chap to sell cows," said the man; "I wonder if you know how many beans make five."

"Two in each hand and one in your mouth," says Jack, as sharp as a needle.

"Right you are," said the man, "and here they are, the very beans themselves," he went on pulling out of his pocket a number of strange-looking beans. "As you are so sharp," says he, "I don't mind doing a swop with you—your cow for these beans."

"Walker!" says Jack; "wouldn't you like it?"

"Ah! You don't know what these beans are," said the man; "if you plant them overnight by morning, they grow right up to the sky."

"Really?" says Jack; "you don't say so."

"Yes, that is so, and if it doesn't turn out to be true, you can have your cow back."

"Right," says Jack, and hands him over Milky-white's halter and pockets the beans.

Back goes Jack home, and as he hadn't gone very far, it wasn't dusk by the time he got to his door.

"What back, Jack?" said his mother; "I see you haven't got Milky-white, so you've sold her. How much did you get for her?"

"You'll never guess, mother," says Jack.

"No, you don't say so. Good boy! Five pounds, ten, fifteen, no, it can't be twenty."

"I told you you couldn't guess what you say to these beans; they're magical; plant them over-night and ____"

"What!" says Jack's mother, "have you been such a fool, such a dolt, such an idiot, to give away my Milky-white, the best milker in the parish, and prime beef to boot, for a set of paltry beans. Take that! Take that! Take that! And as for your precious beans, they go out of the window. And now off with you to bed. Not a sup shall you drink, and not a bit shall you swallow this very night."

So Jack went upstairs to his little room in the attic, sad and sorry he was, to be sure, as much for his mother's sake as for the loss of his supper.

At last, he dropped off to sleep.

When he woke up, the room looked so funny. The sun was shining into part of it, yet all the rest was quite dark and shady. So Jack jumped up and dressed and went to the window. And what do you think he saw? Why the beans his mother had thrown out of the window into the garden had sprung up into a big beanstalk which went up and up and up till it reached the sky. So the man spoke the truth after all.

The beanstalk grew up quite a close past Jack's window, so all he had to do was open it and jump onto the beanstalk, which was made like a big plaited ladder. So Jack climbed, and he climbed, and he climbed, and he climbed, and he climbed, and he climbed, and he climbed till at last, he reached the sky. And when he got there, he found a long broad road going as straight as a dart. So he walked along, and he walked along, and he walked along till he came to a great big tall house, and on the doorstep, there was a great big tall woman.

"Good morning, mum," says Jack, quite polite-like. "Could you be so kind as to give me some breakfast?" For he hadn't had anything to eat, you know, the night before and was as hungry as a hunter.

"It's breakfast you want, is it?" says the big tall woman, "it's breakfast you'll be if you don't move off from here. My man is an ogre, and there's nothing he likes better than boys broiled on toast. You'd better move on, or he'll soon be coming."

"Oh! Please, mum, do give me something to eat, mum. I've had nothing to eat since yesterday morning, really and truly, mum," says Jack. "I may as well be broiled as die of hunger."

The ogre's wife wasn't such a wrong sort, after all. So she took Jack into the kitchen and gave him a junk of bread and cheese and a jug of milk. But Jack hadn't half finished these when thump! Thump! Thump! The whole house began to tremble with the noise of someone coming.

"Goodness gracious me! It's my old man," said the ogre's wife, "what on earth shall I do? Here, come quick and jump in here." And she bundled Jack into the oven just as the ogre came in.

He was a big one, to be sure. At his belt, he had three calves strung up by the heels, and he unhooked them, threw them down on the table, and said: "Here, wife, broil me a couple of these for breakfast. Ah, what's this I smell?

Fee-fi-fo-fum,

I smell the blood of an Englishman,

Be he alive, or be he dead

I'll have his bones to grind my bread."

"Nonsense, dear," said his wife, "you're dreaming. Or perhaps you smell the scraps of that little boy you liked so much for yesterday's dinner. Here, go and have a wash and tidy up, and by the time you come back, your breakfast will be ready for you." So the ogre went off, and Jack was just going to jump out of the oven and run off when the woman told him not. "Wait till he's asleep," says she; "he always has a snooze after breakfast."

Well, the ogre had his breakfast, and after that, he went to a big chest and took out of it a couple of bags of gold and sat down counting them till, at last, his head began to nod, and he began to snore till the whole house shook again.

Then Jack crept out on tiptoe from his oven. As he was passing the ogre, he took one of the bags of gold under his arm, and off he pelters till he came to the beanstalk. Then he threw down the bag of gold, which of course fell into his mother's garden, and then he climbed down and climbed down till at last he got home and told his mother and showed her the gold and said: "Well, mother, wasn't I right about the beans. They are magical, you see."

So they lived on the bag of gold for some time, but at last, they came to an end, so Jack decided to try his luck once more up at the top of the beanstalk. So one fine morning, he got up early and got on to the beanstalk, and he climbed, and he climbed, and he climbed, and he climbed, and he climbed, and he climbed till at last he got on the road again, and came to the great big tall house he had been to before. There, sure enough, was the great big tall woman a-standing on the doorstep.

"Good morning, mum," says Jack, as bold as brass, "could you be so good as to give me something to eat?"

"Go away, my boy," said the big, tall woman, "or else my man will eat you for breakfast. But aren't you the youngster who came here once before? Do you know, that very day, my man missed one of his bags of gold."

"That's strange, mum," says Jack, "I dare say I could tell you something about that, but I'm so hungry I can't speak till I've had something to eat."

The big tall woman was so curious that she took him in and gave him something to eat. But he had scarcely begun munching it as slowly as he could when thump! Thump! Thump! They heard the giant's footsteps, and his wife hid Jack away in the oven.

All happened as it did before. In came the ogre as he did before, said: "Fee-fi-fo-fum," and had his breakfast off three broiled oxen. Then he said: "Wife, bring me the hen that lays the golden eggs." So she brought it, and the ogre said: "Lay," and it laid an egg of gold. And then the ogre began to nod his head and to snore till the house shook.

Then Jack crept out of the oven on tiptoe, caught hold of the golden hen, and was off before you could say "Jack Robinson." But this time, the hen gave a cackle which woke the ogre, and just as Jack got out of the house, he heard him calling: "Wife, wife, what have you done with my golden hen?"

And the wife said: "Why, my dear?"

But that was all Jack heard, for he rushed off to the beanstalk and climbed down like a house on fire. And when he got home, he showed his mother the wonderful hen and said "Lay" to it; it laid a golden egg every time he said "Lay."

Well, Jack was not content, and it wasn't very long before he determined to have another try at his luck up there at the top of the beanstalk. So one fine morning, he got up early and went on to the beanstalk, and he climbed, and he climbed, and he climbed, and he climbed till he got to the top. But this time, he knew better than to go straight to the ogre's house. And when he got near it, he waited behind a bush till he saw the ogre's wife come out with a pail to get some water, and then he crept into the house and got into the copper. He hadn't been there long when he heard a thump! Thump! Thump! as before, and in come the ogre and his wife.

"Fee-fi-fo-fum, I smell the blood of an Englishman," cried out the ogre; "I smell him, wife, I smell him."

"Do you, my dearie?" says the ogre's wife. "Then, if it's that little rogue that stole your gold and the hen that laid the golden eggs, he's sure to have got into the oven." And they both rushed to the oven. But Jack wasn't there, and the ogre's wife said: "There you are again with your fee-fi-fo-fum. Why, of course, it's the laddie you caught last night that I've broiled for your breakfast. How forgetful I am and how careless you are not to tell the difference between a live un and a dead un."

So the ogre sat down to the breakfast and ate it, but now and then he would mutter: "Well, I could have sworn——" and he'd get up and search the larder and the cupboards, and everything, only luckily he didn't think of the copper.

After breakfast, the ogre called out: "Wife, wife, bring me my golden harp." So she brought it and put it on the table before him. Then he said: "Sing!" The golden harp sang most beautifully. And it continued singing till the ogre fell asleep and commenced snoring like thunder.

Then Jack lifted the copper lid very quietly, got down like a mouse, and crept on hands and knees till he got to the table when he got up, caught hold of the golden harp, and dashed with it towards the door. But the harp called out quite loud: "Master! Master!" The ogre woke up just in time to see Jack running off with his harp.

Jack ran as fast as he could, and the ogre came rushing after and would soon caught him. Only Jack had a start and dodged him a bit and knew where he was going. When he got to the beanstalk, the ogre was not more than twenty yards away when suddenly he saw Jack disappear, and when he got up to the end of the road, he saw Jack underneath, climbing down for dear life. Well, the ogre didn't like trusting himself to such a ladder, and he stood and waited so Jack got another start. But just then, the harp cried out: "Master! master!" The ogre swung himself down onto the beanstalk, which shook with his weight. Down climbs Jack, and after him climbs the ogre. By this time, Jack had climbed and climbed down till he was nearly home. So he called out: "Mother! Mother! bring me an axe, bring me an axe." And his mother came rushing out with the axe in her hand, but when she came to the beanstalk, she stood stock still with fright, for there she saw the ogre just coming down below the clouds.

But Jack jumped down, got hold of the axe, and gave a chop at the beanstalk, which cut it half in two. The ogre felt the beanstalk shake and quiver, so he stopped to see what was the matter. Then Jack gave another chop with the axe, cut the beanstalk in two, and began to topple over. Then the ogre fell down and broke his crown, and the beanstalk started toppling.

Then Jack showed his mother his golden harp, and by showing that and selling the golden eggs, Jack and his mother became very rich, and he married a great princess, and they lived happily ever after.

The Fairy Children

From A Dissertation on Fairies.
by Joseph Ritson, Esq.

"Another wonderful thing," says Ralph of Coggeshall, "happened in Suffolk, at St. Mary's of the Wolf-pits. A boy and his sister were found by the inhabitants of that place near the mouth of a pit which is there, they had the form of all their limbs like those of other men, but they were different in the colour of their skin from all the people of our habitable world, for the whole surface of their skin was tinged of green colour. No one could understand their speech.

When they were brought as curiosities to the house of a certain knight, Sir Richard de Calne, at Wikes, they wept bitterly. Bread and victuals were set before them, but they would touch none of them, though they were tormented by great hunger, as the girl afterward acknowledged. At length, when some beans, just cut, with their stalks, were brought into the house, they made signs, with great avidity, that they should be given to them. When they were brought, they opened the stalks instead of the pods, thinking the beans were in the hollow of them. But not finding them there, they began to weep anew. When those who were present saw this, they opened the pods and showed them the naked beans. They fed on these with great delight and tasted no other food for a long time. The boy, however, was always languid and depressed, and he died within a short time.

The girl enjoyed continual good health and, becoming accustomed to various kinds of food, lost completely that green colour and gradually recovered the positive habit of her entire body. She was afterward regenerated by the laver of holy baptism and lived for many years in the service of that knight, as I have frequently heard from him and his family.

Being frequently asked about the people of her country, she asserted that the inhabitants, and all they had in that country, were of green colour and that they saw no sun but enjoyed a degree of light like what is after sunset. Being asked how she came into this country with the aforesaid boy, she replied that, as they were following their flocks, they came to a particular cavern, on entering which they heard a delightful sound of bells, ravished by whose sweetness they went on for a long time wandering on through the cavern until they came to its mouth. When they came out of it, they were struck senseless by the excessive light of the sun and the unusual temperature of the air, and they thus lay for a long time. Being terrified by the noise of those who came on them, they wished to fly, but they could not find the entrance of the cavern before they were caught."

William also tells the story of Newbury, who places it in the reign of King Stephen. He says he long hesitated to believe it but was at length overcome by the weight of evidence. According to him, the place where the children appeared was about four or five miles from Bury-St.-Edmund's. They came in harvest time out of the Wolf-pits. They both lost their green hue, were baptized, and learned English. The boy, who was the younger, died, but the girl married a man at Lenna and lived for many years. They said their country was called St. Martin's Land, as that saint was chiefly worshipped there; that the people were Christians and had churches; that the sun did not rise there, but that there was a bright country which could be seen from theirs, being divided from it by a vast river.

The Ugly Duckling

by Hans Christian Andersen

It was so glorious out in the country; it was summer; the cornfields were yellow, the oats were green, the hay had been put up in stacks in the green meadows, and the stork went about on his long red legs and chattered Egyptian, for this was the language he had learned from his good mother. All around the fields and meadows were great forests, and deep lakes lay in the midst of these forests. Yes, it was right glorious out in the country. In the midst of the sunshine, there lay an old farm, with deep canals about it, and from the wall, down to the water grew great burdocks, so high that little children could stand upright under the loftiest of them. It was just as wild there as in the deepest wood, and here sat a Duck upon her nest; she had to hatch her ducklings, but she was almost tired before the little ones came, and then she seldom had visitors. The other ducks liked to swim about in the canals rather than run up to sit down under burdock and cackle with her.

At last, one eggshell after another burst open. "Piep! piep!" it cried, and in all the eggs, little creatures stuck out their heads.

"Quack! quack!" they said, and they all came quacking out as fast as they could, looking all around them under the green leaves; the mother let them look as much as they chose, for green is good for the eye.

"How wide the world is!" said all the young ones, for they certainly had much more room now than when they were in the eggs.

"D'ye think this is all the world?" said the mother. "That stretches far across the other side of the garden, quite into the parson's field, but I have never been there yet. I hope you are all together," and she stood up. "No, I have not all. The largest egg still lies there. How long is that to last? I am really tired of it." And she sat down again.

"Well, how goes it?" asked an old Duck who

had come to visit her.

"It lasts a long time with that one egg," said the Duck who sat there. "It will not burst. Now, only look at the others; are they not the prettiest little ducks one could possibly see? They are all like their father. The rogue, he never comes to see me."

"Let me see the egg which will not burst," said the old visitor. "You may be sure it is a turkey's egg. I was once cheated in that way and had much anxiety and trouble with the young ones, for they are afraid of the water. Must I say it to you? I could not get them to venture in. I quacked, and I clacked, but it was no use. Let me see the egg. Yes, that's a turkey's egg. Let it lie there, and teach the other children to swim."

"I think I will sit on it a little longer," said the Duck. "I've sat so long now that I can sit a few days more."

"Just as you please," said the old Duck, and she went away.

At last, the great egg burst. "Piep! Piep!" said the little one and crept forth. It was huge and very ugly. The Duck looked at it.

"It's a very large duckling," said she; "none of the others look like that. Can it really be a turkey chick? Well, we shall soon find out. It must go into the water, even if I have to thrust it in myself."

The next day it was bright, beautiful weather; the sun shone on all the green trees. The Mother-Duck went down to the canal with all her family. Splash! she jumped into the water. "Quack! Quack!" she said, and one Duckling after another plunged in. The water closed over their heads, but they came up in an instant and swam capitally; their legs went off themselves, and they were all in the water. The ugly gray Duckling swam with them.

"No, it's not a turkey," said she; "look how well it can use its legs and how straight it holds itself. It is my child! Overall, it's quite pretty if one looks at it rightly. Quack! Quack! Come with me, and I'll lead you out into the great world and present you in the duck yard, but keep close to me so that no one may tread on you, and take care of the cats!"

And so they came into the duck yard. There was a terrible riot in there, for two families were quarreling about an eel's head, and the Cat got it after all.

"See, that's how it goes in the world!" said the Mother-Duck, and she whetted her beak, for she too wanted the eel's head. "Only use your legs," she said. "See that you can bustle about and bow your heads before the old Duck yonder. She's the grandest of all here; she's of Spanish blood—that's why she's so fat, and d'ye see? she has a red rag around her leg; that's something particularly fine, and the greatest distinction a duck can enjoy; it signifies that one does not want to lose her and that she's to be known by the animals and by men too. Shake yourselves—don't turn in your toes; a well-brought-up duck turns its toes quite out, just like father and mother—so! Now bend your necks and say 'Quack!'"

And they did so: but the other ducks round about looked at them and said quite boldly:

"Look there! Now we're to have these hanging on as if there were not enough of us already! And—fie! —how that duckling yonder looks; we won't stand that!" And one Duck flew up at it and bit it in the neck.

"Let it alone," said the mother; "it does not harm anyone."

"Yes, but it's too large and peculiar," said the Duck who had bitten it, "and therefore, it must be put down."

"Those are pretty children that the mother has there," said the old Duck with the rag around her leg. "They're all pretty, but that one; was rather unlucky. I wish she could bear it over again."

"That cannot be done, my lady," replied the Mother-Duck. "It is not pretty, but it has a really good disposition and swims as well as any other; I may even say it swims better. I think it will grow up pretty and become smaller in time; it has lain too long in the egg and therefore is not properly shaped." And then she pinched it in the neck and smoothed its feathers. "Moreover, it is a drake," she said, "and therefore, it is not of so much consequence. I think he will be very strong. He makes his way already."

"The other ducklings are graceful enough," said

the old Duck. "Make yourself at home, and if you find an eel's head, you may bring it to me."

And now they were at home. But the poor Duckling, which had crept last out of the egg, and looked so ugly, was bitten and pushed and jeered, as much by the ducks as by the chickens.

"It is too big!" they all said. And the turkey-cock, who had been born with spurs and therefore thought himself an emperor, blew himself up like a ship in full sail and bore straight down upon it; then he gobbled and grew quite red in the face. The poor Duckling did not know where it should stand or walk; it was quite melancholy because it looked ugly and was the butt of the whole duck yard.

So it went on the first day, and afterward, it worsened. The poor Duckling was hunted about by every one; even its brothers and sisters were quite angry with it and said, "If the cat would only catch you, you ugly creature!" And the mother said, "If you were only far away!" And the ducks bit it, the chickens beat it, and the girl who had to feed the poultry kicked at it with her foot.

Then it ran and flew over the fence, and the little birds in the bushes flew up in fear.

"That is because I am so ugly!" thought the Duckling, and it shut its eyes but flew on farther, and so it came out into the great moor, where the wild ducks lived. Here it lay the whole night long, and it was weary and downcast.

Towards morning the wild ducks flew up and looked at their new companion.

"What sort of a one are you?" they asked, and the Duckling turned in every direction and bowed as well as it could. "You are remarkably ugly!" said the Wild Ducks. "But that is nothing to us, so long as you do not marry into our family."

Poor thing! It certainly did not think of marrying and only hoped to obtain leave to lie among the reeds and drink some of the swamp water.

Thus it lay two whole days; then came thither two wild geese, or, properly speaking, two wild ganders. It was not long since each had crept out of an egg, and that's why they were so saucy.

"Listen, comrade," said one of them. "You're so ugly that I like you. Will you go with us and become a bird of passage? Near here, in another moor, there are a few sweet lovely wild geese, all unmarried and all able to say 'Rap!' You have a chance of making your fortune, ugly as you are."

"Piff! Paff!" resounded through the air, and the two ganders fell down dead in the swamp, and the water became blood red. "Piff! Paff!" it sounded again, and the whole flock of wild geese rose up from the reeds. And then there was another report. A great hunt was going on. The sportsmen were lying in wait all around the moor, and some were even sitting up in the branches of the trees, which spread far over the reeds. The blue smoke rose like clouds among the dark trees and was wafted far away across the water, and the hunting dogs came—splash, splash!—into the swamp, and the rushes and the reeds bent down on every side. That was a fright for the poor Duckling! It turned its head and put it under its wing, but at that moment, a great frightful dog stood close by the Duckling. His tongue hung far out of his mouth, and his eyes gleamed horrible and ugly; he thrust out his nose close against the Duckling, showed his sharp teeth, and—splash, splash!—on he went, without seizing it.

"Oh, Heaven is thanked!" sighed the Duckling. "I am so ugly that even the dog does not like to bite me!"

And so it lay quite quiet while the shots rattled through the reeds and fired gun after gun. At last, late in the day, all was still; but the poor Duckling did not dare to rise up; it waited several hours before it looked round and then hastened away out of the moor as fast as it could. It ran over the field and meadow; there was such a storm raging that it was difficult to get from one place to another.

Towards evening the Duck came to a little miserable peasant's hut. This hut was so dilapidated that it did not know on which side it should fall, and that's why it remained standing. The storm whistled round the Duckling so that the poor creature was obliged to sit down, to stand against it, and the wind blew worse and worse. Then the Duckling noticed that one of the door's hinges had given way, and the door hung so slanting that the Duckling could slip through the crack into the room; that is what it did.

Here lived a woman with her Cat and her Hen. And the Cat, whom she called Sonnie, could arch his back and purr. He could even give out sparks, but one had to stroke his fur the wrong way to make him do it. The Hen had relatively few short legs; therefore, she was called Chickabiddy Short-shanks. She laid good eggs, and the woman loved her like her child.

In the morning, the strange Duckling was noticed, and the Cat began to purr and the Hen cluck.

"What's this?" said the woman, and looked all around, but she could not see well, and therefore she thought the Duckling was a fat duck that had strayed. "This is a rare prize!" she said. "Now I shall have Duck's eggs. I hope it is not a drake. We must try that."

And so the Duckling was admitted on trial for three weeks, but no eggs came. And the Cat was master of the House, and the Hen was the lady, and always said, "We and the world!" for she thought they were half the world and by far the better half.

The Duckling thought one might have a different opinion, but the Hen would not allow it.

"Can you lay eggs?" she asked.

"No."

"Then will you hold your tongue!"

And the Cat said, "Can you curve your back, purr, and give out sparks?"

"No."

"Then you will have no opinion when sensible folks are speaking."

And the Duckling sat in a corner and was melancholy; then the fresh air and the sunshine streamed in, and it was seized with such a strange longing to swim on the water that it could not help telling the Hen of it.

"What are you thinking of?" cried the Hen. "You have nothing to do. That's why you have these fancies. Lay eggs, or purr, and they will pass over."

"But it is so charming to swim on the water!" said the Duckling, "so refreshing to let it close above one's head and to dive down to the bottom."

"Yes, that must be a mighty pleasure, truly," quoth the Hen, "I fancy you must have gone crazy. Ask the Cat about it—he's the cleverest animal I know—ask him if he likes to swim in the water or to dive down—I won't speak about myself. Ask our mistress, the old woman; no one in the world is cleverer than she. Do you think she wants to swim and let the water close above her head?"

"You don't understand me," said the Duckling.

"We don't understand you? Then pray, who is to understand you? You surely don't pretend to be cleverer than the Cat and the woman—I won't say anything of myself. Don't be conceited, child, and thank your Maker for all your kindness. Did you not get into a warm room, and have you not fallen into the company from which you may learn something? But you are a chatterer, and it is not pleasant to associate with you. You may believe me. I speak for your good. I tell you disagreeable things, and by that, one may always know true friends! Only take care that you learn to lay eggs or to purr and give out sparks!"

"I think I will go out into the wide world," said the Duckling.

"Yes, do go," replied the Hen.

And so the Duckling went away. It swam on the water and dived, but every creature slighted it because of its ugliness.

Now came the autumn. The leaves in the forest turned yellow and brown; the wind caught them so that they danced about, and up in the air, it was very cold. The clouds hung low, heavy with hail and snowflakes, and on the fence stood the raven, crying, "Croak! croak!" for mere cold; yes, it was enough to make one feel cold to think of this. The poor little Duckling certainly had not had a good time. One evening—the sun was setting in his beauty—a whole flock of great, handsome birds came out of the bushes. They were dazzlingly white, with long, flexible necks—they were swans. They uttered a very peculiar cry, spread their glorious great wings, and flew away from that cold region to warmer lands and fair open lakes. They mounted so high, so high! The ugly Duckling felt quite strangely as it watched them. It turned round and round in the water like a wheel, stretched out its neck towards them, and uttered such a strange loud cry as frightened itself. Oh! It could not forget those beautiful, happy birds, and so soon as it could see them no longer, it dived down to the very bottom, and when it came up again, it was quite beside itself. It knew not the name of those birds and knew not whither they were flying, but it loved them more than it had ever loved anyone. It was not at all envious of them. How could it think of wishing to possess such loveliness as they had? It would have been glad if only the ducks had endured its company—the poor, ugly creature!

And the winter grew cold, very cold! The Duckling was forced to swim about in the water to prevent the surface from freezing entirely, but every night, the hole in which it swam about became smaller and smaller. It froze so hard that the icy covering crackled again, and the Duckling was obliged to use its legs continually to prevent the hole from freezing up. At last, it became exhausted and lay quite still and thus froze fast into the ice.

Early in the morning, a peasant came by, and when he saw what had happened, he took his wooden shoe, broke the ice crust to pieces, and carried the Duckling home to his wife. Then it came to itself again. The children wanted to play with it, but the Duckling thought they wanted to hurt it and, in its terror, fluttered up into the milk pan, so the milk spurted into the room. The woman clasped her hands, at which the Duckling flew down into the butter tub, into the meal barrel, and out again. How it looked then! The woman screamed and struck at it with the fire tongs; the children tumbled over one another in their efforts to catch the Duckling, and they laughed, and they screamed!—well it was that the door stood open, and the poor creature was able to slip out between the shrubs into the newly-fallen snow—there it lay quite exhausted.

But it would be too melancholy if I were to tell all the misery and care the Duckling had to endure in the hard winter. It lay out on the moor among the reeds when the sun began to shine again and the larks to sing. It was a beautiful spring.

Then all at once, the Duckling could flap its wings. They beat the air more strongly than before and bore it firmly away; before it knew how all this happened, it found itself in a great garden, where the elder trees smelt sweet and bent their long green branches down to the canal that wound through the region. Oh, here it was so beautiful, such a gladness of spring! And from the thicket came three glorious white swans; they rustled their wings and swam lightly on the water. The Duckling knew the splendid creatures and felt oppressed by a peculiar sadness.

"I will fly away to them, to the royal birds, and they will beat me because I that am so ugly, dare to come near them. But it is all the same. Better to be killed by them than pursued by ducks, beaten by fowls, and pushed about by the girl who takes care of the poultry yard and to suffer hunger in winter!" And it flew out into the water and swam towards the beautiful swans; these looked at it and came sailing down upon it with outspread wings. "Kill me!" said the poor creature and bent its head down upon the water, expecting nothing but death. But what was this that it saw in the clear water? It beheld its own image, and, lo! It was no longer a clumsy dark-gray bird, ugly and hateful to look at, but a—swan!

It matters nothing if one is born in a duck yard if one has only lain in a swan's egg.

It felt quite glad at all the need and misfortune it had suffered. Now it realized its happiness in all the splendor that surrounded it. And the great swans swam round it and stroked it with their beaks.

In the garden came little children, who threw bread and corn into the water, and the youngest cried, "There is a new one!" The other children shouted joyously, "Yes, a new one has arrived!" And they clapped their hands and danced about and ran to their father and mother, and bread and cake were thrown into the water; and they all said, "The new one is the most beautiful of all! so young and handsome!" and the old swans bowed their heads before him. Then he felt quite ashamed and hid his head under his wings, for he did not know what to do; he was so happy and yet not at all proud. He thought he had been persecuted and despised, and now he heard them saying he was the most beautiful of all birds. Even the elder tree bent its branches straight down into the water before him, and the sun shone warm and mild. Then his wings rustled, he lifted his slender neck, and cried rejoicingly from the depths of his heart:

"I never dreamed of so much happiness when I was the Ugly Duckling!"

The Magic Jar

by Juliana Horatia Ewing

There was once a young fellow fortune had blessed with a good mother, a clever head, and a strong body. But beyond this, she had not much favoured him; though able and willing to work, he often had little to do and less to eat. But his mother had taught him to be contented with his lot and to feel for others. Moreover, from her, he inherited a great love for flowers.

One day, when his pockets were emptiest, a fair was held in the neighboring town, and he must need to go as well as the rest, though he had no money to spend. But he stuck a buttercup in his cap, for which he had nothing to pay, and strode along as merrily as the most.

Towards evening some of the merrymakers became riotous; a party of them fell upon an old Jew who was keeping a stall of glass and china and would smash his stock. Now, as the Jew stood before his booth beseeching them to spare his property, up came the strong young man, with the flower still unwithered in his cap, and he took the old Jew's part and defended him. For from childhood, his mother had taught him to feel for others.

So those who would have ill-treated the old Jew now moved off, and the young man stayed with him till he had packed up his wares.

Then the Jew turned towards him and said, "My son, who delivers the oppressed and has respect unto the aged, needs no reward, for the blessing of Him that blesseth is about him. Nevertheless, that I may not seem ungrateful, choose, I pray thee, one of these china jars; and take it to thee for thine own. If thou shalt choose well, it may be of more use to thee than presently appears."

The young man examined the jars, which were highly ornamented with many figures and devices, but he chose a comparatively plain one; only it had a bunch of flowers painted on the front, round which was a pretty device in spots or circles of gold.

Then said the Jew, "My son, why have you chosen this jar when there are others so much finer?"

The young man said, "Because the flowers please me, and I love flowers."

Then said the Jew, "Happy is he whose tastes are simple! Moreover, herein is rare wisdom, and thou hast gained that which is the most valuable of my possessions. This jar has properties that I will further explain to thee. It was given to me by a wise woman, subject to this condition, that I must expose it for sale from sunrise to sunset at the yearly fair. When I understood this, I took counsel with myself on how to preserve it; I bought other china jars of more apparent value and marked them all with the same price. I said, 'There is no man who does not desire to get as much as he can for his money. Therefore, my jar is safe from its contrast with these others.' And it was even so; for truly, many have desired to buy the jar because of the delicate beauty of the flowers, if I would have sold it for less than others which seemed more valuable."

"Many times it has been almost gone, but when I have shown the others at the same price, my customers have reviled me, saying, 'Dog of a Jew, dost thou, ask as much for this as for these others Which are manifestly worth double?' and they have either departed, cursing me, and taking nothing; or they have bought one of the more richly decorated jars at the same price. For surely in most men, the spirit of covetousness is stronger than the love of beauty, and they desire to get much for their money than to obtain that which is suitable and convenient."

"But in thee, O young man! I have beheld rare wisdom. To choose that which is good in thine eyes, and suitable to thy needs, rather than that which satisfieth the lust of over-reaching; and lo! what I have so long kept from thousands, has become thine!"

Then the young man wished to restore to the Jew the jar he valued so highly and to choose another.

But the Jew refused, saying, "A gift cannot be recalled. Moreover, I will now explain to thee its uses. Within the jar lies a toad whose spit is poison. But it will never spit at its master. Every evening thou must feed it with bread and milk when it falls asleep, and at sunrise, in the morning, it will awake and breathe heavily against the side of the jar, which will thus become warm. As it warms, the flowers will blossom out and become real and full of perfume, and thou wilt can pluck them without diminishing their number.

Moreover, these twelve round spots of gold will drop off and become twelve gold pieces, which will be thine. And thus, it will be every day. Only thou must thyself rise with the sun and gather the flowers and the gold with thine own hands. Furthermore, the flowers and gilding will be as before when the jar cools. Fare thee well."

And even as he spoke, the Jew lifted the huge china crate onto his back and disappeared among the crowd.

All came about as the Jew had promised. As he had twelve gold pieces a day, the young man now wanted for nothing, besides which he had fresh flowers on his table all year round.

It is well said, "Thy business is my business, and the business of all beside," for every man's affairs are his neighbors' property. Thus, all those who lived near the young man were perplexed that he had such beautiful flowers in all seasons and esteemed it as an injury to themselves that he should have them and give no explanation as to whence they came.

At last, it came to the ears of the king, and he also was disturbed. For he was curious and fond of prying into small matters; a taste which ill becomes those of high position. But the king had no child to succeed him, and he was always suspecting those about him of plotting to obtain the crown, and thus he came to be forever prying into the affairs of his subjects.

When he heard of the young man who had flowers on his table all year round, he desired one of his officers to question him about how he obtained them. But the young man contrived to evade his questions, and the matter was at rest for a while.

Then the king sent another messenger with orders to press the young man more closely, and because the young man disdained to tell a lie, he said, "I get the flowers from yon china jar."

Then the messenger returned and said to the king, "The young man says that he gets the flowers from a certain china jar that stands in his room."

Then said the king, "Bring the contents of the jar hither to me." And the messenger returned and brought the toad.

But when the king laid hold upon the toad, it spat in his face; he was poisoned and died.

Then the toad sat upon the king's mouth and would not be enticed away. And everyone feared touching it because it spat poison. And they called the wise men of the council; they performed certain rites to charm the toad, yet it would not go.

But after three days, the master of the toad came to the palace, and without saying who he was, he desired to be permitted to try and get the toad from the king's corpse.

And when he was taken into the king's chamber, he stood and beckoned to the toad, saying, "The person of the king and the bodies of the dead are sacred, wherefore come away."

And the toad crawled from the king's face and came to him, and did not spit at him; and he put it back into the jar.

Then said the wise men, "There is no one so fit to succeed to the kingdom as this man is; both for the wisdom of speech and the power of command."

And what they said pleased the people, and the young man was king. And in due time, he married an amiable and talented princess and had children. And he ruled the kingdom well and wisely and was beloved till his death.

Now when, after the lapse of many years, he died, there was great grief among the people, and his body was laid out in his room, and the people were permitted to come and look upon his face for the last time.

And among the crowd, there appeared an aged Jew. And he did not weep as did the others, but he came and stood by the bier and gazed upon the face of the dead king in silence. And after a while, he exclaimed and said:

"Oh, wonderful spectacle! A man, and not covetous. A ruler, and not oppressive. Contented in poverty and moderate in wealth. Elect of the people and beloved to the end!"

And when he had said this, he again became silent and stood as one astonished.

And no one knew when he came in nor perceived when he departed.

But when they came to search for the china jar,
it was gone and could never afterward be found.

Catskin

by Joseph Jacobs

Well, there was once a gentleman who had good lands and houses, and he wanted to have a son to be heir to them. So when his wife brought him a daughter, bonny as bonny could be, he cared nought for her and said, "Let me never see her face."

So she grew up a bonny girl, though her father never set eyes on her until she was fifteen years old and ready to marry. But her father said, "Let her marry the first that comes for her." And when this was known, who should be first but a nasty rough old man. So she didn't know what to do, and went to the henwife and asked her advice. The henwife said, "Say you will not take him unless they give you a coat of silver cloth." Well, they gave her a coat of silver cloth, but she wouldn't take him for all that but went again to the henwife, who said, "Say you will not take him unless they give you a coat of beaten gold." Well, they gave her a coat of beaten gold, but still, she would not take him, but went to the henwife, who said, "Say you will not take him unless they give you a coat made of the feathers of all the birds of the air." So they sent a man with a great heap of pease, and the man cried to all the birds of the air, "Each bird take a pea, and put down a feather." So each bird took a pea and put down one of its feathers: and they took all the feathers and made a coat of them and gave it to her; but still, she would not, but asked the henwife once again, who said, "Say they must first make you a coat of catskin." So they made her a coat of Catskin; she put it on, tied up her other coats, and ran away into the woods.

So she went along and went along and went along till she came to the end of the wood and saw a fine castle. So there she hid her delicate dresses, went up to the castle gates, and asked for work. The lady of the castle saw her and told her, "I'm sorry I have no better place, but if you like, you may be our scullion." So down she went into the kitchen, and they called her Catskin because of her dress. But the cook was cruel to her and led her to a sad life.

Well, it happened soon after that the young lord of the castle was coming home, and there was to be a grand ball in honour of the occasion. And when they were speaking about it among the servants, "Dear me, Mrs. Cook," said Catskin, "how much I should like to go."

"What! You dirty impudent slut," said the cook, "go among all the fine lords and ladies with your filthy Catskin? a fine figure you'd cut!" She took a water basin and dashed with it into Catskin's face. But she only briskly shook her ears and said nothing.

When the day of the ball arrived, Catskin slipped out of the house and went to the edge of the forest where she had hidden her dresses. So she bathed herself in a crystal waterfall, put on her coat of silver cloth, and hastened away to the ball. As soon as she entered, all were overcome by her beauty and grace, while the young lord at once lost his heart to her. He asked her to be his partner for the first dance, and he would dance with none other the live-long night.

When it came to parting time, the young lord said, "Pray to tell me, fair maid, where you live." But Catskin curtsied and said:

"Kind sir, if the truth I must tell,

I dwell at the 'Basin of Water' sign."

Then she flew from the castle, donned her

catskin robe again, and slipped into the scullery again, unbeknown to the cook.

The young lord went the next day to his mother, the lady of the castle, and declared he would wed none other but the lady of the silver dress and would never rest till he had found her. So another ball was soon arranged, hoping the beautiful maid would appear again. So Catskin said to the cook, "Oh, how I should like to go!" The cook screamed in a rage, "What, you, you dirty impudent slut! you would cut a fine figure among all the fine lords and ladies." And with that, she up with a ladle and broke it across Catskin's back. But she only shook her ears and ran off to the forest, where she first bathed and then put on her coat of beaten gold, and off she went to the ballroom.

As soon as she entered, all eyes were upon her; the young lord recognised her as the "Basin of Water" lady, claimed her hand for the first dance, and did not leave her till the last. When that came, he again asked her where she lived. But all that she would say was:

"Kind sir, if the truth I must tell,

At the sign of the 'Broken Ladle,' I dwell."

And with that, she curtsied and flew off the ball with her golden robe, on with her Catskin, and into the scullery without the cook's knowing.

The next day when the young lord could not find where was the sign of the "Basin of Water" or the "Broken Ladle," he begged his mother to have another grand ball so that he might meet the beautiful maid once more.

All happened as before. Catskin told the cook how much she would like to go to the ball. The cook called her "a dirty slut," and broke the skimmer across her head. But she only shook her ears and went off to the forest, where she first bathed in the crystal spring, then donned her coat of feathers, and then off to the ballroom.

When she entered, everyone was surprised at a beautiful face and form dressed in so rich and rare a dress; but the young lord soon recognised his gorgeous sweetheart and would dance with none but her the whole evening. When the ball came to an end, he pressed her to tell him where she lived, but all she would answer was:

"Kind sir, if the truth I must tell,

At the 'Broken Skimmer sign,' I dwell;"

And with that, she curtsied and was off to the forest. But this time, the young lord followed her and watched her change her delicate dress of feathers for her catskin dress, and then he knew her for his scullery-maid.

The next day he went to his mother, the lady of the castle, and told her that he wished to marry the scullery-maid, Catskin. "Never," said the lady and rushed from the room. Well, the young lord was so grieved that he took to his bed and was very ill. The doctor tried to cure him, but he would not take any medicine unless from the hands of Catskin. So the doctor went to the lady of the castle and told her her son would die if she did not consent to his marriage with Catskin. So she had to give way and summoned Catskin to her. But she put on her coat of beaten gold and went to the lady, who soon was glad to wed her son to so beautiful a maid.

Well, so they were married, and after a time, a dear little son came to them and grew up a bonny lad; and one day, when he was four years old, a beggar woman came to the door, so Lady Catskin gave some money to the little lord and told him to go and give it to the beggar woman. So he went and gave it but put it into the hand of the woman's child, who leaned forward and kissed the little lord. Now the wicked old cook—why hadn't she been sent away?—was looking on, so she said, "Only see how beggars' brats take to one another." This insult went to Catskin's heart, so she went to her husband, the young lord, and told him all about her father and begged he would go and find out what had become of her parents. So they set out in the lord's grand coach and traveled through the forest till they came to Catskin's father's house and put up near an inn where Catskin stopped while her husband went to see if her father would own her. Now her father had never had any other child, and his wife had died, so he was all alone in the world and sate, moping and miserable. When the young lord came in, he hardly looked up till he saw a chair close up to him and asked him: "Pray, sir, had you not once a young daughter whom you would never see or own?"

The old gentleman said: "It is true; I am a hardened sinner. But I would give all my worldly goods if I could see her once before I die." Then the young lord told him what had happened to Catskin, took him to the inn, and brought his father-in-law to his castle, where they lived happily ever afterward.

The Blackberry Elf

by Mrs Molesworth

Ora and Hilary were staying in the country with their cousins. It was a new part of the world to them, for their own home, though not actually in a town, was not far from one and therefore far less rich in wildflowers and mushrooms and blackberries and all such delightful things than the real country place where these fortunate cousins lived.

Had it not been for the newness and the freedom of it all, they might have found it a little dull, for there was only one child in the family near their ages—Nora was eight and Hilary six—and this was a boy of seven called Cecil. Cecil was much younger than his brothers and sisters and seemed even younger than his age, for he was small, delicate, and very quiet. Hilary, a great big strong fellow, seemed much older; indeed, if you had seen the two together, you would certainly have guessed that Cecil and not his cousin was the, so to say, town-bred boy. Cecil had never been so happy in his life as since the two little visitors had come to stay with him. They seemed to find out all sorts of new things that had never struck him before; pleasures and interests springing all about and close at hand which he had never thought of.

They found everything delightful; as the summer gradually faded into autumn and the bright flowers grew scarcer and less tempting to gather, the wild fruit, in its turn, began to ripen. Day by day, the children watched the blackberries with the greatest eagerness, as the small red heads steadily got rounder and deeper in colour, till, at last, one day, some of the big people said in the children's hearing, "a couple of days' sunshine and the blackberries will be at their prime; there's a splendid show of them this year."

Nora and Hilary could scarcely keep jumping with joy, making Cecil nearly as eager as themselves. The sun seemed to enter into their feelings, for the very next morning, he showed a more smiling face than for some time past and continued in this amiable humor for several days so that the children were able on the third day to set off, armed with baskets nearly as big as themselves, for a regular good blackberrying.

All went well for some time. They had been told where and how far they might go, and though it took somewhat longer than they had expected to fill even one of the baskets, they worked on cheerfully, nowise disheartened, chattering to each other from time to time, when a strange thing happened.

Nora was saying that the only thing she was ever afraid of in the woods was "snakes," and Cecil was assuring her that he was sure there were none in "our woods," when she was startled by her giving a little scream.

"What's the matter?" he called out, half thinking that a snake had appeared after all.

"Hush, Cecil, oh, hush!" said Nora in a low and startled voice; "come here, and you, Hilary, come close here, but don't make any noise."

Wondering and frightened, the two boys crept through the bushes to her side.

"What is it, Nora?" they both whispered in an awestruck tone.

"I don't know," she replied. "Cecil, do you know of anything queer in these woods? Are there any dwarfs or—or creatures like in fairy stories? I am sure I saw a very, very little black or dark-brown man with a red jacket and cap—he wasn't as high as up to my waist

—scrambling among the bushes over there and picking and eating blackberries."

Cecil and Hilary stared at her.

"You must have fancied it, Nora," said Cecil. "I never heard of a—" but he was interrupted by a smothered scream.

"There, there," whispered Nora, clutching hold of both the boys, "there he is again!"

And sure enough, there "he" was, and just precisely as Nora had described him. A tiny dark-brown creature, like a wee old man, with a little red jacket and a small red skull cap on the top of his head. He seemed to have come up suddenly from among the bushes; he was holding the branch of a blackberry tree in one hand and greedily plucking and eating the fruit as fast as he could.

"Who can he be?" said Nora, who had grown very pale.

"I wish I'd take a gun here," said Hilary, who was rather given to boasting.

"Nonsense," said Nora, "if he's some kind of a man—and he can't be an animal—animals don't wear jackets and caps—it would be very wrong, and if he's a —a wood spirit, or anything like that, shooting would be no good."

But she and Hilary had raised their voices in this discussion without knowing it. Suddenly the small man turned round, placed one hand behind his big black ear as if listening, and then, seemingly catching sight of the children, sprang forward, stretching out his two long arms before him curiously towards the little group.

A group no longer—with a scream or three screams joined into one, the children had turned and fled. How they got through the thick growing bushes without being torn to pieces, I am sure I cannot tell. Fear lends wings, I suppose. However that may be, I know it was in a wonderfully short time that they found themselves, panting and shaking, breathless and trembling, but safe, inside the shelter of their garden gate.

"Oh, Nora!"

"Oh, Cecil!"

"Oh, Hilary!"

"I never was so frightened in my life," each exclaimed.

"If we hadn't all seen it, we might think it was fancy," said Nora.

"I'm afraid the big ones will say it's fancy as it is," said Cecil, "and they will laugh at us."

"Then we won't tell them," said Nora, "at least we'll wait for a little and see. But I daren't go into the woods again; I daren't."

"Not without a gun," said Hilary.

"Rubbish," said Nora.

They kept their own counsel all that day, though strongly tempted to confide in one or other of the big ones. But after dinner that evening, Cecil's father called them to him when they went into dessert.

"I've got a story which will amuse you, children," he said. "I was riding past Welby's farm this morning, and Welby was quite full of a present his sailor son has sent him. It is a monkey—the funniest little fellow possible. He arrived dressed in a red jacket and cap and was soon as friendly as possible with them all, he says. But the queerest thing is this. Last week Tom Welby took the monkey for a walk in the woods and gave him some blackberries. Mr. Monkey seemed to like them very much, and the next morning he disappeared to the Welbys' consternation. They were sure he was stolen or lost. But late in the afternoon, he returned home in very good humour. And the next morning off, he went again, to come home just like the day before. They couldn't make it out, but Tom was determined to find out, so he watched Mr. Monkey, and where do you think he was? In the woods gathering blackberries on his account, 'like a Christian,' said old Welby, enjoying himself thoroughly. And now he goes off every morning regularly and comes home when the afternoon gets chilly. It's most amusing, isn't it?"

The children looked at each other, but for a moment, none of them spoke. Then, at last, Nora burst out.

"Uncle, we saw him this morning. But—we were very silly—"

"We thought he was a wood spirit—a—a—I can't remember the name," said Cecil.

"I wanted to shoot him," said Hilary.

At this, there was a shout of laughter all around the table. The children hesitated, then they looked at each other again and burst out laughing too.

"Why didn't you tell us?" asked big sister Mabel.

"We thought you'd laugh at us," they said.

"And after all, we have laughed at you, but I don't think you're any the worse," said Mabel smiling, as she kissed their little flushed faces.

On the Way to The Sun

by Mrs. W. K. Clifford

He had journeyed a long way and was very tired. It seemed like a dream when he stood up after sleeping in the field, looked over the wall, and saw the garden, flowers, and the children playing. He looked at the long road behind him, the dark wood, and the barren hills; it was the world he belonged to. He looked at the garden before him, at the big house, the terrace, and the steps that led down to the smooth lawn—it was the world that belonged to the children.

"Poor boy," said the elder child, "I will get you something to eat."

"But where did he come from?" the gardener asked.

"We do not know," the child answered, "but he is starving, and mother says we may give him some food."

"I will take him some milk," said the little one; in one hand, she carried a mug, and with the other, she pulled along her little broken cart.

"But what is he called?" asked the gardener.

"We do not know," the little one answered, "but he is very thirsty, and mother says we may give him some milk."

"Where is he going?" asked the gardener.

"We do not know," the children said, "but he is exhausted."

When the boy had rested well, he got up, saying, "I must not stay any longer," and turned to go on his way.

"What have you to do?" the children asked.

"I am one of the crew and must help to make the world go round," he answered.

"Why do we not help too?"

"You are the passengers."

"How far have you to go?" they asked.

"Oh, a long way!" he answered. "On and on until I can touch the sun."

"Will you touch it?" they said, awestruck.

"I dare say I shall tire long before I get there," he answered sadly. "Perhaps without knowing it, though, I shall reach it in my sleep," he added. But they hardly heard the last words, for he was already far off.

"Why did you talk to him?" the gardener said. "He is just a working boy."

"And we do nothing! It was very good of him to notice us," they said humbly.

"Good!" said the gardener in despair. "Why, there is a great difference between you and him."

"There was only a wall," they answered. "Who set it up?" they asked curiously.

"Why, the builders, of course. Men set it up."

"And who will pull it down?"

"It will not want any pulling down," the man answered grimly. "Time will do that."

As the children returned to their play, they looked up at the light towards which the boy was journeying.

"Perhaps we too shall reach it someday," they said.

The Girl Who Owned a Bear

by L. Frank Baum

Mamma had gone downtown to shop. She had asked Nora to look after Jane Gladys, and Nora promised she would. But it was her afternoon for polishing the silver, so she stayed in the pantry and left Jane Gladys to amuse herself alone in the big sitting room upstairs.

The little girl did not mind being alone, for she was working on her first piece of embroidery—a sofa pillow for papa's birthday present. So she crept into the big bay window and curled herself up on the broad sill while she bent her brown head over her work.

Soon the door opened and closed again quietly. Jane Gladys thought it was Nora, so she didn't look up until she had taken a couple more stitches on a forget-me-not. Then she raised her eyes and was astonished to find a strange man in the middle of the room who regarded her earnestly.

He was short and fat and seemed to be breathing heavily from climbing stairs. He held a work silk hat in one hand, and underneath his other elbow was tucked a good-sized book. He was dressed in a black suit that looked old and rather shabby, and his head was bald upon the top.

"Excuse me," he said while the child gazed at him in solemn surprise. "Are you Jane Gladys Brown?"

"Yes, sir," she answered.

"Very good; very good, indeed!" he remarked with a queer smile. "I've had quite a hunt to find you, but I've succeeded at last."

"How did you get in?" inquired Jane Gladys, growing distrust of her visitor.

"That is a secret," he said mysteriously.

This was enough to put the girl on her guard. She looked at the man, and the man looked at her, and both looks were grave and somewhat anxious.

"What do you want?" she asked, straightening herself with a dignified air.

"Ah!—now we are coming to business," said the man briskly. "I'm going to be quite frank with you. To begin with, your father has abused me in a most ungentlemanly manner."

Jane Gladys got off the window sill and pointed her small finger at the door.

"Leave this room' meejitly!" she cried, her voice trembling with anger. "My papa is the best man in the world. He never bused anybody!"

"Allow me to explain, please," said the visitor, without paying attention to her request to go away. "Your father may be very kind to you, for you are his little girl, you know. But when he's downtown in his office, he's inclined to be rather severe, especially on book agents. I called on him the other day and asked him to buy the 'Complete Works of Peter Smith,' What do you suppose he did?"

She said nothing.

"Why," continued the man, with growing excitement, "he ordered me from his office and had me put out of the building by the janitor! What do you think of such treatment as that from the 'best papa in the world,' eh?"

"I think he was quite right," said Jane Gladys.

"Oh, you do? Well," said the man, "I resolved to be revenged for the insult. So, as your father is big and strong and a dangerous man, I have decided to be revenged upon his little girl."

Jane Gladys shivered.

"What are you going to do?" she asked.

"I'm going to present you with this book," he answered, taking it from under his arm. Then he sat down on the edge of a chair, placed his hat on the rug, and drew a fountain pen from his vest pocket.

"I'll write your name in it," said he. "How do you spell Gladys?"

"G-l-a-d-y-s," she replied.

"Thank you. Now this," he continued, rising and handing her the book with a bow, "is my revenge for your father's treatment of me. Perhaps he'll be sorry he didn't buy the 'Complete Works of Peter Smith.' Good-by, my dear."

He walked to the door, gave her another bow, and left the room, and Jane Gladys could see that he was laughing to himself as if very much amused.

When the door had closed behind the queer little man, the child sat down in the window again and glanced at the book. It had a red and yellow cover, and the word "Thingamajigs" was across the front in big letters.

Then she opened it curiously and saw her name written in black letters upon the first white leaf.

"He was a funny little man," she said thoughtfully.

She turned the next leaf and saw a big picture of a clown dressed in green, red, and yellow with a white face with three-cornered spots of red on each cheek and over the eyes. While she looked at this, the book trembled in her hands, the leaf crackled and creaked, and suddenly the clown jumped out of it and stood upon the floor beside her, becoming instantly as big as any ordinary clown.

After stretching his arms and legs and yawning in a rather impolite manner, he gave a silly chuckle and said:

"This is better! You don't know how cramped one gets, standing so long upon a page of flat paper."

Perhaps you can imagine how startled Jane Gladys was and how she stared at the clown who had just leaped out of the book.

"You didn't expect anything of this sort, did you?" he asked, leering at her in clown fashion. Then he turned around to look at the room, and Jane Gladys laughed despite her astonishment.

"What amuses you?" demanded the clown.

"Why, your back is all white!" cried the girl. "You're only a clown in front of you."

"Quite likely," he returned in an annoyed tone. "The artist made a front view of me. He wasn't expected to make the back of me, for that was against the book's page."

"But it makes you look so funny!" said Jane Gladys, laughing until her eyes were moist with tears.

The clown looked sulky and sat down on a chair so she couldn't see his back.

"I'm not the only thing in the book," he remarked

crossly.

This reminded her to turn another page, and she had scarcely noted that it contained the picture of a monkey when the animal sprang from the book with a great crumpling of paper and landed upon the window seat beside her.

"He-he-he-he-he!" chattered the creature, springing to the girl's shoulder and then to the center table. "This is great fun! Now I can be a real monkey instead of a picture of one."

"Real monkeys can't talk," said Jane Gladys reprovingly.

"How do you know? Have you ever been one yourself?" inquired the animal, and then he laughed loudly, and the clown laughed, too, as if he enjoyed the remark.

The girl was quite bewildered by this time. She thoughtlessly turned another leaf, and before she had time to look twice, a gray donkey leaped from the book and stumbled from the window seat to the floor with a great clatter.

"You're clumsy enough, I'm sure!" the child indignantly, for the beast had nearly upset her.

"Clumsy! And why not?" demanded the donkey with an angry voice. "If the fool artist had drawn you out of perspective, as I did, I guess you'd be clumsy yourself."

"What's wrong with you?" asked Jane Gladys.

"My front and rear legs on the left side are nearly six

inches too short; that's what's the matter! If that artist didn't know how to draw properly, why did he try to make a donkey?"

"I don't know," replied the child, seeing an answer was expected.

"I can hardly stand up," grumbled the donkey, "and the least little thing will topple me over."

"Don't mind that," said the monkey, making a spring at the chandelier and swinging from it by his tail until Jane Gladys feared he would knock all the globes off; "the same artist has made my ears as big as that clown's and everyone knows a monkey hasn't any ears to speak of—much less to draw."

"He should be prosecuted," remarked the clown gloomily. "I haven't any back."

Jane Gladys looked from one to the other with a puzzled expression upon her sweet face and turned another page of the book.

Swift as a flash, a tawney, spotted leopard sprang over her shoulder, which landed upon the back of a big leather armchair and turned upon the others with a fierce movement.

The monkey climbed to the top of the chandelier and chattered with fright. The donkey tried to run and straightway tipped over on his left side. The clown grew paler than ever, but he sat still in his chair and gave a low whistle of surprise.

The leopard crouched upon the back of the chair,

lashed his tail from side to side, and glared at all of them by turns, including Jane Gladys.

"Which of us are you going to attack first?" asked the donkey, trying hard to get upon his feet again.

"I can't attack any of you," snarled the leopard. "The artist made my mouth shut, so I haven't any teeth, and he forgot to make my claws. But I'm a frightful looking creature, nevertheless; am I not?"

"Oh, yes," said the clown indifferently. "I suppose you're frightful looking enough. But if you have no teeth or claws, we don't mind your looks."

This annoyed the leopard so that he growled horribly, and the monkey laughed at him.

Just then, the book slipped from the girl's lap, and as she moved to catch it, one of the pages near the back opened wide. She caught a glimpse of a fierce grizzly bear looking at her from the page and quickly threw the book from her. It fell with a crash in the middle of the room, but beside it stood the great grizzly, who had wrenched himself from the page before the book closed.

"Now," cried the leopard from his perch, "you'd better look out for yourselves! You can't laugh at him as you did at me. The bear has both claws and teeth."

"Indeed I have," said the bear in a low, deep, growling voice. "And I know how to use them, too. If you read that book, you'll find I'm described as a horrible, cruel, and remorseless grizzly whose only life business is to eat up little girls—shoes, dresses, ribbons, and all! And then, the author says, I smack my lips and glory in my wickedness."

"That's awful!" said the donkey, sitting upon his haunches and shaking his head sadly. "What do you suppose possessed the author to make you so hungry for girls? Do you eat animals, also?"

"The author does not mention my eating anything but little girls," replied the bear.

"Very good," remarked the clown, drawing a long breath of relief. "you may begin eating Jane Gladys as soon as you wish. She laughed because I had no back."

"And she laughed because my legs are out of perspective," brayed the donkey.

"But you also deserve to be eaten," screamed the leopard from the back of the leather chair, "for you laughed and poked fun at me because I had no claws nor teeth! Don't you suppose, Mr. Grizzly, you could manage to eat a clown, a donkey, and a monkey after you finish the girl?"

"Perhaps so, and a leopard into the bargain," growled the bear. "It will depend on how hungry I am. But I must first begin with the little girl because the author says I prefer girls to anything."

Jane Gladys was much frightened on hearing this conversation, and she began to realize what the man meant when he said he gave her the book to be revenged. Surely papa would be sorry he hadn't bought the "Complete Works of Peter Smith" when he came

home and found his little girl eaten up by a grizzly bear
—shoes, dress, ribbons and all!

The bear stood up and balanced himself on his rear
legs.

"This is how I look in the book," he said. "Now watch
me eat the little girl."

He advanced slowly toward Jane Gladys, and the
monkey, the leopard, the donkey, and the clown all
stood around in a circle and watched the bear with
much interest.

But before the grizzly reached her, the child had a
sudden thought and cried out:

"Stop! You mustn't eat me. It would be wrong."

"Why?" asked the bear in surprise.

"Because I own you. You're my private property," she
answered.

"I don't see how you make that out," said the bear in a
disappointed tone.

"Why the book was given to me; my name's on the
front leaf. And you belong, by rights, in the book. So
you mustn't dare to eat your owner!"

The grizzly hesitated.

"Can any of you read?" he asked.

"I can," said the clown.

"Then see if she speaks the truth. Is her name really in
the book?"

The clown picked it up and looked at the name.

"It is," said he. "'Jane Gladys Brown;' written quite plainly in big letters."

The bear sighed.

"Then, of course, I can't eat her," he decided. "That author is as disappointing as most authors are."

"But he's not as bad as the artist," exclaimed the donkey, who was still trying to stand up straight.

"The fault lies with yourselves," said Jane Gladys severely. "Why didn't you stay in the book where you were put?"

The animals foolishly looked at each other, and the clown blushed under his white paint.

"Really—" began the bear, and then he stopped short.

The doorbell rang loudly.

"It's mamma!" cried Jane Gladys, springing to her feet. "She's come home at last. Now, you stupid creatures—"

But she was interrupted by them all making a rush for the book. There was a swish and a buzz and a rustling of leaves, and an instant later, the book lay on the floor looking just like any other book while Jane Gladys' strange companions had all disappeared.

The Twelve Dancing Princesses

by Brothers Grimm

There was a king who had twelve beautiful daughters. They slept in twelve beds all in one room; and when they went to bed, the doors were shut and locked up; but every morning, their shoes were found to be quite worn through as if they had been danced in all night; and yet nobody could find out how it happened, or where they had been.

Then the king made it known to all the land that if any person could discover the secret and find out where it was that the princesses danced in the night, he should have the one he liked best for his wife and should be king after his death; but whoever tried and failed, after three days and nights, should be put to death.

A king's son soon came. He was well entertained and, in the evening, was taken to the chamber next to the one where the princesses lay in their twelve beds. There he was to sit and watch where they went dancing, and the door of his chamber was left open so that nothing might pass without his hearing it. But the king's son soon fell asleep, and when he awoke in the morning, he found that the princesses had all been dancing, for the soles of their shoes were full of holes. The same thing happened on the second and third nights: the king ordered his head to be cut off. After he came several others, but they had all the same luck and all lost their lives in the same manner.

Now it chanced that an old soldier, who had been wounded in battle and could fight no longer, passed through the country where this king reigned: and as he was traveling through a wood, he met an old woman who asked him where he was going. 'I hardly know where I am going or what I had better do,' said the soldier, 'but I think I should like very well to find out where the princesses dance, and then I might be a king in time.' 'Well,' said the old dame, 'that is no tough task: only take care not to drink any of the wine that one of the princesses will bring to you in the evening, and as soon as she leaves, you pretend to be fast asleep.'

Then she gave him a cloak and said, 'As soon as you put that on, you will become invisible, and you will then be able to follow the princesses wherever they go.' When the soldier heard all this good counsel, he determined to try his luck: so he went to the king and said he was willing to undertake the task.

He was as well received as the others had been, and the king ordered fine royal robes to be given him, and when the evening came, he was led to the outer chamber. Just as he was going to lie down, the eldest of the princesses brought him a cup of wine; but the soldier threw it all away secretly, taking care not to drink a drop. Then he laid himself on his bed and began to snore loudly for a little while as if fast asleep. When the twelve princesses heard this, they laughed heartily; the eldest said, 'This fellow too might have done a wiser thing than lose his life in this way!' Then they rose, opened their drawers and boxes, took out all their fine clothes, dressed at the glass, and skipped about as if they were eager to begin dancing. But the youngest said, 'I don't know how it is; while you are so happy, I feel very uneasy; I am sure some mischance will befall us.' 'You simpleton,' said the eldest, 'you are always afraid; have you forgotten how many kings' sons have already watched in vain? And as for this soldier, even if

I had not given him his sleeping draught, he would have slept soundly enough.'

When they were all ready, they went and looked at the soldier; but he snored on and did not stir hand or foot: so they thought they were pretty safe, and the eldest went up to her bed and clapped her hands, and the bed sank into the floor, and a trap-door flew open. The soldier saw them going down through the trap-door one after another, the eldest leading the way; and thinking he had no time to lose, he jumped up, put on the cloak which the old woman had given him, and followed them; but in the middle of the stairs he trod on the gown of the youngest princess, and she cried out to her sisters, 'All is not right; someone took hold of my gown.' 'You silly creature!' said the eldest, 'it is nothing but a nail in the wall.' Then down they all went, and at the bottom, they found themselves in a most delightful grove of trees; the leaves were all silver, glittered, and sparkled beautifully. The soldier wished to take away some token of the place, so he broke off a little branch, and a loud noise came from the tree. Then the youngest daughter said again, 'I am sure all is not right—did not you hear that noise? That never happened before.' But the eldest said, 'It is only our princes who are shouting for joy at our approach.'

Then they came to another grove of trees, where all the leaves were of gold, and afterward to a third, where the leaves were all glittering diamonds. And the soldier broke a branch from each; and every time there was a loud noise, which made the youngest sister tremble with fear; but the eldest still said it was only the princes, who were crying for joy. So they went on till they came to a great lake, and at the side of the lake, there lay twelve little boats with twelve handsome princes, who seemed to be waiting there for the princesses.

One of the princesses went into each boat, and the soldier stepped into the same boat with the youngest. As they were rowing over the lake, the prince who was in the boat with the youngest princess and the soldier said, 'I do not know why it is, but though I am rowing with all my might, we do not get on so fast as usual, and I am quite tired: the boat seems very heavy today.' 'It is only the heat of the weather,' said the princess: 'I feel it very warm too.'

On the other side of the lake stood a fine illuminated castle, from which came the merry music of horns and trumpets. There they all landed and went into the castle, and each prince danced with his princess; and the soldier, who was all the time invisible, danced with them too; and when any of the princesses had a cup of wine set by her, he drank it all up, so that when she put the cup to her mouth, it was empty. At this, too, the youngest sister was frightened, but the eldest always silenced her. They danced until three o'clock in the morning, and then all their shoes were worn out, so they were obliged to leave. The princes rowed them back again over the lake (but this time, the soldier placed himself in the boat with the eldest princess), and on the opposite shore, they took leave of each other, the princesses promising to come again the next night.

When they came to the stairs, the soldier ran on before the princesses and laid himself down; and as the twelve sisters slowly came up very much tired, they heard him snoring in his bed; so they said, 'Now all is quite safe'; then they undressed, put away their fine clothes, pulled off their shoes, and went to bed. In the morning, the soldier said nothing about what had happened but determined to see more of this strange adventure and went again the second and third night; everything happened just as before; the princesses danced each time till their shoes were worn to pieces and then returned home. However, on the third night, the soldier carried away one of the golden cups as a token of where he had been.

As soon as the time came when he was to declare the secret, he was taken before the king with the three branches and the golden cup; and the twelve princesses stood listening behind the door to hear what he would say. And when the king asked him. 'Where do my twelve daughters dance at night?' he answered, 'With twelve princes in a castle underground.' And then he told the king all that had happened and showed him the three branches and the golden cup he had brought. Then the king called for the princesses and asked them whether what the soldier said was true: and when they saw that they were discovered and that it was useless to deny what had happened, they confessed it all. And the king asked the soldier which of them he would choose for his wife; and he answered, 'I am not very young so that I will have the eldest.'—And they were married that very day, and the soldier was chosen to be the king's heir.

Mr. Wardle's Servant Joe

by Charles Dickens
Edited By Rev. Jesse Lyman Hurlbut, D.D.

An old country gentleman named Wardle had a servant of whom he was very proud, not because of the latter's diligence but because Joe, commonly called the "Fat Boy," was a character that could not be matched anywhere in the world. When our story opens, Mr. Pickwick of London, and three others from his literary club, are traveling in search of adventure. With Mr. Pickwick, the founder and head of the Pickwick Club, were Mr. Tupman, whose great weakness for the ladies brought him frequent troubles, Mr. Winkle, whose desire to appear as a sport brought much ridicule upon himself, and Mr. Snodgrass, whose poetic nature induced him to write many romantic verses which amused his friends and all who read them. These four Pickwickians were introduced one day to Mr. Wardle, his aged sister Miss Rachel Wardle, and his two daughters, Emily and Isabella, as they were looking at some army reviews from their coach. Mr. Wardle hospitably asked Mr. Pickwick and his friends to join them in the coach.

"Come up here! Mr. Pickwick," said Mr. Wardle, "come along, sir. Joe! Drat, that boy! He's gone to sleep again. Joe let down the steps and opened the carriage door. Come ahead, room for two of you inside and one outside. Joe, make room for one. Put this gentleman on the box!" Mr. Wardle mounted with a bit of help, and the fat boy, where he was, fell fast asleep.

One rank of soldiers after another passed, firing over the heads of another level, and when the cannon went off, the air resounded with the screams of ladies. Mr. Snodgrass needed to support one of the Misses Wardle with his arm. Their maidenly aunt was in such a dreadful state of nervous alarm that Mr. Tupman found that he was obliged to put his arm around her waist to keep her up. Everyone was excited except for the fat boy, who slept as soundly as if the roaring of cannon were his ordinary lullaby.

"Joe! Joe!" called Mr. Wardle. "Drat, that boy! He's gone asleep again. Pinch him in the leg, if you please. Nothing else wakens him. Thank you. Get out the lunch, Joe." The fat boy, who Mr. Winkle had effectually aroused, proceeded to unpack the hamper more quickly than could have been expected from his previous inactivity.

"Now, Joe, knives and forks." The knives and forks were handed in, and each was furnished with these valuable implements.

"Now Joe, the fowls. Drat, that boy! He's gone asleep again. Joe! Joe!" With numerous taps on the head with a stick, the fat boy, with some difficulty, was awakened. "Go hand in the eatables." There was something in the sound of the last word which aroused him. He jumped up with reddened eyes, which twinkled behind his mountainous cheeks, and feasted upon the food as he unpacked it from the basket.

"Now make haste," said Mr. Wardle, for the fat boy was hanging fondly over a chicken he seemed unable to part with. The boy sighed deeply and, casting an ardent gaze upon its plumpness, unwillingly handed it to his master.

"A very extraordinary boy, that," said Mr. Pickwick. "Does he always sleep in this way?"

"Sleep!" said the old gentleman. "He's always

sleeping. He goes on errands fast asleep and snores as he waits at the table."

"How very odd," said Mr. Pickwick.

"Ah! odd indeed," returned the old gentleman. "I'm proud of that boy. I wouldn't part with him on any account. He's a natural curiosity. Here, Joe, take these things away and open another bottle. Do you hear?" The fat boy, aroused, opened his eyes, started and finished the piece of pie he was in the act of eating when he fell fast asleep, and slowly obeyed his master's orders, looking intently upon the remains of the feast as he removed the plates and stowed them in the hamper. At last, Mr. Wardle and his party mounted the coach and prepared to drive off.

"Now mind," he said, as he shook hands with Mr. Pickwick, "we expect to see you all tomorrow. You have the address?"

"Manor Farm, Dingley Dell," said Mr. Pickwick, consulting his pocketbook.

"That's it," said the old gentleman. "You must come for at least a week. If you are traveling to get country life, come to me, and I will give you plenty of it. Joe! Drat, that boy, he's gone to sleep again. Help put in the horses." The horses were put in, the driver mounted, and the boy clambered up by his side. The farewells were exchanged, and the carriage rolled off. As the Pickwickians turned around to take a last glimpse of it, the setting sun cast a red gold upon the faces of their entertainers and fell upon the form of the fat boy. His head was sunk upon his bosom, and he slumbered again.

After some amusing difficulties, which we have no space to describe here, Mr. Pickwick and his friends arrived safely at the country home of Mr. Wardle. The time passed very pleasantly.

One day some of the men decided upon a shooting trip, and Mr. Winkle did not admit that he knew nothing about guns to maintain his reputation as a sport. Mr. Pickwick, early in the morning, seeing Mr. Wardle carrying a gun, asked what they would do.

"Why, your friend and I are going out rook shooting. He's a perfect shot, isn't he?" said Mr. Wardle.

"I have heard him say he's a capital one," replied Mr. Pickwick, "but I never saw him aim at anything."

"Well," said the host, "I wish Mr. Tupman would join us. Joe! Joe!" The fat boy who, under the exciting influences of the morning, did not appear to be more than three parts and a fraction asleep, emerged from the house. "Go up and call Mr. Tupman, and tell him he will find us waiting."

At last, the party started, Mr. Tupman having joined them. Some boys, who were with them, discovered a tree with a nest in one of the branches, and when all was ready, Mr. Wardle was persuaded to shoot first. In violent conversation, the boys shouted and shook a unit with a nest on it, and a half-dozen young rooks flew out to ask what the matter was. Mr. Wardle leveled his gun and fired; down fell one, and off flew the others.

"Pick him up, Joe," said the old gentleman. As he advanced, there was a smile upon the youth's face, for an indistinct vision of rook pie floated through his imagination. He laughed as he retired with the bird. It was a plump one.

"Now, Mr. Winkle," said the host, reloading his gun, "fire away." Mr. Winkle advanced and raised his rifle. Mr. Pickwick and his friends crouched involuntarily to escape damage from the heavy fall of birds, which they felt pretty confident would be caused by their friend's skill. There was a solemn pause, a shout, a flapping of wings.

Mr. Winkle closed his eyes and fired; there was a scream from an individual, not a rook. Mr. Tupman had saved the lives of innumerable birds by receiving a portion of the charge in his left arm. Though it was a slight wound, Mr. Tupman made a great fuss about it, and everyone was horror-stricken. He was partly carried to the house. The unmarried aunt uttered a piercing scream, burst into a hysterical laugh, and fell backward into the arms of her nieces. She recovered, screamed again, laughed again, and fainted again.

"Calm yourself," said Mr. Tupman, affected almost to tears by this expression of sympathy. "Dear, the dear Madam, calm yourself."

"You are not dead?" exclaimed the hysterical lady. "Say you are not dead!"

"Don't be a fool, Rachel," said Mr. Winkle. "What the mischief is the use of his saying he isn't dead?"

"No! No! I am not," said Mr. Tupman. "I require no assistance but yours. Let me lean on your arm," he added in a whisper. Miss Rachel advanced and offered her arm. They turned into the breakfast parlor. Mr. Tupman gently pressed her hands to his lips and sunk upon the sofa. Presently the others left him to her tender mercies. That afternoon Mr. Tupman, much affected by the extreme tenderness of Miss Rachel, suggested that as he was feeling much better, they take a short stroll in the garden. There was a bower at the farther end, all honeysuckles and creeping plants, and somehow they unconsciously wandered in its direction and sat down on a bench within.

"Miss Wardle," said Mr. Tupman, "you are an angel." Miss Rachel blushed very becomingly. Much more conversation of this nature followed until, finally, Mr. Tupman proceeded to do what his enthusiastic emotions prompted and what were (for all we know, for we are but little acquainted with such matters) what people in such circumstances always do. She started, and he, throwing his arms around her neck, imprinted upon her lips numerous kisses, which, after a good show of struggling and resistance, she received so passively that there is no telling how many more Mr. Tupman might have bestowed if the lady had not given a remarkably unaffected start and exclaimed: "Mr. Tupman, we are observed! We are discovered!"

Mr. Tupman looked around. The fat boy was perfectly motionless, with his large, circular eyes staring into the arbor but without the slightest expression on his face.

Mr. Tupman gazed at the fat boy, and the fat boy stared at him, but the longer Mr. Tupman observed the utter vacancy of the fat boy's face, the more convinced he became that he either did not know or did not understand anything that had been happening. Under this impression, he said with great fierceness: "What do you want here?"

"Supper is ready, sir," was the prompt reply.

"Have you just come here?" inquired Mr. Tupman with a piercing look.

"Just," replied the fat boy. Mr. Tupman looked at him hard again, but there was no wink of his eye or a movement in his face. Mr. Tupman took the arm of the spinster aunt and walked toward the house. The fat boy followed behind.

"He knows nothing of what has happened," he whispered.

"Nothing," said the spinster aunt. There was a sound behind them as of an imperfectly suppressed chuckle. Mr. Tupman turned sharply around.

No, it could not have been the fat boy. There was not a gleam of joy or anything but feeding in his whole visage. "He must have been fast asleep," whispered Mr. Tupman.

"I have not the least doubt of it," replied Miss Rachel, and they both laughed heartily. Mr. Tupman was wrong. The fat boy, for once, had not been fast asleep. He was awake, wide awake to everything that had happened.

The day following, Joe saw his mistress, Mr. Wardle's aged mother, sitting in the arbor. Without saying a word, he walked up to her, stood perfectly still, and said nothing.

The old lady was easily frightened, as most old ladies are, and her first impression was that Joe was about to do her some bodily harm with a view of stealing what money she might have with her. She, therefore, watched his motions, or rather lack of motions, with feelings of intense terror, which were in no degree lessened by his finally coming close to her and shouting in her ear, for she was very deaf, "Missus!"

"Well, Joe," said the trembling old lady, "I am sure I have been a good mistress to you." He nodded. "You have always been treated very kindly?" He nodded. "You have never had too much to do?" He nodded. "You have always had enough to eat?" This last was an appeal to the fat boy's most sensitive feelings. He seemed touched as he replied, "I know I have."

"Then what do you want to do now?"

"I want to make yo' flesh creep," replied the boy. This sounded like a very blood-thirsty method of showing one's gratitude, and so the old lady was as much frightened as before. "What do you think I saw in this arbor last night?" inquired the boy.

"Mercies, what?" screamed the old lady, alarmed at the mysterious manner of the corpulent youth.

"A strange gentleman as had his arm around her, a kissin' and huggin'."

"Who, Joe, who? None of the servants, I hope?"

"Worser than that," roared the fat boy in the old lady's ear.

"None of my granddaughters."

"Worser than that," said Joe.

"Worse than that?" said the old lady, who had thought this the extreme limit. "Who was it, Joe? I insist upon knowing!"

The fat boy looked cautiously about and, having finished his survey, shouted in the old lady's ear, "Miss Rachel!"

"What?" said the old lady shrilly, "speak louder!"

"Miss Rachel," roared the fat boy.

"My daughter?" The succession of nods the fat boy gave by permission could not be doubted. "And she allowed him?" exclaimed the old lady. A grin stole over the fat boy's features as he said, "I see her a kissin' of him again!" Joe's voice of necessity had been so loud that another party in the garden could not help hearing the entire conversation. If they could have seen the expression on the old lady's face at this time, a sudden burst of laughter would probably have betrayed them. Fragments of angry sentences drifted to them through the leaves, such as "Without my permission!" "At her time of life!" "Might have waited until I was dead," etc. Then they heard the heels of the fat boy's foot crunching the gravel as he retired and left the old lady alone.

Mr. Tupman would probably have found himself in considerable trouble if one of his friends, who had overheard the conversation, had not told Mrs. Wardle that perhaps Joe had dreamed the entire incident, which did not seem improbable. She watched Mr. Tupman at supper that evening, but this gentleman, having been warned, paid no attention to Miss Rachel. The old lady was finally persuaded that it was all a mistake.

Finally, the visit of Mr. Pickwick and his friends ended, and it was several months before they again partook of Mr. Wardle's hospitality. The Pickwickians had arrived at the Inn near Mr. Wardle's place for dinner before completing the rest of their journey to Dingley Dell. Mr. Pickwick had brought several barrels of oysters and some special wine as a gift to his host, and he stood examining his packages to see that they had all arrived when he felt gently pulled by the skirts of his coat. Looking around, he discovered that the individual who used this means of drawing his attention was no other than Mr. Wardle's favorite page, the fat boy.

"Aha!" said Mr. Pickwick.

"Ah!" said the fat boy, and as he said it, he glanced from the wine to the oysters and chuckled joyously. He was more overweight than ever.

"Well, you look rosy enough, my young friend," said Mr. Pickwick.

"I have been sitting in front of the fire," replied the fat boy, who had indeed heated himself to the color of a new chimney pot in an hour's nap. "Master sent me over with the cart to carry your luggage over to the house." Mr. Pickwick called his man, Sam Weller, and said, "Help Mr. Wardle's servant put the packages into the cart and then ride on with him. We prefer to walk." Having given this direction, Mr. Pickwick and his three friends walked briskly away, leaving Mr. Weller and the fat boy face to face for the first time. Sam looked at the fat boy with great astonishment but without saying a word and began to put the things rapidly upon the cart while Joe stood calmly by and seemed to think it an exciting sort of thing to see Mr. Weller working by himself.

"There," said Sam, "everything packed at last. There they are."

"Yes," said the fat boy in a cheerful tone, "there they are."

"Well, young twenty stone," said Sam. "You're a nice specimen, you are."

"Thankee," said the fat boy.

"You ain't got nothing on your mind as makes you fret yourself, have you?" inquired Sam.

"Not as I know of," replied the boy.

"I should rather have thought, to look at you, that you were a laborin' under a disappointing love affair with some young woman," said Sam. "Well, young boa-constrictor," said Sam, "I'm glad to hear it. Do you ever drink anythin'?"

"I like eatin' better," replied the boy.

"Ah!" said Sam. "I should ha' 'sposed that, but I 'spose you were never cold with all them elastic fixtures?"

"Was sometimes," replied the boy, "I like a drop of something good."

"Ah! you do, do you," said Sam, "come this way." Then after a short interruption, they got into the cart.

"You can drive, can you?" said the fat boy.

"I should rather think so," replied Sam.

"Well then," said the fat boy, putting the reins in his hands and pointing up a lane, "it's as straight as you can drive. You can't miss it." With these words, the fat boy laid himself affectionately down by the side of the provisions and, placing an oyster barrel under his head for a pillow, fell asleep instantly.

"Well," said Sam, "of all the boys ever I set my eyes on —wake up, young dropsy." But as young dropsy could not be awakened, Sam Weller set himself down in front of the cart, started the old horse with a jerk of the rein, and jogged steadily toward Manor Farm.

The White Cat

by the Comtesse d'Aulnoy

There was once a king with three sons, all remarkably handsome in their persons and their tempers, brave and noble. Some wicked courtiers made the king believe that the princes were impatient to wear the crown and were contriving a plot to deprive him of his scepter and kingdom. The king felt he was growing old; but as he found himself as capable of governing as he had ever been, he had no inclination to resign his power; and therefore, that he might pass the rest of his days peaceably, he determined to employ the princes in such a manner, as at once to give each of them the hope of succeeding to the crown, and fill up the time they might otherwise spend in so undutiful a manner. He sent them to his cabinet, and after conversing with them kindly, he added: "You must be sensible, my dear children, that my great age prevents me from attending so closely as I have hitherto done to state affairs. I fear this may be harmful to my subjects; I, therefore, desire to place my crown on the head of one of you, but it is no more than just that in return for such a present, you should procure me some amusement in my retirement before I leave the Capital forever. I cannot help thinking that a little dog that is handsome, faithful, and engaging would be the very thing to make me happy, so without bestowing a preference on either of you, I declare that he who brings me the most perfect little dog shall be my successor." The princes were much surprised at the fancy of their father to have a little dog. Yet, they accepted the proposition with pleasure: and accordingly, after taking leave of the king, who presented them with an abundance of money and jewels and appointed that day twelvemonth for their return, they set off on their travels.

Before taking leave of each other, however, they took some refreshments together in an old palace about three miles out of town, where they agreed to meet in the same place on that day twelvemonth and go all together with their presents to court. They also decided to change their names so that they might be unknown to everyone in their travels.

Each took a different road, but it is intended to relate

the adventures of only the youngest, who was the most handsome, most amiable, and accomplished prince that had ever been seen. No day passed, as he traveled from town to town, that he did not buy all the handsome dogs that fell in his way; and as soon as he saw one that was more handsome than those he had before, he made a present of the last; for twenty servants would have been scarcely sufficient to take care of all the dogs he was continually buying.

At length, wandering, he knew not whither he found himself in a forest; night suddenly came on, with it a violent thunder, lightning, and rain storm. To add to his perplexity, he lost his path and could find no way out of the forest. After he had groped about for a long time, he perceived a light, which made him suppose that he was not far from some house: he accordingly pursued his way towards it and, in a short time, found himself at the gates of the most magnificent palace he ever beheld. The door that opened into it was made of gold, covered with sapphire stones, which cast so resplendent a brightness over everything around that the strongest eyesight could scarcely bear to look at it. This was the light the prince had seen from the forest. The walls of the building were of transparent porcelain, variously colored, and represented the history of all the fairies that had existed from the beginning of the world. The prince coming back to the golden door, observed a deer's foot fastened to a chain of diamonds; he could not help wondering at the magnificence he beheld and the security in which the inhabitants seemed to live;

"for," said he to himself, "nothing can be easier than for thieves to steal this chain, and as many of the sapphire stones as would make their fortunes." He pulled the chain and heard a bell, the sound of which was exquisite. In a few moments, the door was opened; but he perceived nothing but twelve hands in the air, each holding a torch. The prince was so astonished that he durst not move a step; when he felt himself gently pushed on by some other hands from behind him. He walked on, in great perplexity, till he entered a vestibule inlaid with porphyry and lapis-stone. There the most melodious voice he had ever heard chanted the following words:

"Welcome, prince, no danger, fear,

Mirth and love attend you here;

You shall break the magic spell,

That on a beauteous lady fell.

"Welcome, prince, no danger, fear,

Mirth and love attend you here,"

The prince now advanced with confidence, wondering what these words could mean; the hands moved him forward towards a large door of coral, which opened of itself to give him admittance into a splendid apartment built of mother-of-pearl, through which he passed into others so richly adorned with paintings and jewels, and so resplendently lighted with thousands of lamps, girandoles, and lusters, that the prince imagined he must be in an enchanted palace.

When he had passed through sixty apartments, all equally splendid, he was stopped by the hands, and a large easy chair advanced of itself towards the chimney. The hands, which he observed were extremely white and delicate, took off his wet clothes, supplied their place with the finest linen imaginable, and then added a commodious wrapping-gown embroidered with the brightest gold and all over enriched with pearls. The hands next brought him an elegant dressing table and combed his hair so very gently that he scarcely felt their touch. They held before him a beautiful basin filled with perfumes for him to wash his face and hands and afterward took off the wrapping gown and dressed him in a suit of clothes of still more extraordinary splendor. When his dress was complete, they conducted him to an apartment he had not yet seen and was magnificently furnished. There was a table spread for a repast, and everything upon it was of the purest gold adorned with jewels. The prince observed two covers set and was wondering who was to be his companion when his attention was suddenly caught by a small figure, not a foot high, who just then entered the room and advanced towards him. It had on a long black veil and was supported by two cats dressed in mourning and with swords by their sides: they were followed by a numerous retinue of cats, some carrying cages full of rats and others mousetraps full of mice.

The prince was at a loss for what to think. The little figure now approached and threw aside her veil. He beheld a most beautiful white cat. She seemed young and melancholy, addressing herself to the prince. She said, "Young prince, you are welcome; your presence affords me the greatest pleasure." "Madam," replied the prince, "I would fain thank you for your generosity, nor can I help to observe that you must be an extraordinary creature to possess with your present form the gift of speech and the magnificent palace I have seen." "All this is very true," answered the beautiful cat, "but, prince, I am not fond of talking, and least of all do I like compliments; let us sit down to supper." The trunkless hands then placed the dishes on the table, and the prince and white cat seated themselves. The first dish was a pie made of young pigeons, and the next was a fricassee of the fattest mice. The view of the one made the prince almost afraid to taste the other till the white cat, who guessed his thoughts, assured him that there were certain dishes at a table in which there was not a morsel of either rat or mouse, which had been dressed on purpose for him. Accordingly, he ate heartily of such as she recommended. When supper was over, the prince perceived that the white cat had a portrait set in gold hanging to one of her feet. He begged her permission to look at it; when, to his astonishment, he saw the portrait of a handsome young man that exactly resembled himself! He thought there was something very extraordinary in all this: yet, as the white cat sighed and looked very sorrowful, he did not venture to ask any questions. He conversed with her on different subjects and found her extremely well-versed in everything that was passing in the world. When the night was far advanced, the white cat wished him a good night, and the hands conducted him to his bed-chamber, which was different still from anything he had seen in the palace, being hung with the wings of butterflies mixed with the most curious feathers. His bed was of gauze, festooned with bunches of the gayest ribands, and the looking glasses reached from the floor to the ceiling. The prince was undressed and put into bed by the hands without speaking. He, however, slept little and, in the morning, was awakened by a confused noise. The hands took him out of bed and put on him a handsome hunting jacket. He looked into the courtyard and perceived more than five hundred cats, busily employed in preparing for the field, for this was a day of the festival. Presently the white cat came to his apartment and politely inquired about his health. She invited him to partake of their amusement. The prince willingly accepted, mounted a wooden horse, richly caparisoned, which had been prepared for him, and which he was assured would gallop to admiration. The beautiful white cat mounted a monkey dressed in a dragoon's bonnet, which made her look so fierce that all the rats and mice ran away with the utmost terror.

Everything being ready, the horns sounded, and away they went; no hunting was ever more agreeable; the cats ran faster than the hares and rabbits, and when they caught any, they were hunted in the presence of the white cat and a thousand cunning tricks were played. Nor were the birds in safety, for the monkey made nothing of climbing up the trees, with the white cat on his back, to the nest of the young eagles. When the hunting was over, the whole entourage returned to the palace. The white cat immediately exchanged her dragoon's cap for the veil and sat down to supper with the prince. Being very hungry, he ate heartily and, afterward, partook with her of the most delicious liqueurs, which often made him forget that he was to procure a little dog for the old king. He thought no longer of anything but of pleasing the sweet little creature who received him so courteously; accordingly, every day was spent in new amusements. The prince had almost forgotten his country and relations and sometimes even regretted that he was not a cat, so great was his affection for his mewing companions. "Alas!" said he to the white cat, "how will it afflict me to leave you, whom I love so much! Either make yourself a lady or make me a cat." She smiled at the prince's wish but made him scarcely any reply. At length, the twelvemonth was nearly expired; the white cat, who knew the very day when the prince was to reach his father's palace, reminded him that he had but three days longer to look for a perfect little dog. The prince, astonished at his forgetfulness, began to afflict himself; when the cat told him not to be so sorrowful since she would not only provide him with a little dog but also with a wooden horse which should convey him safely in less than twelve hours. "Look here," said she, showing him an acorn, "this contains what you desire." The prince put the acorn to his ear and heard the barking of a little dog. Transported with joy, he thanked the cat a thousand times, and the next day, bidding her tenderly adieu, he set out on his return.

The prince arrived first at the place of rendezvous and was soon joined by his brothers; they mutually embraced and began to give an account of their success; when the youngest showed them only a little mongrel cur, telling them he thought it could not fail to please the king from its extraordinary beauty, the brothers trod on each other's toes under the table; as much as to say, we have not much to fear from this sorry looking animal. The next day they went together to the palace. The dogs of the two elder princes were lying on cushions and so curiously wrapped around with embroidered quilts that one would scarcely venture to touch them. The youngest produced his cur, dirty all over, and all wondered how the prince could hope to receive a crown for such a present. The king examined the two little dogs of the elder princes and declared he thought them so equally beautiful that he knew not to which, with justice, he could give the preference. They accordingly began to dispute; when the youngest prince, taking his acorn from his pocket, soon ended their contention for a little dog that could easily go through the smallest ring and was a miracle of beauty. The king could not possibly hesitate in declaring his satisfaction; yet, as he was not more inclined than the year before to part with his crown, he could think of nothing more to his purpose than telling his sons that he was extremely obliged to them for the pains they had taken; and that since they had succeeded so well, he could not but wish they would make a second attempt; he, therefore, begged they would take another year for procuring him a piece of cambric, so fine as to be drawn through the eye of a small needle.

The three princes thought this very hard, yet they obeyed the king's command. The two eldest took different roads, and the youngest remounted his wooden horse and, in a short time, arrived at the palace of his beloved white cat, who received him with the greatest joy while the trunkless hands helped him to dismount, and provided him with immediate refreshments; after which the prince gave the white cat an account of the admiration which had been bestowed on the beautiful little dog, and informed her of his father's farther injunction. "Make yourself perfectly easy, dear prince," said she, "I have in my palace some cats that are perfectly clever in making such cambric as the king requires; so you have nothing to do but to give me the pleasure of your company while it is making, and I will procure you all the amusement possible." She accordingly ordered the most curious fireworks to be played off in the sight of the window of the apartment in which they were sitting, and nothing but festivity and rejoicing was heard throughout the palace for the prince's return. As the white cat continually gave proofs of an excellent understanding, the prince was by no means tired of her company; she talked with him of state affairs, of theatres, of fashions; in short, she was at a loss on no subject whatever; so that when the prince was alone, he had plenty of amusement in thinking how it could possibly be that a small white cat could be endowed with all the powers of human creatures.

The twelvemonth in this manner again passed

insensibly away, but the cat took care to remind the prince of his duty in proper time. "For once, my prince," said she, "I will have the pleasure of equipping you as suits your high rank;" when looking into the courtyard, he saw a superb car ornamented all over with gold, silver, pearls, and diamonds, drawn by twelve horses as white as snow, and harnessed in the most sumptuous trappings. Behind the car, a thousand guards richly apparelled were waiting to attend to the prince's person. She then presented him with a nut: "You will find in it," said she, "the piece of cambric I promised you. Do not break the shell till you are in the presence of the king, your father." Then, to prevent the acknowledgments the prince was about to offer, she hastily bade him adieu. Nothing could exceed the speed with which the snow-white horses conveyed this fortunate prince to his father's palace, where his brothers had just arrived before him. They embraced each other and demanded an immediate audience from the king, who received them with the greatest kindness. The princes hastened to place the curious present he had required them to procure at the feet of his majesty. The eldest produced a piece of cambric that was so extremely fine that his friends did not doubt it was passing the eye of the needle, which was now delivered to the king, having been kept locked up in the custody of his majesty's treasurer all the time, Everyone supposed he would certainly obtain the crown. But when the king tried to draw it through the eye of the needle, it would not pass, though it failed very little. Then came the second prince, who was sure of obtaining the crown as his brother had done, but, alas! With no better success: for though his piece of cambric was exquisitely fine, it could not be drawn through the eye of the needle. It was now the youngest prince's turn, who accordingly advanced, and opening an elegant little box inlaid with jewels, he took out a walnut and cracked the shell, imagining he should immediately perceive his piece of cambric; but what was his astonishment to see nothing but a filbert! He did not, however, lose his hopes; he cracked the filbert, and it presented him with a cherry stone. The lords of the court, who had assembled to witness this extraordinary trial, could not, any more than the princes, his brothers, refrain from laughing to think he should be so silly as to claim with them the crown on no better pretensions. The prince, however, cracked the cherry stone, which was filled with a kernel: he divided it and found in the middle a grain of wheat and, in that grain, a millet seed. He was now absolutely confounded and could not help muttering between his teeth: "O white cat, white cat, thou hast deceived me!" At this instant, he felt his hand scratched by the claw of a cat: upon which he again took courage, and opening the grain of millet seed, to the astonishment of all present, he drew forth a piece of cambric four hundred yards long, and fine enough to be drawn with perfect ease through the eye of the needle. When the king found he had no pretext left for refusing the crown to his youngest son, he sighed deeply, and it was easy to be seen that he was sorry for the prince's success. "My sons," said he, "it is so gratifying to the heart of a father to receive proofs of his children's love and obedience that I cannot refuse myself the satisfaction of requiring of you one more. You must undertake another expedition, and whichever brings me the most beautiful lady by the end of a year shall marry her and obtain my crown."

So they again took leave of the king and each other and set out without delay, and in less than twelve hours, our young prince arrived in his splendid car at the palace of his dear white cat. Everything went on as before till the end of another year. At length, only one day remained of the year when the white cat thus addressed him: "Tomorrow, my prince, you must present yourself at your father's palace and give him proof of your obedience. It depends only on yourself to conduct thither the most beautiful princess ever yet beheld, for the time is come when the enchantment by which I am bound may be ended. You must cut off my head and tail," continued she, "and throw them into the fire." "I!" said the prince hastily, "I cut off your head and tail! You surely mean to try my affection, which beautiful cat is truly yours." "You mistake me, generous prince," said she, "I do not doubt your regard, but if you wish to see me in any other form than a cat, you must consent to do as I desire. Then you will have done me a service I shall never be able sufficiently to repay." The prince's eyes filled with tears as she spoke, yet he considered himself obliged to undertake the dreadful task, and the cat continued to press him with greater eagerness. With a trembling hand, he drew his sword, cut off her head and tail, and threw them into the fire. No sooner was this done than the most beautiful lady his eyes had ever seen stood before him: and before he had sufficiently recovered from his surprise to speak to her, a long train of attendants, who, at the same moment as their mistress, were changed to their natural shapes, came to offer their congratulations to the queen, and inquire her commands. She received them with the greatest kindness and ordered them to withdraw. She thus addressed the astonished prince. "Do not imagine, dear prince, that I have always been a cat or that I am of obscure birth. My father was the monarch of six kingdoms; he tenderly loved my mother, leaving her always at liberty to follow her inclinations. Her prevailing passion was to travel; and a short time before my birth, having heard of some fairies who were in possession of the largest gardens filled with the most delicious fruits, she had so strong a desire to eat some of them that she set out for the country in which they lived. She arrived at their abode, which she found to be a magnificent palace, on all sides glittering with gold and precious stones. She knocked a long time at the gates, but no one came, nor could she perceive the least sign that it had any inhabitant. The difficulty, however, increased the violence of my mother's longing, for she saw the tops of the trees above the garden walls loaded with the most luscious fruits. The queen, in despair, ordered her attendants to place tents close to the palace door; but having waited six weeks without seeing anyone pass the gates, she fell sick of vexation, and her life was despaired of.

"One night, as she lay half asleep, she turned herself about, and, opening her eyes, perceived a little old woman, very ugly and deformed, seated in the easy chair by her bedside. 'I, and my sister fairies,' said she, 'take it very ill that your majesty should so obstinately persist in getting some of our fruit; but since so precious a life is at stake, we consent to give you as much as you can carry away, provided you will give us in return what we shall ask.' 'Ah! a kind fairy,' cried the queen, 'I will give you anything I possess, even my very kingdoms, on condition that I eat of your fruit.' The old fairy then informed the queen that what they required was that she would give them the child she was going to have as soon as she should be born, adding that every possible care should be taken of her and that she should become the most accomplished princess. The queen replied that however cruel the condition was, she must accept it since nothing but the fruit could save her life. In short, dear prince," continued the lady, "my mother instantly got out of bed, was dressed by her attendants, entered the palace, and satisfied her longing. When the queen had eaten her fill, she ordered four thousand mules to be procured and loaded with the fruit, which had the virtue of continuing all year round in a state of perfection. Thus provided, she returned to the king, my father, who, with the whole court, received her with rejoicings, as it was before imagined she would die of disappointment. All this time, the queen said nothing to my father of the promise she had made to give her daughter to the fairies; so that, when the time came that she expected my birth, she grew very melancholy; till, at length, being pressed by the king, she declared to him the truth. Nothing could exceed his affliction when he heard that his only child, when born, was to be given to the fairies. He bore it, however, as well as he could, for fear of adding to my mother's grief; and believing he should find some means of keeping me in a place of safety, which the fairies would not be able to approach. As soon as I was born, he had me conveyed to a tower in the palace, to which there were twenty flights of stairs and a door to each, of which my father kept the key so that none came near me without his consent. When the fairies heard of what had been done, they sent first to demand me. On my father's refusal, they let loose a monstrous dragon who devoured men, women, and children, and the breath of whose nostrils destroyed everything it came near so that the trees and plants began to die in great abundance. The grief of the king at seeing this could scarcely be equaled, and finding that his whole kingdom would be reduced to famine in a short time, he consented to give me into their hands. I was laid in a mother-of-pearl cradle ornamented with gold and jewels and carried to their palace when the dragon immediately disappeared. The fairies placed me in a tower of their palace, elegantly furnished, but to which there was no door so that whoever approached was obliged to come by the windows, which were a great height from the ground: from these, I had the liberty of getting out into a delightful garden, in which were baths, and every sort of cooling fruit. In this place was I educated by the fairies, who behaved to me with the greatest kindness; my clothes were splendid, and I was instructed in every kind of accomplishment. In short, prince, if I had never seen anyone but themselves, I should have remained very happy. One of the windows of my tower overlooked a long avenue shaded with trees so that I had never seen in it a human creature. One day, however, as I was talking at this window with my parrot, I perceived a young gentleman listening to our conversation. As I had never seen a man but in pictures, I was not sorry for the opportunity of gratifying my curiosity. I thought him a very pleasing object, and he at length bowed in the most respectful manner without daring to speak, for he knew that I was in the palace of the fairies. When it grew dark, he went away, and I vainly endeavored to see which road he took. The following day, as soon as it was light, I again placed myself at the window and saw that the gentleman had returned to the same place. He now spoke to me through a speaking trumpet and informed me he thought me a most charming lady and that he should be very unhappy if he did not pass his life in my company.

"I resolved to find some means of escaping from my tower with the engaging prince I had seen. I was not long in devising a means to execute my project. I begged the fairies to bring me a netting needle, a mesh, and some cord, saying I wished to make some nets to amuse myself with catching birds at my window. They readily complied with this, and I completed a ladder long enough to reach the ground in a short time. I now sent my parrot to the prince to beg he would come to his usual place, as I wished to speak with him. He did not fail and, finding the ladder, mounted it, and quickly entered my tower. This at first alarmed me, but the charms of his conversation had restored me to tranquillity when all at once the window opened, and the fairy Violent, mounted on the dragon's back, rushed into the tower. My beloved prince thought of nothing but how to defend me from their fury; for I had had time to relate to him my story previous to this cruel interruption, but their numbers overpowered him, and the fairy Violent had the barbarity to command the dragon to devour my prince before my eyes. In my despair, I would have thrown myself also into the mouth of the horrible monster, but this they took care to prevent, saying my life should be preserved for greater punishment. The fairy touched me with her wand, and I instantly became a white cat. She next conducted me to this palace, which belonged to my father, and gave me a train of cats for my attendants, together with the twelve hands which waited on your highness. She then informed me of my birth and the death of my parents and pronounced upon me what she imagined the greatest of maledictions: That I should not be restored to my natural figure till a young prince, the perfect resemblance of him I had lost, should cut off my head and tail. You are that perfect resemblance; accordingly, you have ended the enchantment. I need not add that I already love you more than my life. Let us, therefore, hasten to the palace of the king, your father, and obtain his approbation to our marriage."

The prince and princess set out side by side in a car of still greater splendor than before and reached the palace just as the two brothers had arrived with two beautiful princesses. The king, hearing that each of his sons had succeeded in finding what he had required, again began to think of some new expedient to delay the time of his resigning his crown. Still, when the whole court was with the king assembled to pass judgment, the princess who accompanied the youngest, perceiving his thoughts by his countenance, stepped majestically forward and thus addressed him: "What pity that your majesty, who is so capable of governing, should think of resigning the crown! I am fortunate enough to have six kingdoms in my possession; permit me to bestow one on each of the eldest princes and to enjoy the remaining four in the society of the youngest. And may it please your majesty to keep your own kingdom and make no decision concerning the beauty of three princesses, who, without such a proof of your majesty's preference, will no doubt live happily together!" The air resounded with the applauses of the assembly. The young prince and princess embraced the king and, next, their brothers and sisters; the three weddings immediately took place, and the kingdoms were divided as the princess had proposed

Little Dorrit

By Charles Dickens

Many years ago, when people could be imprisoned for debt, a poor gentleman, unfortunate enough to lose all his money, was brought to the Marshalsea prison. As there seemed no prospect of being able to pay his debts, his wife and their two little children came to live there with him. The elder child was a boy of three; the younger a little girl of two years old, and another little girl was born not long after. The three children played in the courtyard and were happy, on the whole, for they were too young to remember a happier state of things.

But the youngest child, who had never been outside the prison walls, was a thoughtful little creature and wondered what the outside world could be like. Her great friend, the turnkey, who was also her godfather, became very fond of her, and as soon as she could walk and talk, he bought a little armchair and stood it by his fire at the lodge, and coaxed her with cheap toys to come and sit with him.

One day, she was sitting in the lodge gazing wistfully up at the sky through the barred window. The turnkey, after watching her some time, said:—

"Thinking of the fields, ain't you?"

"Where are they?" she asked.

"Why, they're—over there, my dear," said the turnkey, waving his key vaguely, "just about there."

"Does anybody open them and shut them? Are they locked?"

"Well," said the turnkey, discomfited, "not in general."

"Are they pretty, Bob?" She called him Bob because he wished it.

"Lovely. Full of flowers. There are buttercups, and

there are daisies, and there's—" here he hesitated, not knowing the names of many flowers—"there are dandelions and all manner of games."

"Is it very pleasant to be there, Bob?"

"Prime," said the turnkey.

"Was father ever there?"

"Hem!" coughed the turnkey. "O yes, he was there, sometimes."

"Is he sorry not to be there now?"

"N—not particular," said the turnkey.

"Nor any of the people?" she asked, glancing at the listless crowd within. "O, are you quite sure and certain, Bob?"

At this point, Bob gave in and changed the subject. But after this chat, the turnkey and little Amy would go out on his free Sunday afternoons to some meadows or green lanes, and she would pick grass and flowers to bring home while he smoked his pipe.

When Amy was only eight years old, her mother died. The poor father was more helpless and broken down than ever, and as Fanny was a careless child and Edward idle, the little one, who had the bravest and most faithful heart, was inspired by her love and unselfishness to be the little mother of the forlorn family, and struggled to get some little education for herself and her brother and sister. She went as often as she could to an evening school outside and got her brother and sister sent to a day school at intervals for three or four years. At thirteen, she could read and keep accounts. Once, amongst the debtors, a dancing master came in, and as Fanny had a great desire to learn dancing, little Amy went timidly to the new prisoner and said,

"If you please, I was born here, sir."

"Oh! You are the young lady, are you?" said he.

"Yes, sir."

"And what can I do for you?"

"Nothing for me, sir, thank you; but if, while you stay here, you could be so kind as to teach my sister cheap."

"My child, I'll teach her for nothing," said the dancing master.

Fanny was a very apt pupil, and the good-natured dancing master went on giving her lessons even after his release. Amy was so encouraged with the success of her attempt that, when a milliner came in, she went to her on her own behalf and begged her to teach her.

"I am afraid you are so weak, you see," the milliner objected.

"I don't think I am weak, ma'am."

"And you are so very, very little, you see," the milliner still objected.

"Yes, I am afraid I am very little indeed," returned the child, and began to sob, so that the milliner was touched, took her in hand and made her a clever workwoman.

But the father could not bear the idea that his children should work for a living, so they had to keep it all secret. Fanny became a dancer and lived with a poor old uncle, who played the clarionet at the small theatre where Fanny was engaged. Amy, or little Dorrit as she was generally called, her father's name Dorrit, earned small sums by going out to do needlework. She got Edward into many situations, but he was an idle, careless fellow and always came back to be a burden and care for his poor little sister. At last, she saved up enough to send him out to Canada.

"God bless you, dear Tip" (his name had been shortened to Tip), "don't be too proud to come and see us when you have made your fortune," she said.

But Tip only went as far as Liverpool and appeared once more before his poor little second mother, in rags, and with no shoes.

In the end, after another trial, Tip returned, telling Amy that this time he was "one of the regulars."

"Oh! Don't say you are a prisoner, Tip. Don't, don't!"

But he was—and Amy nearly broke her heart. So with all these cares and worries, struggling bravely, little Dorrit passed the first twenty-two years of her life. Then the son of a lady, Mrs. Clennem, to whose house Amy went to do needlework, was interested in the pale, patient little creature and, learning her history resolved to do his best to try and get her father released and to help them all.

One day when he was walking home with little Dorrit, a voice was heard calling, "Little Mother, Little Mother," and a strange figure came bouncing up to them and fell, scattering her basketful of potatoes on the ground. "Oh, Maggie," said Little Dorrit, "what a clumsy child you are!"

She was about eight and twenty, with large bones, large features, large hands and feet, large eyes, and no hair. Little Dorrit told Mr. Clennem that Maggie was the granddaughter of her old nurse and that her grandmother had been very unkind to her and beat her. "When Maggie was ten years old, she had a fever, and she has never grown older."

"Ten years old," said Maggie. "But what a nice hospital! So comfortable, wasn't it? Such an Ev'nly place! Such beds there are there! Such lemonades! Such oranges! Such delicious broth and wine! Such chicking! Oh, AIN'T it a delightful place to stop at!"

"Then, when she came out, her grandmother did not know what to do with her and was very unkind. But after some time, Maggie tried to improve and was very attentive and industrious, and now she can earn her own living entirely, sir!"

Little Dorrit did not say who had taken pains to teach and encourage the poor half-witted creature, but Mr. Clennem guessed from the name Little Mother and the fondness of the poor creature for Amy.

Thanks to Mr. Clennem, a great change took place in the fortunes of the family, and not long after this wretched night, it was discovered that Mr. Dorrit was the owner of a large property, and they became very rich.

When, in his turn, Mr. Clennem became a prisoner in the Marshalsea, little Dorrit came to comfort and console him, and after many changes of fortune, she became his wife, and they lived happily ever after

Why Rabbits Have Short Tails

by Abbie Phillips Walker

Bunny Rabbit was sitting in his yard one day, thinking very hard, when his grandfather came along.

"Why are you so quiet and sober, grandson?" he inquired.

"I am wondering, grandfather," said Bunny, "why we have such long ears and so short a tail. I should think it would be much better if it were just the other way about."

"Of course; of course," said Grandfather Rabbit, bobbing his ears back and forth. "We all think we could have made a better rabbit if we had been consulted. But let me tell you why your tail is short, and your ears are long, and then you will learn you are better off now than was your great-grandfather's great-grandfather, who had a long tail and short ears."

It did not take Bunny Rabbit long to find a nice soft seat for his grandfather and to sit close and very still, with his ears sticking up to listen, for he dearly loved the stories his grandfather told.

"Once upon a time," began Grandfather Rabbit, just as all grandfathers start a story—"a long, long time ago, there lived in some woods a rabbit. He had a long tail and short ears, just as all the rabbits in those days had.

"One day, he ran over the hill to the garden where Mr. Man lived. He should have been very careful, but he wasn't, and when he crawled under the rail fence around the garden, didn't Mr. Dog see him and begin to bark and chase Short Ears, as he was called?

"Short Ear was a good runner, and it was lucky he was, or there would be an end to this story right here. Through the garden, he ran under cover of the vegetable leaves, and when he got out, he was a good bit ahead of Mr. Dog.

"Over the field, they ran, and under the stone wall went Short Ears, and over it went Mr. Dog. Down the road they ran lickety-split, and into his house ran Short Ears just as Mr. Dog came into the yard.

"Short Ears had no time to lose, I can tell you. He slammed the door, and what do you suppose happened?"

Bunny Rabbit was so interested in his grandfather's story that he only started; he did not answer. So his grandfather went on.

"Why Short Ears slammed that door right on his long tail, and he was held fast, with his tail hanging outside."

"Oh! Oh! Oh!" cried Bunny Rabbit, feeling his stubby little tail to be sure it was safe behind him.

"What did poor Short Ears do then?" he asked.

"He could not do a thing, for Mr. Dog was right in the yard and running straight for the door," said Grandfather Rabbit.

Bunny Rabbit sat closer to his grandfather, and his ears grew longer as he listened.

"Yes," said Grandfather Rabbit, "Short Ears was in a bad fix, as you can see. He could not open the door to get his tail out because Mr. Dog would come in and catch him.

"He did not have long to think about it, for the next thing he knew, Mr. Dog grabbed at his tail, and off it came right up to the door. And off he ran. For, you see, he thought he had Short Ears on the end of the tail, and he did not stop to look. He just ran.

"When his tail broke off, over went Short Ears on the floor, for that set him free. 'Oh, dear! Oh, dear! What shall I do?' he cried when he jumped up and looked in the mirror and saw that his long tail was gone and all that remained was a little stubby tail, just like yours.

"First, he ran to the medicine closet and got some salve and a soft piece of cloth. But he found he could not reach the end of his tail—it was too short.

"His first thought was to run over to his cousin. Rabbit's house was not far-off, but when he started toward the door, he remembered Mr. Dog.

"Short Ears leaned his head to the crack in the door and listened hard. His ears were short, you remember, but not so short that he heard Mr. Dog barking.

"Nearer and nearer came the bark. Short Ears locked the door, ran to the windows, fastened them, and drew the shades, and then he ran into the closet and closed the door.

"Away back he crept under his Sunday clothes, where he was sure no one would find him, and there he sat and listened and listened and listened.

"Mr. Dog barked and jumped about outside the house, for he was very much upset when he found that he did not have Short Ears on the end of the tail he carried off.

"But it was no use. He could not get into Short Ears' house, and at last, he gave it up and ran off home, barking all the way.

"Short Ears listened, and though Mr. Dog's tones grew fainter and fainter, Short Ears was surprised to find he could hear the barking, though it was a long way off.

"After it was dark, he came out of the closet and crept into his bed without even thinking of the end of his tail. He was so tired and worn out listening.

"And now, what do you think had happened to him, and what do you think he saw when he looked in the mirror in the morning to brush his hair?"

Bunny Rabbit shook his head. "I don't know, grandfather," he said. "What had happened to Short Ears?"

"His ears had grown long. He had listened so hard to the barking of Mr. Dog," said Grandfather Rabbit. "And from that day, all the Rabbit family have had short tails and long ears, which is just as it should be, for we can hear Mr. Dog a long way off, and we do not have the bother of looking after a long tail when we run to cover. So don't wish to have yours changed again, for you see now that you are better off than poor Short Ears was, don't you?"

Bunny Rabbit said he did and should never wish for a long tail and short ears again. And he didn't.

Little Nell

By Charles Dickens

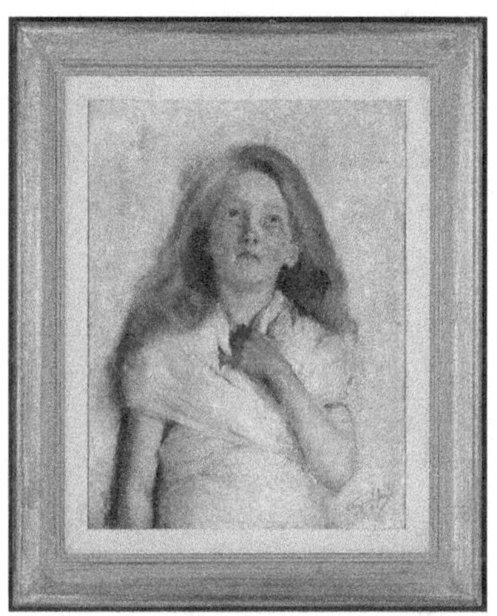

The house was one of those receptacles for old and curious things, which seem to crouch in odd corners of the town, and in the old, dark, murky rooms, there lived alone together an old man and a child—his grandchild, little Nell. Solitary and monotonous as was her life, the innocent and cheerful spirit of the child found happiness in all things, and through the dim rooms of the old curiosity shop, little Nell went singing, moving with gay and lightsome step.

But gradually, over the old man, to whom she was so tenderly attached, there stole a sad change. He became thoughtful, gloomy, and wretched. He had no sleep or rest but that which he took by the day in his easy chair, for every night, and all night long, he was away from home.

At last, a raging fever seized him, and as he lay delirious or insensible through many weeks, Nell learned that the house which sheltered them was theirs no longer; that in the future, they would be very poor; that they would scarcely have bread to eat.

At length, the old man began to mend, but his mind was weakened. As the time drew near when they must leave the house, he did not refer to the necessity of finding other shelters. But a change came upon him one evening as he and Nell sat silently together.

"Let us speak softly, Nell," he said. "Hush! for if they knew our purpose, they would say that I was mad and take thee from me. We will not stop here another day. We will travel afoot through the fields and woods and trust ourselves to God in the places where He dwells."

The child's heart beat high with hope and confidence. To her, it seemed they might beg their way from door to door in happiness, so they were together.

When the day began to glimmer, they stole out of the

house and, passing into the street, stood still.

"Which way?" asked the child.

The old man looked irresolutely and helplessly at her and shook his head. It was plain that she was thenceforth his guide and leader. The child felt it but had no doubts or misgivings, and putting her hand in his, led him gently away.

They passed through the long, deserted streets until these streets dwindled, and the open country was about them. They walked all day and slept that night at a small cottage where beds were left to travelers. The sun was setting on the second day of their journey when, following a path that led to the town where they were to spend the night, they fell in with two traveling showmen bound for the races at a neighboring town.

They made two long days' journey with their new companions. The men were rough and strange in their ways, but they were kindly, too. In the bewildering noise and movement of the race course, where she tried to sell some little nosegays, Nell would have clung to them for protection had she not learned that these men suspected that she and the old man had left their home secretly and that they meant to take steps to have them sent back and taken care of. Separation from her grandfather was the greatest evil Nell could dread. She seized her opportunity to evade the watchfulness of the two men, and hand in hand, she and the old man fled away together.

That night they reached a little village in a woody

hollow. The village schoolmaster, attracted by the child's sweetness and modesty, gave them lodging for the night, nor would he let them leave him until two days more had passed.

They journeyed on when the time came that they must wander forth again by pleasant country lanes. The afternoon had worn away into a beautiful evening when they went to a caravan drawn up by the road. It was a smart little house upon wheels, and at the door sat a stout and comfortable lady, taking tea. The tea things were set out upon a drum, covered with a white napkin. And there, as if at the most convenient table in the world, sat this roving lady, taking her tea and enjoying the prospect. Of this stout lady, Nell ventured to ask how far it was to the neighboring town. And the lady, noticing that the tired child could hardly repress a tear at hearing that eight weary miles lay still before them, not only gave them tea but offered to take them on in the caravan.

Now, this lady of the caravan was the owner of a wax-work show, and her name was Mrs. Jarley. She offered Nell employment in pointing out the figures in the wax-work show to the visitors who came to see it, promising both board and lodging for the child and her grandfather and some small sum of money in return. Nell was thankful to accept this offer, and for some time, her life and that of the poor, vacant, fond old man passed quietly and almost happily.

One night Nell and her grandfather went out to walk. A terrible thunderstorm came on, and they were forced to take refuge in a small public house where men played cards. The old man watched them with increasing interest and excitement until his appearance completely changed. His face was flushed and eager, his teeth set. He seized Nell's little purse and, in spite of her entreaties, joined in the game, gambling with such a savage thirst for gain that the distressed and frightened child could almost better have borne to see him dead. The night was far advanced before the play ended, and they were forced to remain there until morning. And in the night, the child was awakened from her troubled sleep to find a figure in the room. It was her grandfather himself, his white face pinched and sharpened by the greediness which made his eyes unnaturally bright, counting the money of which his hands were robbing her.

Evening after evening, after that night, the old man would steal away, not to return until the night was far spent, demanding, wildly, money. And at last, there came an hour when the child overheard him, tempted beyond his feeble powers of resistance, undertake to find more money to feed the desperate passion which had laid hold upon his weakness by robbing Mrs. Jarley.

That night the child took her grandfather by the hand and led him forth; sustained by one idea—that they were flying from disgrace and crime and that her grandfather's preservation must depend solely upon her firmness; the old man following as though she had been an angel messenger sent to lead him where she would.

They slept in the open air that night, and on the following morning, some men offered to take them a long distance on their barge. These men, though they were not unkindly, drank and quarreled among themselves to Nell's inexpressible terror. It rained, too, heavily, and she was wet and cold. At last, they reached the great city where the barge was bound, and here they wandered up and down, being now penniless, and watched the faces of those who passed, to find a ray of encouragement or hope among them.

They laid down that night, and the next night too, with nothing between them and the sky; a penny loaf was all they had had that day, and when the third morning came, it found the child much weaker, yet she made no complaint. Faint and spiritless as they were, the streets were insupportable; and the child, throughout the remainder of that harrowing day, compelled herself to press on that they might reach the country. The evening was drawing on; they dragged themselves through the last street. Seeing a traveler on foot before them, she shot on before her grandfather and began in a few faint words to implore the stranger's help. He turned his head, and the child uttered a wild shriek and fell senseless at his feet. It was the village schoolmaster who had been so kind to them before.

The good man took her in his arms and quickly carried her to a little inn hard by, where she was tenderly put to bed and where a doctor arrived quickly. The schoolmaster, as it appeared, was on his way to a new home. And when the child had recovered somewhat from her exhaustion, it was arranged that she and her grandfather should accompany him to the village whither he was bound and that he should endeavor to find them some humble occupation by which they could exist.

It was a secluded village, lying among the quiet country scenes Nell loved. And here, her grandfather being tranquil and at rest, a great peace fell upon the child's spirit. Often she would steal into the church and sit down among the quiet figures carved upon the tombs. What if the spot awakened thoughts of death? It would be no pain to sleep here. The time was drawing nearer every day when Nell was to rest indeed. She never murmured or complained but faded like a light upon a summer's evening and died. Day after day and all day long, the old man, broken-hearted and with no love or care for anything in life, would sit beside her grave with her straw hat and the little basket she had been used to carrying, waiting till she should come to him again. At last, they found him lying dead on the stone. And in the church where they had often prayed and mused and lingered, hand in hand, the child and the old man slept together.

Brother and Sister

by Andrew Lang

Brother took sister by the hand and said: 'Look here; we haven't had one happy hour since our mother died. Our stepmother beats us regularly every day, and if we dare go near her, she kicks us away. We never get anything but hard, dry crusts to eat —why the dog under the table is better off than we are? She does throw him a good morsel or two now and then. Oh, dear! If our own dear mother only knew all about it! Come along, and let us go together into the wide world.'

So off they started through fields and meadows, over hedges and ditches, and walked the whole day long, and when it rained, sister said:

'Heaven and our hearts are weeping together.'

Towards evening they came to a large forest and were so tired out from hunger and their long walk, as well as all their trouble, that they crept into a hollow tree and soon fell fast asleep.

The next morning, when they woke up, the sun was already high in the heavens and shining bright and warmly into the tree. Then said, brother:

'I'm so thirsty, sister; if I did but knew where to find a little stream, I'd go and have a drink. I do believe I hear one.' He jumped up, took sister by the hand, and they set off to hunt for the brook.

Their cruel stepmother was, in reality, a witch, and she knew perfectly well that the two children had run away. She had crept secretly after them and had cast her spells over all the streams in the forest.

Presently the children found a little brook dancing and glittering over the stones, and brother was eager to drink of it, but as it rushed past, sister heard it murmuring:

'Who drinks of me will be a tiger! Who drinks of me will be a tiger!'

So she cried out, 'Oh! Dear brother, pray you don't drink, or you'll be turned into a wild beast and tear me to pieces.'

Brother was dreadfully thirsty, but he did not drink.

'Very well,' said he, 'I'll wait till we come to the next spring.'

When they came to the second brook, sister heard it repeating too:

'Who drinks of me will be a wolf! Who drinks of me will be a wolf!'

And she cried, 'Oh! Brother, pray you don't drink here either, or you'll be turned into a wolf and eat me up.'

Again brother did not drink, but he said:

'Well, I'll wait a little longer till we reach the next stream, but whatever you say, I must drink, for I can no longer bear this thirst.'

And when they got to the third brook, sister heard it say as it rushed past:

'Who drinks of me will be a roe! who drinks of me will be a roe!'

And she begged, 'Ah! Brother, don't drink yet, or you'll become a roe and run away from me.'

But her brother was already kneeling by the brook and bending over it to drink, and, sure enough, no sooner had his lips touched the water than he fell on the grass and transformed into a little Roebuck.

Sister cried bitterly over her poor bewitched brother, and the little Roe wept too and sat sadly by her side. At last, the girl said:

'Never mind, dear little fawn, I will never forsake you,' She took off her golden garter and tied it around Roe's neck.

Then she plucked rushes and plaited a soft cord of them, which she fastened to the collar. When she did this, she led the Roe farther and farther, right into the forest's depths.

After they had gone a long, long way, they came to a little house, and when the girl looked into it, she found it was quite empty, and she thought, 'perhaps we might stay and live here.'

So she hunted up leaves and moss to make a soft bed for the little Roe, and every morning and evening, she went out and gathered roots, nuts, and berries for herself and tender young grass for the fawn. And he fed from her hand, played around her, and seemed quite happy. In the evening, when sister was tired, she said her prayers and then laid her head on the fawn's back and fell sound asleep with it as a pillow. And if brother had but kept his natural form, really, it would have been a most delightful kind of life.

They had been living for some time in the forest in this way when it came to pass that the King of that country had a great hunt through the woods. Then the whole forest rang with such a blowing of horns, baying of dogs, and joyful cries of huntsmen, that the little Roe heard it and longed to join in too.

'Ah!' said his sister, 'do let me go off to the hunt! I

can't keep still any longer.'

And he begged and prayed till, at last, she consented.

'But,' said she, 'mind you come back in the evening. I shall lock my door fast for fear of those wild huntsmen, so, to make sure of my knowing you, knock at the door and say, "My sister dear, open; I'm here." If you don't speak, I shan't open the door.'

So off sprang the little Roe, and he felt quite well and happy in the free open air.

The King and his huntsmen soon saw the beautiful creature and started in pursuit, but they could not come up with it, and whenever they thought they were sure to catch it, it bounded off to one side into the bushes and disappeared. When night came on, it ran home and, knocking at the door of the little house, cried:

'My sister dear, open; I'm here.' The door opened, and he ran in and rested all night on his soft mossy bed.

The next morning the hunt began again, and as soon as the little Roe heard the horns and the 'Ho! Ho!' of the huntsmen, he could not rest another moment and said:

'Sister, open the door. I must get out.'

So sister opened the door and said, 'Now mind and get back by nightfall, and say your little rhyme.'

As soon as the King and his huntsmen saw the Roe with the golden collar, they all rode off after it, but it was far too quick and handy for them. This went on all day, but as evening came on, the huntsmen gradually encircled the Roe, and one of them wounded it slightly in the foot, so it limped and ran off slowly.

Then the huntsman stole after it as far as the little house and heard it call out, 'My sister dear, open; I'm here,' He saw the door open and close immediately after the fawn had run in.

The huntsman remembered all this carefully, went straight to the King, and told him all he had seen and heard.

'Tomorrow, we will hunt again,' said the King.

Poor sister was frightened when she saw how her little fawn had been wounded. She washed off the blood, bound up the injured foot with herbs, and said: 'Now, dear, go and lie down and rest so that your wound may heal.'

The wound was so slight that it was quite well the next day, and the little Roe did not feel it at all. No sooner did it hear the sounds of hunting in the forest than it cried:

'I can't stand this. I must be there too; I'll take care they shan't catch me.'

Sister began crying and said, 'They are certain to kill you, and then I shall be left alone in the forest and forsaken by everyone. I can't and won't let you out.'

'Then I shall die of grief,' replied the Roe, 'for when I hear that horn, I feel as if I must jump right out of my skin.'

So at last, when sister found nothing else to be done,

she opened the door with a heavy heart, and the Roe darted forth full of glee and health into the forest.

As soon as the King saw the Roe, he said to his huntsman, 'Now then, give chase to it all day till evening, but the mind and be careful not to hurt it.'

When the sun had set, the King said to his huntsman, 'Now come and show me the little house in the wood.'

And when he got to the house, he knocked at the door and said, 'My sister dear, open; I'm here.' Then the door opened, the King walked in, and there stood the loveliest maiden he had ever seen.

The girl was startled when she saw a man with a gold crown on his head walk in instead of the little Roe she expected. But the King looked kindly at her, held his hand, and said, 'Will you come with me to my castle and be my dear wife?'

'Oh yes!' replied the maiden, 'but you must let my Roe come too. I could not possibly forsake it.'

'It shall stay with you as long as you live and shall want for nothing,' the King promised.

In the meantime, the Roe came bounding in, and sister tied the rush cord once more to its collar, took the end in her hand, and so they left the little house in the forest together.

The King lifted the lonely maiden onto his horse and led her to his castle, where the wedding was celebrated with the greatest splendor. The Roe was petted, caressed, and ran about in the palace gardens.

Now all this time, the wicked stepmother, who had been the cause of these poor children's misfortunes and trying adventures, was feeling fully persuaded that sister had been torn to pieces by wild beasts and brother shot to death in the shape of a Roe. When she heard how happy and prosperous they were, her heart was filled with envy and hatred, and she could think of nothing but how to bring some fresh misfortune on them. Her own daughter, who was as hideous as night and had only one eye, reproached her by saying, 'It is I who ought to have had this good luck and been Queen.'

'Be quiet, will you,' said the old woman; 'when the time comes, I shall be at hand.'

After some time, it happened one day when the King was out hunting that the Queen gave birth to a beautiful little boy. The old witch thought there was a good chance for her, so she took the form of the lady in waiting and, hurrying into the room where the Queen lay in her bed, called out, 'The bath is quite ready; it will help to make you strong again. Let us be quick, for fear the water should get cold.' Her daughter was at hand, too, and between them, they carried the Queen, who was still very weak, into the bathroom and laid her in the bath; then they locked the door and ran away.

They took care beforehand to make a blazing hot fire under the bath so that the lovely young Queen might be suffocated.

As soon as they were sure this was the case, the old

witch tied a cap on her daughter's head and laid her in the Queen's bed. She managed, too, to make her figure and general appearance look like the Queen's, but even her power could not restore the eye she had lost, so she made her lie on the side of the missing eye to prevent the King's noticing anything.

In the evening, when the King came home and heard the news of his son's birth, he was full of delight and insisted on going at once to his dear wife's bedside to see how she was getting on. But the old witch cried out, 'Take care and keep the curtains drawn; don't let the light get into the Queen's eyes; she must be kept perfectly quiet.' So the King went away and never knew that it was a false Queen who lay in the bed.

When midnight came, and everyone in the palace was sound asleep, the nurse who alone watched by the baby's cradle in the nursery saw the door open gently and who should come in but the real Queen. She lifted the child from its cradle, laid it on her arm, and nursed it for some time. Then she carefully shook up the pillows of the little bed, laid the baby down, and tucked the coverlet around him. She did not forget the little Roe either but went to the corner where it lay and gently stroked its back. Then she silently left the room, and the next morning when the nurse asked the sentries if they had seen anyone go into the castle that night, they all said, 'No, we saw no one at all.'

For many nights the Queen came in the same way, but she never spoke a word, and the nurse was too frightened to say anything about her visits.

After some little time had elapsed, the Queen spoke one night and said:

'Is my child well? Is my Roe well?

I'll come back twice and then farewell.'

The nurse did not answer, but as soon as the Queen had disappeared, she went to the King and told him everything. The King exclaimed, 'Good heavens! What do you say? I will watch myself tonight by the child's bed.'

When the evening came, he went to the nursery, and at midnight the Queen appeared and said:

'Is my child well? Is my Roe well?

I'll come back once and then farewell.'

And she nursed and petted the child as usual before she disappeared. The King dared not trust himself to speak to her, but he kept watch the following night again.

That night when the Queen came, she said:

'Is my child well? Is my Roe well?

I've come this once, and now farewell.'

Then the King could restrain himself no longer but sprang to her side and cried, 'You can be no one but my dear wife!'

'Yes,' said she, 'I am your dear wife!' At that exact moment, she was restored to life and as fresh and well and rosy as ever. Then she told the King all the cruel things the wicked witch and her daughter had done.

The King had them both arrested at once and brought to trial, and they were condemned to death. The daughter was led into the forest, where the wild beasts tore her to pieces, and the old witch was burnt at stake.

As soon as she was reduced to ashes, the spell was taken off the little Roe, and he was restored to his natural shape once more, so brother and sister lived happily ever after.

Rushen Coatie

by Joseph Jacobs

There was once a king and a queen, as many a one has been; few have we seen, and as few may we see. But the queen died, leaving only one bonny girl, and she told her on her death-bed: "My dear, after I am gone, there will come to you a little red calf, and whenever you want anything, speak to it, and it will give it to you."

After a while, the king married an ill-natured wife

again, with three ugly daughters of her own. And they hated the king's daughter because she was so bonny. So they took all her fine clothes away and gave her only a coat made of rushes. So they called her Rushen Coatie and made her sit in the kitchen nook amid the ashes. And when dinner-time came, the nasty stepmother sent her a thimbleful of broth, a grain of barley, a thread of meat, and a crumb of bread. But when she had eaten all this, she was just as hungry as before, so she said: "Oh! how I wish I had something to eat." Just then, who should come in but a little red calf and said to her: "Put your finger into my left ear." She did so and found some nice bread. Then the calf told her to put her finger into its right ear, and she found some cheese there and made a good meal of the bread and cheese. And so it went on from day to day.

Now the king's wife thought Rushen Coatie would soon die from the scanty food she got, and she was surprised to see her as lively and healthy as ever. So she set one of her ugly daughters on the watch at meal times to find out how Rushen Coatie got enough to live on. The daughter soon found out that the red calf gave food to Rushen Coatie and told her mother. So her mother went to the king and told him she was longing to have a sweetbread from a red calf. Then the king sent for his butcher and had the little red calf killed. And when Rushen Coatie heard of it, she sat down and wept by its side, but the dead calf said:

"Take me up, bone by bone,

And put me beneath a yon grey stone;

When there is aught you want

Tell it to me, and I'll grant."

So she did so but could not find the shank bone of the calf.

Now the very next Sunday was Yuletide, and all the folk was going to church in their best clothes, so Rushen Coatie said: "Oh! I should like to go to church, too," but the three ugly sisters said: "What would you do at the church, you nasty thing? You must bide at home and make the dinner." And the king's wife said: "And this is what you must make the soup of, a thimbleful of water, a grain of barley, and a crumb of bread."

When they all went to church, Rushen Coatie sat down and wept, but looking up, who should she see coming in limping, lamping, with a shank wanting, but the dear red calf? And the red calf said to her: "Do not sit there weeping, but go, put on these clothes, and above all, put on this pair of glass slippers, and go your way to church."

"But what will become of the dinner?" said Rushen Coatie.

"Oh, do not fash about that," said the red calf, "all you have to do is to say to the fire:

"'Every peat make t'other burn,

Every spit makes another turn,

Every pot makes another play,

Till I come from church this good Yuleday,'

and be off to church with you. But mind you come home first."

So Rushen Coatie said this and went off to church, and she was the grandest and finest lady there. There happened to be a young prince there, and he fell in love with her at once. But she came away before service was over, and was home before the rest, and had off her fine clothes and on with her Rushen coatie, and she found the calf had covered the table, and the dinner was ready, and everything was in good order when the rest came home. The three sisters said to Rushen Coatie: "Eh, lassie if you had seen the bonny fine lady in the church today that the young prince fell in love with!" Then she said: "Oh! I wish you would let me go with you to the church tomorrow," for they used to go for three days together to church at Yuletide.

But they said: "What should the like of you do at church, nasty thing? The kitchen nook is good enough for you."

So the next day, they all went to church, and Rushen Coatie was left behind to make dinner out of a thimbleful of water, a grain of barley, a crumb of bread, and a thread of meat. But the red calf came to her help again, gave her finer clothes than before, and she went to church, where all the world was looking at her and wondering where such a grand lady came from, and the prince fell more in love with her than ever and tried to find out where she went to. But she was too quick for him and got home long before the rest, and the red calf had the dinner ready.

The next day the calf dressed her in even grander clothes than before, and she went to the church. And the young prince was there again, and this time he put a guard at the door to keep her, but she took a hop and a run and jumped over their heads, and as she did so, down fell one of her glass slippers. You may be sure she didn't wait to pick it up, but off she ran home, as fast as she could go, on with the rushen coatie, and the calf had all things ready.

Then the young prince proclaimed that whoever could put on the glass slipper should be his bride. All the ladies of his court went and tried to put on the slipper. And they tried and tried and tried, but it was too small for them all. Then he ordered one of his ambassadors to mount a fleet horse, ride through the kingdom, and find an owner for the glass shoe. He rode, and he rode to town and castle and made all the ladies try to put on the shoe. Many tried to get it on that she might be the prince's bride. But no, it wouldn't do, and many a one wept, I warrant because she couldn't get on the bonny glass shoe. The ambassador rode on and on till he came at the very last to the house where there were the three ugly sisters. The first two tried it, and it wouldn't do, and the queen, mad with spite, hacked off the toes and heels of the third sister, and she could then put the slipper on, and the prince was brought to marry her, for he had to keep his promise. The ugly sister was dressed all in her best and was put up behind the prince on horseback, and off they rode in great gallantry. But ye all know, pride must have a fall, for as they rode along, a raven sang out of a bush—

"Hackèd Heels and Pinchèd Toes

Behind the young prince rides,

But Pretty Feet and Little Feet

Behind the cauldron bides."

"What's that the birdie sings?" said the young prince.

"Nasty, lying thing," said the step-sister, "never mind what it says."

But the prince looked down and saw the slipper dripping with blood, so he rode back and put her down. Then he said, "There must be someone that the slipper has not been tried on."

"Oh, no," said they, "there's none but a dirty thing that sits in the kitchen nook and wears a rushen coatie."

But the prince was determined to try it on Rushen Coatie, but she ran away to the grey stone, where the red calf dressed her in her bravest dress, and she went to the prince and the slipper jumped out of his pocket onto her foot, fitting her without any chipping or paring. So the prince married her that day, and they lived happily ever after.

The Queen Bee

By Brothers Grimm

Two kings' sons once upon a time went into the world to seek their fortunes, but they soon fell into a wasteful foolish way of living, so they could not return home again. Then their brother, who was a little insignificant dwarf, went out to seek his brothers: but when he had found them, they only laughed at him, thinking that he, who was so young and simple, should try to travel through the world, when they, who were so much wiser, had been unable to get on. However, they all embarked on their journey together and finally came to an ant hill. The two elder brothers would have pulled it down to see how the poor ants, in their fright, would run about and carry off their eggs. But the little dwarf said, 'Let the poor things enjoy themselves. I will not suffer you to trouble them.'

So on they went and came to a lake where many, many ducks were swimming about. The two brothers wanted to catch two and roast them. But the dwarf said, 'Let the poor things enjoy themselves. You shall not kill them.' Next, they came to a bees'-nest in a hollow tree, and there was so much honey that it ran down the trunk; the two brothers wanted to light a fire under the tree and kill the bees to get their honey. But the dwarf held them back and said, 'Let the pretty insects enjoy themselves. I cannot let you burn them.'

At length, the three brothers came to a castle: and as they passed by the stables, they saw fine horses standing there, but all were of marble, and no man was to be seen. Then they went through all the rooms till they came to a door on which were three locks: but in the middle of the door was a wicket so they could look into the next room. There they saw a little grey old man sitting at a table, and they called to him once or twice, but he did not hear: however, they called a third time, and then he rose and came out to them.

He said nothing but took hold of them and led them

to a beautiful table covered with all sorts of good things: and when they had eaten and drunk, he showed each of them to a bed-chamber.

The following day he came to the eldest and took him to a marble table, where there were three tablets containing an account of how the castle might be disenchanted. The first tablet said: 'In the wood, under the moss, lie a thousand pearls belonging to the king's daughter; they must all be found: and if one be missing by set of sun, he who seeks them will be turned into marble.'

The eldest brother set out and sought for the pearls the whole day: but the evening came, and he had not found the first hundred: so he was turned into stone as the tablet had foretold.

The next day the second brother undertook the task, but he succeeded no better than the first, for he could only find the double hundred of the pearls, and he was turned into stone.

At last, came the little dwarf's turn; and he looked in the moss, but it was so hard to find the pearls, and the job was so tiresome!—so he sat down upon a stone and cried. And as he sat there, the king of the ants (whose life he had saved) came to help him with five thousand ants; and it was not long before they had found all the pearls and laid them in a heap.

The second tablet said: 'The key of the princess's bed-chamber must be fished up out of the lake.' And as the dwarf came to the brink of it, he saw the two ducks whose lives he had saved swimming about; and they dived down and soon brought in the key from the bottom.

The third task was the hardest. It was to choose the youngest and the best of the king's three daughters. Now they were all beautiful and all exactly alike: but he was told that the eldest had eaten a piece of sugar, the next some sweet syrup, and the youngest a spoonful of honey; so he was to guess which it had eaten the honey.

Then came the queen of the bees, who the little dwarf had saved from the fire, and she tried the lips of all three, but at last, she sat upon the lips of the one that had eaten the honey: and so the dwarf knew which was the youngest. Thus the spell was broken, and all who had been turned into stones awoke and took their proper forms. And the dwarf married the youngest and the best of the princesses and was king after her father's death, but his two brothers married the other two sisters.

Kind William and the Water Sprite

By Juliana Horatia Ewing

There once lived a poor weaver whose wife died a few years after marriage. He was now alone in the world except for their child, who was a very quick and industrious little lad and of such an obliging disposition that he gained the nickname of Kind

William.

On his seventh birthday, his father gave him a little net with a long handle, and with this, Kind William betook himself to a shallow part of the river to fish. After wandering on for some time, he found a quiet pool dammed in by stones, and here he dipped for the minnows that darted about in the clear brown water. He caught nothing at the first and second casts, but with the third, he landed no less than twenty-one little fishes and minnows he had never seen, for as they leaped and struggled in the net, they shone with them alternate tints of green and gold.

He was gazing at them with wonder and delight when a voice behind him cried, in piteous tones—

"Oh, my little sisters! Oh, my little sisters!"

Kind William turned round and saw, sitting on a rock that stood out of the stream, a young girl weeping bitterly. She had a beautiful face, abundant yellow hair of great length, and such uncommon brightness that even in the shade, it shone like gold. She was dressed in green grass, and from her knees downwards, she was hidden by the clumps of fern and rushes that grew by the stream.

"What ails you, my little lass?" said Kind William.

But the maid only wept more bitterly and, wringing her hands, repeated, "Oh, my little sisters! Oh, my little sisters!" presently adding in the same tone, "The little fishes! Oh, the little fishes!"

"Dry your eyes, and I will give you half of them," said the good-natured child, "and if you have no net, you shall fish with me this afternoon."

But the maid's sobs redoubled at this proposal, and she prayed and begged with a frantic eagerness that he would throw the fish back into the river. For some time, Kind William would not consent to throw away his prize, but at last, he yielded to her excessive grief and emptied the net into the pool, where the glittering fishes were soon lost to sight under the sand and pebbles.

The girl now laughed and clapped her hands.

"This good deed you shall never rue, Kind William," said she, "and even now, it shall repay you threefold. How many fish did you catch?"

"Twenty-one," said Kind William, not without regret in his tone.

The maid at once began to pull hairs out of her head and did not stop till she had counted sixty-three and laid them together in her fingers. She then began to wind the lock up into a curl, which took far longer to wind than the sixty-three hairs had taken to pull. Kind William never could tell how long her hair was, for after it reached her knees, he lost sight of it among the fern, but he began to suspect that she was no trustworthy village maid but a water sprite, and he heartily wished himself safe at home.

"Now," said she, when the lock was wound, "will you promise me three things?"

"If I can do so without sin," said Kind William.

"First," she continued, holding out the lock of hair, "will you keep this carefully and never give it away? It will be for your good."

"One never gives away gifts," said Kind William, "I promise that."

"The second thing is to spare what you have spared. Fish up and down the river at your will, but swear never to cast net in this pool again."

"One should not do a kindness by halves," said Kind William. "I promise that also."

"Thirdly, you must never tell what you have now seen and heard till thrice seven years have passed. And now come hither, my child, and give me your little finger, that I may see if you can keep a secret."

But by this time, Kind William's hairs were standing on end, and he gave the last promise more from fear than from any other motive and seized his net to go.

"No hurry, no hurry," said the maiden (and the words sounded like the rippling of a brook over pebbles). Then bending towards him, with a strange smile, she added, "You are afraid that I shall pinch too hard, my pretty boy. Well, give me a farewell kiss before you go."

"I kiss none but the miller's lass," said Kind William, sturdily, for she was his little sweetheart. Besides, he feared the water witch would enchant and draw him down. At his answer, she laughed till the echoes rang, but Kind William shuddered to hear that the echoes seemed to come from the river instead of from the hills; and they rang in his ears like a distant torrent leaping over rocks.

"Then listen to my song," said the water sprite. With which she drew some of her golden hairs over her arm and tuning them as if they had been the strings of a harp, she began to sing:

"Warp of woolen and woof of gold: When seven and seven and seven are told."

But when Kind William heard that the river was running with the tune's cadence, he could no longer bear it and took to his heels. When he had run a few yards, he heard a splash as if a salmon had jumped, and on looking back, he found that the yellow-haired maiden was gone.

Kind William was trustworthy and obliging, and he kept his word. He said nothing of his adventure. He put the yellow lock into an old china teapot that had stood untouched on the mantelpiece for years. And fishing up and down the river, he never again cast a net into the haunted pool. And over time, the whole affair passed from his mind.

Fourteen years went by, and Kind William was Kind William still. He was as obliging as ever and still loved the miller's daughter, who, for her part, had not forgotten her old playmate. But the miller's memory was not so good, for the fourteen years had been prosperous with him, and he was rich, whereas they had only brought bad trade and poverty to the weaver and his son. So the lovers were not even allowed to speak to each other.

One evening Kind William wandered by the riverside, lamenting his hard fate. It was his twenty-first birthday, and he might not even receive the good wishes of the day from his old playmate. It was just growing dusk, a time when prudent bodies hurry home from the neighbourhood of fairy rings, sprite-haunted streams, and the like, and Kind William was beginning to quicken his pace when a voice from behind him sang:

"Warp of woolen and woof of gold: When seven and seven and seven are told."

Kind William felt sure that he had heard this before, though he could not recall when or where; but suspecting that it was no human voice that sang, he hurried home without looking behind him. Before he reached the house, he remembered all and that his promise of secrecy expired on this very day.

Meanwhile, the old weaver had been sadly preparing the loom to weave a small stock of yarn, which he had received in payment for some work. He had set up the warp and was about to fill the shuttle when his son came in, told the story, and repeated the water sprite's song.

"Where is the lock of hair, my son?" asked the old man.

"In the teapot still, if you have not touched it," said

Kind William, "but the dust of fourteen years must have destroyed all gloss and colour."

On searching the teapot, however, the lock of hair was found to be as bright as ever, and it lay in the weaver's hand like a coil of gold.

"It is the song that puzzles me," said Kind William. "Seven, and seven, and seven make twenty-one. Now that is just my age."

"There is your warp of woolen if that is anything," added the weaver, gazing at the loom with a melancholy air.

"And this is golden enough," laughed Kind William, pointing to the curl. "Come, father, let us see how far one hair will go on the shuttle." And suiting the action to the word, he began to wind. He wound the shuttle full, then sat down to the loom and started throwing.

The result was a fabric of such beauty that the Weavers shouted with amazement, and one single hair served for the woof of the whole piece.

Before long, there was not a town name or a fine country lady but must need have a dress of the new stuff, and before the sixty-three hairs were used up, the fortunes of the weaver and his son were made.

About this time, the miller's memory became more precise, and he was often heard to speak of an old boy-and-girl love between his dear daughter and the wealthy manufacturer of the golden cloth. Within a year and a day, Kind William married his sweetheart, and as money sticks to money, he added the old miller's riches to his own.

Moreover, there is every reason to believe that he and his wife lived happily to the end of their days.

And what became of the water sprite?

That you must ask somebody else, for I do not know.

The Princess and the Pea

by Hans Christian Andersen

Once, a prince wanted to marry a princess; but she was to be an actual princess. So he traveled about, all through the world, to find a real one, but everywhere there was something in the way. There were enough princesses, but whether they were real, he could not quite make out: there was always something that did not seem quite right. So he came home again and was quite sad: for he wished so much to have an actual princess. One evening a terrible storm came on. It lightened and thundered, and the rain streamed down; it was quite fearful! Then there was a knocking at the town gate, and the old king went out to open it.

It was a princess who stood outside the gate. But, mercy! How she looked, from the rain and the rough weather! The water ran down from her hair and clothes; it ran in at the points of her shoes and out at the heels, yet she declared that she was an actual princess.

"Yes, we will soon find that out," thought the old queen. But she said nothing, only went into the bedchamber, took all the bedding off, and put a pea on the flooring of the bedstead; then she took twenty mattresses and laid them upon the pea, and then twenty eider-down beds upon the mattresses. On this, the princess had to lie all night. In the morning, she was asked how she had slept.

"Oh, miserably!" said the princess. "I scarcely closed my eyes all night long. Goodness knows what was in my bed. I lay upon something hard so that I am black and blue all over. It is quite dreadful!"

Now they saw that she was an actual princess, for she had felt the pea through the twenty mattresses and the twenty eider-down beds. No one but an actual princess could be so delicate.

So the prince took her for his wife, for now, he knew

that he had an actual princess; the pea was put in the museum, and it is there now unless somebody has carried it off.

Look at you, and this is a true story.

Greta and the Black Cat

by Abbie Phillips Walke

One day a woodsman named Peter was chopping down a tree when he saw a bundle swinging from one of the branches. Dropping his ax, he climbed up, and to his surprise, when he opened the pile, he found a baby girl asleep in it. Peter hurried home with the baby to his wife. "Look, Martha," he said. "I have found a baby girl to be a sister to our son Robert. We will name her Greta, and they shall grow up as brother and sister."

But Martha did not want the baby. "We have three mouths to feed now," she grumbled. "Why should we care for a child we know nothing of?"

But Peter would not hear of putting the child out of doors, so Greta lived with Peter and Martha and grew up with Robert.

Poor little Greta had anything but happy life, for Martha treated her kindly only when Peter was in sight, and that was seldom.

Robert, seeing that his mother did not treat Greta well, began to order her to wait upon him as soon as he was old enough and treated her as a servant.

Greta had to weed the garden and bring in the water and the wood. She had to wash the dishes, make the beds, and do all the work except when Peter was home.

One day when Peter was going to the woods, he told Robert to chop a pile of wood in the yard and have it finished by the time he came home.

When Peter was out of sight, Robert told Greta to chop the wood. "That is what you are here for—to do the work," said Robert. "The bears would have eaten you up if we had not taken you in. Now go to work and chop that wood."

Greta began to cry and said she could not handle the ax; she was too small. But Martha boxed her ears and told her she should not have dinner if she did not do as Robert told her.

Greta went to the woodpile and picked up the ax,

but it was no use. She could not chop the wood. And fearing a beating if she did not do it, Greta ran away. On and on, she ran until she came to a turn in the road, which led into a forest. She decided to stop for the night, lying down by a rock, when she heard a pitiful "meow."

Looking in the bushes, Greta saw a big black cat holding up one paw as though it was hurt. "Poor pussy!" said Greta, taking the cat in her arms. "You look as unhappy as I feel. Let me bind up your paw."

Greta tore off a piece of her dress and bound up the cat's paw, and then, to her surprise, the black cat spoke to her.

"Come with me, and I will show you where to sleep. You will have to carry me, for my paw is very painful," said the cat.

Greta picked up the cat, too surprised to be frightened, and went through the woods as the cat directed her.

When they reached a big rock with an opening, the cat said: "Here is my home. Take me in, and you will find a place to sleep and food."

Creeping in on her hands and knees with the cat under her arm, Greta found herself in a big room with a table in the center and on it plenty of food.

In one corner of the room was a bed; on this, Greta saw a queer-looking old woman with a hooked nose.

She was asleep and did not notice them until the cat

said, "Eat your supper."

Up jumped the queer-looking old woman when she heard this, for she was the witch.

"You, and a mortal with you," she screamed as she reached for her crooked stick.

Greta ran to the door, for she thought the old witch was about to strike her; but the black cat, who was sitting on the floor nearby where Greta had put it, said: "Don't you dare touch this girl; she has saved my life, and from this hour you are in my power, for a mortal has held me in her arms.

"If you would live, call the good fairy that has been looking for me all these years. I shall find her, anyway, but it will save time if you use your magic power, and you will regret it if you do not obey me."

When the old witch heard this, she began to tremble and hobbled to the cave door and tapped it three times with her crooked stick.

The rock opened so she could walk out, and Greta followed to see what she did, for she was no longer afraid; she knew the black cat would protect her.

The old witch gave a peculiar cry when she was outside, and Greta saw the next instant a tiny creature dressed in pink gauze, holding a wand of gold in one little hand, standing on a bush beside the old witch.

"Here I am, Witch Terrible," said the fairy. "What can I do for you? You must be in great danger, or you would not have called for one of us."

When it heard the fairy speak, the cat ran out of the cave, limping, and lay down in front of the fairy. "Help me, my good fairy," said the black cat. "I am the Prince for whom you have looked so long. The old witch changed me into a black cat and took away my power to speak until I was held in the arms of a mortal.

"I know her secret, and, though she dared not kill me, she wanted me to die, so she turned me into the forest to starve, and if it had not been for this girl, good fairy, the old witch would have had her wish granted.

"When she changed me into a black cat, she said I should never speak until a mortal held me and that I could not regain my shape until a fairy changed me, but something has happened since then, and to save herself, she obeyed me and called you, for I know her secret, and that is why I did not have to hunt for you, my good fairy."

The fairy touched the black cat with her wand, and Greta saw a handsome man dressed in black velvet with gold trimmings in place of the big black cat. "Now tell me the secret you know about the witch," said the fairy.

The old witch threw up her arms and cried for mercy. "Remember, I called the fairy," she said; "you would have hunted a long time if I had not. Be merciful!"

"I shall not forget," said the Prince. "This woman is only half a witch," he said. "She is part mortal, and every night at midnight, she has to become a mortal for an hour because she tried to change a water nymph into a frog. The river god, the water nymph's father, called on a mighty ogre, his friend, and the ogre was about to change her into a rock, but she begged so hard he made her half-mortal and left her to her fate."

"Which means she can never leave this forest," said the fairy, "and as she does many of her magic deeds at night when she rides abroad on her broomstick, she is not a very powerful witch."

"Yes, that is it," said the Prince, "and she does not want it known among the fairies, goblins, or any of the magic-power folks. That is the mercy for which she begs.

"I hope you will keep her secret, good fairy, for she saved me so much time and trouble in calling you."

"I will keep her secret from all but the fairies, but one of the fairy family will come here every night to make sure no mortal has been harmed by her, for someone might stray in here just as this girl did and be changed into some other form."

"I have one more favor to ask of you, good fairy," said the Prince. "I wish to make this girl my wife if she marries me, and I would like to have the proper clothes for a princess so that I may take her to my palace at once."

"What do you say, my dear?" asked the fairy. "Will you marry the Prince?"

Greta felt she must be dreaming, but she was sure

she would love the handsome Prince if she were awake, so she told the fairy she would, and the next instant, her ragged clothes dropped from her. She stood before the Prince in a beautiful green velvet riding-habit, with a long feather in her hat, looking every inch a princess.

That night a great feast was held at the palace of the Prince in honor of his return and to celebrate their wedding, and the very next day, Greta and the Prince rode to the home where she had once lived to give Peter a bag of gold.

"He was the only person who ever treated me kindly until I met you," Greta told the Prince, "and I shall never forget him."

Martha or her son Robert did not recognize Greta, for they little thought the beautiful Princess was the poor girl that had once been their slave. But Peter, who had loved her, looked after the coach as it rolled away. "It looked a little like her," he said, "but it could not be." Greta and the Prince sent many gifts to Peter, and in his old age, he was given a comfortable house and plenty to eat, and though Martha and Robert shared his good fortune, they never knew who sent it.

The Prince told Peter who the Princess was one day because the poor old man had never ceased to sorrow. After all, Greta could not be found, but not a word did he tell of this to Robert or Martha, but he kept his secret all to himself as long as he lived.

The Boy and Little Great Lady

by Mrs. W. K. Clifford

She was always called the "little great lady," for she lived in a grand house and was very rich. He was a strange boy; the great little lady never knew whence he came or whither he went. She only saw him when the snow lay deep upon the ground. Then in the early morning, he swept a pathway to the stable where she had once kept a white rabbit. When it was finished, she came down the steps in her white dress and little thin shoes with bows and walked slowly along the pathway. It was always swept so dry she might have worn paper shoes without getting them wet. At the far end, he always stood waiting till she came, smiled and said, "Thank you, little boy," and passed on. Then he was no longer seen till the next snowy morning when again he swept the pathway, and again the great little lady came down the steps in her dainty shoes and went to the stable.

But at last, one morning, when the snow lay white and thick and she came down the steps, there was no pathway as usual. The little boy stood leaning on a spade, and his feet were buried deep in the snow.

"Where is your broom? And where is the pathway to the rabbit house?" she asked.

"The rabbit is dead, and the broom is worn out," he answered, "and I am tired of making pathways that lead to empty houses."

"But why have you done it so long?" she asked.

"You have bows on your shoes," he said, "and they are so thin you could not walk over the snow in them— why, you would catch your death of cold," he added scornfully.

"What would you do if I wore boots?"

"I should learn how to build ships, paint pictures, or write books. But I should not think of you so much," he said.

The great little lady answered eagerly, "Go and learn how to do all those things; I will wait till you come back and tell me what you have done," She turned and went into the house.

"Goodbye," the boy said, as he stood watching for a moment the closed door; "dear little great lady, goodbye." And he went along the unmade pathway beyond the empty rabbit house.

Jenny Wren

by Charles Dickens, Edited by Jesse Lyman

Walking into the city one holiday a great many years ago, a gentleman ran up the steps of a tall house in the neighborhood of St. Mary Axe. The lower windows were those of a counting house, but the blinds, like those of the entire front of the house, were drawn down.

The gentleman knocked and rang several times before anyone came, but an old man finally opened the door. "What were you up to that you did not hear me?" said Mr. Fledgeby irritably.

"I was taking the air at the top of the house, sir," said the old man meekly, "it being a holiday. What might you please want, sir?"

"Humph! Holiday indeed," grumbled his master, a toy merchant, amongst other things. He then seated himself in the counting house and gave the old man—a Jew and Riah by name—directions about the dressing of some dolls about which he had come to speak, and, as he rose to go, exclaimed—

"By-the-by by, how do you take the air? Do you stick your head out of a chimney pot?"

"No, sir, I have made a little garden on the leads."

"Let's look it at," said Mr. Fledgeby.

"Sir, I have company there," returned Riah hesitating, "but will you please come up and see them?"

Mr. Fledgeby nodded, and, passing his master with a bow, the old man led the way up flight after flight of stairs till they arrived at the housetop. Two girls bending over books were seated on a carpet and leaning against a chimney stack. Some humble creepers were trained around the chimney pots, evergreens were placed around the roof, and a few more books, a basket of gaily colored scraps, bits of tinsel, and another of ordinary print stuff lay near. One of the girls rose on seeing that Riah had brought a visitor, but the other remarked, "I'm the person of the house downstairs, but I can't get up, whoever you are because my back is bad and my legs are queer."

"This is my master," said Riah, speaking to the two girls, "and this," he added, turning to Mr. Fledgeby, "is Miss Jenny Wren; she lives in this house and is a clever little dressmaker for little people. Her friend Lizzie," continued Riah, introducing the second girl. "They are both good girls, and as busy as they are good; in spare moments, they come up here and take to book learning."

"We are glad to come up here for rest, sir," said Lizzie, with a grateful look at the old Jew. "No one can tell the rest what this place is to us."

"Humph!" said Mr. Fledgeby, looking round, "Humph!" He was so surprised that he couldn't get beyond that word, and as he went down again, the old chimney pots in their black cowls seemed to turn round and look after him as if they were saying "Humph" too.

Lizzie, the elder of these two girls, was strong and handsome, but little Jenny Wren, whom she loved and protected, was small and deformed. However, she had a beautiful little face and the most prolonged and loveliest golden hair in the world, which fell about her like a cloak of shining curls as though to hide the poor little misshapen figure.

The Jew Riah and Lizzie were always kind and gentle to Jenny Wren, who called him her godfather.

She had a father, who shared her poor little rooms, whom she called her child, for he was a bad, drunken, worthless old man, and the poor girl had to care for him and earn money to keep them both. She suffered greatly, for the poor little bent back constantly ached sadly and was often weary from constant work. Still, it was only on rare occasions when alone or with her friend Lizzie, who often brought her work and sat in Jenny's room, that the brave child ever complained of her hard lot. Sometimes the two girls, Jenny helping herself with a crutch, would walk about the fashionable streets to note how the great folks were dressed. As they walked along, Jenny would tell her friend about the fancies she had when sitting alone at her work. "I imagine birds till I can hear them sing," she said one day, "and flowers till I can smell them. And the beautiful children that come to me in the early mornings! They are quite different from other children, not like me, never cold, or anxious, or tired, or hungry, never any pain; they come in numbers, in long bright slanting rows, all dressed in white and shiny heads. 'Who is this in pain?' they say, and they sweep around and about me, take me up in their arms, and I feel so light, and all the pain goes. I know they are coming a long way off by hearing them say, 'Who is this in pain?' and I answer, 'Oh my blessed children, it's poor me! have pity on me, and take me up, and then the pain will go."

Lizzie sat stroking and brushing the beautiful hair while the tired little dressmaker leaned against her when they were at home again, and as she kissed her goodnight, a miserable old man stumbled into the room. "How's my Jenny Wren, best of children?" he mumbled as he shuffled unsteadily towards her, but Jenny pointed her small finger towards him, exclaiming —"Go along with you, you bad, wicked old child, you troublesome, wicked old thing, I know where you have been, I know your tricks and your manners." The wretched man began to whimper like a scolded child. "Slave, slave, slave, from morning to night," went on Jenny, still shaking her finger at him, "and all for this; ain't you ashamed of yourself, you disgraceful boy?"

"Yes; my dear, yes," stammered the tipsy old father, tumbling into a corner. Thus was the poor little dolls' dressmaker dragged down day by day by the very hands that should have cared for and held her up; poor, poor little dolls' dressmaker! One day when Jenny was on her way home with Riah, who had accompanied her on one of her walks to the West End, they came into a small crowd of people. A drunk man had been knocked down and badly hurt. "Let us see what it is!" said Jenny, coming swiftly forward on her crutches. The next moment she exclaimed—"Oh, gentlemen—gentlemen, he is my child. He belongs to me, my poor, bad old child!"

"Your child—belongs to you," repeated the man who was about to lift the helpless figure onto a stretcher, which had been brought for the purpose. "Aye, it's old Dolls—tipsy old Dolls," cried someone in the crowd, for it was by this name that they knew the old man.

"He's her father, sir," said Riah in a low tone to the doctor, who was now bending over the stretcher.

"So much the worse," answered the doctor, "for the man is dead."

Yes, "Mr. Dolls" was dead, and many were the dresses that the weary fingers of the sorrowful little worker must make to pay for his humble funeral and buy a black dress for herself. Riah sat by her in her poor room, saying a word of comfort now and then, and Lizzie came and went and did all manner of little things to help her, but often the tears rolled down onto her work. "My poor child," she said to Riah, "my poor old child, and to think I scolded him so."

"You were always a good, brave, patient girl," returned Riah, smiling a little over her quaint fancy about her child, "always good and patient, however, tired."

And so the poor little "person of the house" was left alone but for the faithful affection of the kind Jew and her friend Lizzie. Her room grew pretty and comfortable, for she was in great request in her "profession," as she called it, and there was now no one to spend and waste her earnings. But nothing could make her life otherwise than a suffering one till the happy morning when her child angels visited her for the last time and carried her away to the land where all such pain as hers is healed forever.

The Fish and The Ring

by Joseph Jacobs

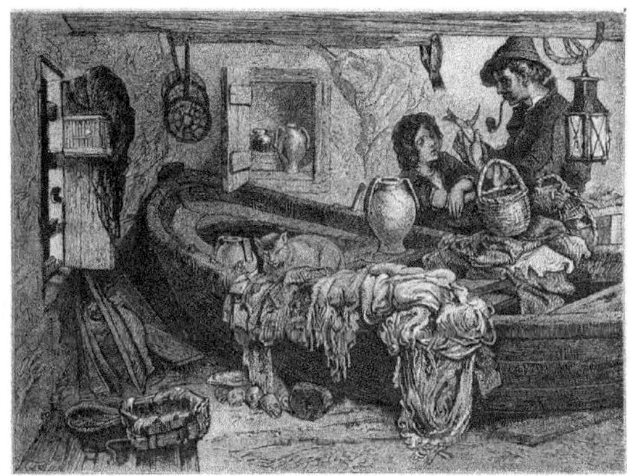

Once upon a time, there was a mighty baron in the North Country who was a great magician that knew everything that would come to pass. So one day, when his little boy was four years old, he looked into the Book of Fate to see what would happen to him. And to his dismay, he found that his son would wed a lowly maid that had just been born in a house under the shadow of York Minster. Now the

Baron knew the little girl's father was very, very poor, and he already had five children. So he called for his horse, rode into York, passed by the father's house, and saw him sitting by the door, sad. So he dismounted, went up to him, and said: "What is the matter, my good man?" And the man said: "Well, your honour, the fact is, I've five children already, and now a sixth's come, a little lass, and where to get the bread from to fill their mouths, that's more than I can say."

"Don't be downhearted, my man," said the Baron. "If that's your trouble, I can help you. I'll take away the last little one, and you won't have to bother about her."

"Thank you kindly, sir," said the man, and he went in and brought out the lass and gave her to the Baron, who mounted his horse and rode away with her. And when he got by the bank of the river Ouse, he threw the little thing into the river and rode off to his castle.

But the little lass didn't sink; her clothes kept her up for a time, and she floated, and she floated, till she was cast ashore just in front of a fisherman's hut. There the fisherman found her, took pity on the poor little thing, and took her into his house, and she lived there till she was fifteen years old and a fine, handsome girl.

One day, the Baron went out hunting with some companions along the banks of the River Ouse and stopped at the fisherman's hut to get a drink, and the girl came out to give it to them. They all noticed her beauty, and one said to the Baron: "You can read fates, Baron. Whom will she marry, d'ye think?"

"Oh! That's easy to guess," said the Baron; "some yokel or other. But I'll cast her horoscope. Come here, girl, and tell me on what day you were born?"

"I don't know, sir," said the girl, "I was picked up just here after having been brought down by the river about fifteen years ago."

Then the Baron knew who she was, and when they went away, he rode back and said to the girl: "Hark ye, girl, I will make your fortune. Take this letter to my brother in Scarborough, and you will be settled for life." And the girl took the letter and said she would go. Now, this was what he had written in the letter:

"Dear Brother,—Take the bearer and put her to death immediately.

"Yours affectionately,

"Albert."

So soon after, the girl set out for Scarborough and slept for the night at a little inn. Now that very night, a band of robbers broke into the inn and searched the girl, who had no money, and only the letter. So they opened this and read it and thought it a shame. The captain of the robbers took a pen and paper and wrote this letter:

"Dear Brother,—Take the bearer and marry her to my son immediately.

"Yours affectionately,

"Albert."

And then he gave it to the girl, bidding her begone. So she went on to the Baron's brother at Scarborough, a noble knight with whom the Baron's son was staying. When she gave the letter to his brother, he ordered the wedding to be prepared at once, and they were married that very day.

Soon after, the Baron came to his brother's castle, and it was his surprise to find that the very thing he had plotted against had come to pass. But he was not to be put off that way, and he took out the girl for a walk, as he said, along the cliffs. And when he got her all alone, he took her by the arms and was going to throw her over. But she begged hard for her life. "I have not done anything," she said: "if you only spare me, I will do whatever you wish. I will never see you or your son again till you desire it." Then the Baron took off his gold ring and threw it into the sea, saying: "Never let me see your face till you can show me that ring," and he let her go.

The poor girl wandered on and on till, at last, she came to a great noble's castle, and she asked to have some work given to her; and they made her the scullion girl of the castle, for she had been used to such work in the fisherman's hut.

Now one day, who should she see coming up to the noble's house but the Baron and his brother and his son, her husband? She didn't know what to do but thought they would not see her in the castle kitchen. So she went back to her work with a sigh and set to cleaning a big giant fish that was to be boiled for their dinner.

And, as she was cleaning it, she saw something shine inside it, and what do you think she found? There was the Baron's ring, the one he had thrown over the cliff at Scarborough. She was right. Glad to see it, and you may be sure. Then she cooked the fish as nicely as possible and served it up. When the fish came to the table, the guests liked it so well that they asked the noble who cooked it. He said he didn't know but called to his servants: "Ho, there, send up the cook that cooked that fine fish." So they went down to the kitchen and told the girl she was wanted in the hall. Then she washed and tidied herself, put the Baron's gold ring on her thumb, and went up into the hall.

When the banqueters saw such a beautiful young cook, they were surprised. But the Baron was in a tower of a temper and started up as if he would do her some violence. So the girl went up to him with her hand and the ring and put it down before him on the table. Then, at last, the Baron saw that no one could fight against Fate, and he handed her to a seat and announced to all the company that this was his son's faithful wife; and he took her and his son home to his castle, and they all lived as happy as could be ever afterward.

One Eye, Two Eyes, Three Eyes

by Brothers Grimm

There was once a woman with three daughters, of whom the eldest was named "One Eye" because she had only one Eye in the middle of her forehead. The second had two eyes, like other people, and she was called "Two Eyes." The youngest had three eyes, two like her second sister and one in the middle of her forehead, like the eldest, and she bore the name "Three Eyes."

Now because little Two Eyes looked like other people, her mother and sisters could not endure her. They told her, "You are not better than common folks with your two eyes; you don't belong to us."

So they pushed her about, threw all their old clothes to her for her to wear, gave her only the pieces left to eat, and did everything they could to make her miserable. It so happened that little Two Eyes was sent into the fields to take care of the goats, and she was often starving, although her sisters had as much as they liked to eat. So one day, she sat on a mound in the field and began to weep and cry so bitterly that two little rivulets flowed from her eyes. Once, amid her sorrow, she looked up and saw a woman standing near her who said, "What are you weeping for, little Two Eyes?"

"I cannot help weeping," she replied; "for because I have two eyes, like other people, my mother and sisters cannot bear me; they push me about from one corner to another and make us wear their old clothes, and give me nothing to eat but what is left, so that I am always hungry. Today they gave me so little that I am nearly starved."

"Dry up your tears, little Two Eyes," said the wise woman; "I will tell you something to do which will prevent you from ever being hungry again. You have only to say to your goat:

"'Little goat, if you're able, Pray deck out my table,'

"and immediately, there will be a pretty little table before you were full of all sorts of good things for you to eat, as much as you like. And when you have had enough, and you do not want the table anymore, you need only say:

"'Little goat, when you're able, Remove my nice table,'

"and it will vanish from your eyes."

Then the wise woman went away. "Now," thought little Two Eyes, "I will try if what she says is true, for I am starving," so she said:

"Little goat, if you're able, Pray deck out my table."

The words were scarcely spoken when a beautiful little table stood before her; it had a white cloth, plates, knives and forks, silver spoons, and such a delicious dinner, smoking hot as if it had just come from the kitchen. Then little Two Eyes sat down and said the shortest grace she knew—"Pray God to be our guest for all time. Amen"—before she allowed herself to taste anything. But oh, how she did enjoy her dinner! and when she had finished, she said, as the wise woman had taught her:

"Little goat, when you're able, Remove my nice table."

In a moment, the table and everything upon it had disappeared. "That is a pleasant way to keep house," said little Two Eyes, and felt quite contented and happy. In the evening, when she went home with the goat, she found an earthenware dish with some scraps which her sisters had left for her, but she did not touch them. The following day she went away with the goat, leaving them behind where they had been placed for her. The first and second times that she did so, the sisters did not notice it; but when they found it happened every day, they said one to the other, "There is something strange about little Two Eyes, she leaves her supper every day, and all that has been put for her has been wasted; she must get food somewhere else."

So they determined to find out the truth, and they arranged that when Two Eyes took her goat to the field, One Eye should go with her to take particular notice of what she did and discover if anything was brought for her to eat and drink.

So when Two Eyes started with her goat, One Eye said to her, "I am going with you today to see if the goat gets her food properly while you are watching the rest."

But Two Eyes knew what she had in her mind. So she drove the goat into the long grass and said, "Come, One Eye, let us sit down here and rest, and I will sing to you."

One Eye seated herself, and, not accustomed to walking so far or to be out in the sun's heat, she began to feel tired, and as little Two Eyes kept on singing, she closed her one Eye and fell fast asleep.

When Two Eyes saw this, she knew that One Eye

could not betray her, so she said:

"Little goat, if you can, Come and deck my pretty table."

She seated herself when it appeared and ate and drank very quickly, and when she had finished, she said:

"Little goat, come and clear away my table when you are able."

It vanished in the twinkling of an eye, and then Two Eyes woke up One Eye and said, "Little One Eye, you are a clever one to watch goats; for, while you are asleep, they might be running all over the world. Come, let us go home!"

So they went to the house, and little Two Eyes again left the scraps on the dish untouched, and One Eye could not tell her mother whether little Two Eyes had eaten anything in the field, for she said to excuse herself, "I was asleep."

The next day the mother said to Three Eyes, "You must go to the field this time and find out whether there is anyone who brings food to little Two Eyes, for she must eat and drink secretly."

So when little Two Eyes started with her goat, Three Eyes followed and said, "I am going with you today to see if the goats are properly fed and watched."

But Two Eyes knew her thoughts, so she led the goat through the long grass to tire Three Eyes, and at last, she said, "Let us sit down here and rest, and I will sing to you, Three Eyes."

She was glad to sit down, for the walk and the sun's heat had really tired her; as her sister continued her song, she was obliged to close two of her eyes, and they slept, but not the third. Three Eyes was wide awake with one Eye and heard and saw all that Two Eyes did; for poor little Two Eyes, thinking she was asleep, said her speech to the goat, and the table came with all the good things on it and was carried away when Two Eyes had eaten enough. The cunning Three Eyes saw it all with her one Eye. But she pretended to be asleep when her sister came to wake her and told her she was going home.

That evening, when little Two Eyes again left the supper they placed aside for her, Three Eyes said to her mother, "I know where the proud thing gets her good eating and drinking," and then she described all she had seen in the field. "I saw it all with one eye," she said, "for she had made my other two eyes close with her fine singing, but luckily the one in my forehead remained open."

Then the envious mother cried to poor little Two Eyes, "You wish to have better food than we, do you? You shall lose your wish!" She took up a butcher's knife, went out, and stuck the excellent little goat in the heart, and it fell dead.

When little Two Eyes saw this, she went out into the field, seated herself on a mound, and wept most bitter tears.

Presently the wise woman stood before her and said, "Little Two Eyes, why do you weep?"

"Ah!" she replied, "I must weep. The goat, which spread my table so beautifully every day, has been killed by my mother, and I shall have again to suffer from hunger and sorrow."

"Little Two Eyes," said the wise woman, "I will give you some good advice. Go home, ask your sister to give you the inside of the slaughtered goat, and then go and bury it in the ground in front of the house door."

On saying this, the wise woman vanished.

Little Two Eyes went home quickly and said to her sister, "Dear sister, give me some part of my poor goat. I don't want anything valuable; only give me the inside."

Her sister laughed and said, "Of course, you can have that if you don't want anything else."

So little Two Eyes took the inside and, in the evening, when all was quiet, buried it in the ground outside the house door, as the wise woman had told her to do.

The following day, when they all rose and looked out of the window, there stood a most beautiful tree with leaves of silver and apples of gold hanging between them. Nothing in the wide world could be more beautiful or more costly. None of them knew how the tree could come there in one night except little Two Eyes. She supposed it had grown up from the goat inside, for it stood over where she had buried it in the earth.

Then said the mother to little One Eye, "Climb up, my child, and break off some of the fruit from the tree."

One Eye climbed up, but when she tried to catch a branch and pluck one of the apples, it escaped from her hand, and so it happened every time she attempted, and, do what she would, she could not reach one.

"Three Eyes," said the mother, "climb up, and try what you can do; perhaps you will be able to see better with your three eyes than One Eye can."

One Eye slid down from the tree, and Three Eyes climbed up. But Three Eyes was not more skillful; with all her efforts, she could not draw the branches, nor the fruit, near enough to pluck even a leaf, for they sprang back as she put out her hand.

At last, the mother was impatient and climbed up herself, but with no more success, for, as she appeared to grasp a branch or fruit, her hand closed upon thin air.

"May I try?" said little Two Eyes; "perhaps I may succeed."

"You, indeed!" cried her sisters; "you, with your two eyes, what can you do?"

But Two Eyes climbed up, and the golden apples did not fly back from her when she touched them but almost laid themselves on her hand, and she plucked them one after another till she carried down her little apron full.

The mother took them from her and gave them to her sisters, as she said little Two Eyes did not handle them properly; but this was only from jealousy because little Two Eyes was the only one who could reach the fruit, and she went into the house feeling more spiteful to her than ever.

While all three sisters were standing under the tree together, a young knight rode by. "Run away, quick, and hide, little Two Eyes; hide somewhere, for we shall be quite ashamed for you to be seen." Then they pushed the poor girl, in great haste, under an empty cask, which stood near the tree, and several of the golden apples that she had plucked along with her.

As the knight came nearer, they saw he was a handsome man; presently, he halted and looked with wonder and pleasure at the beautiful tree with its silver leaves and golden fruit.

At last, he spoke to the sisters and asked: "To whom does this beautiful tree belong? If a man possessed only one branch, he might obtain all he wished for in the world."

"This tree belongs to us," said the two sisters, "and we will break off a branch for you if you like." They gave themselves a great deal of trouble in trying to do as they offered, but all to no purpose, for the branches and the fruit evaded their efforts and sprung back at every touch.

"This is wonderful," exclaimed the knight, "that the tree should belong to you, yet you cannot gather even a branch."

They persisted, however, in declaring that the tree

was their property. At this moment, little Two Eyes, angry because her sisters had not told the truth, caused two golden apples to slip out from under the cask, and they rolled on till they reached the feet of the knight's horse. When he saw them, he asked in astonishment where they came from.

The two ugly maidens replied that they had another sister, but they dared not let him see her, for she had only two eyes, like ordinary people, and was named little Two Eyes.

But the knight felt very anxious to see her and called out, "Little Two Eyes, come here." Then came Two Eyes, quite comforted from the empty cask, and the knight was astonished to find her so beautiful.

Then he said, "Little Two Eyes, can you break off a tree branch for me?"

"Oh yes," she replied, "I can, very easily, for the tree belongs to me." And she climbed up and, without any trouble, broke off a branch with its silver leaves and golden fruit and gave it to the knight.

He looked down at her as she stood by his horse and said: "Little Two Eyes, what shall I give you for this?"

"Ah!" she answered, "I suffer from hunger and thirst, and sorrow, and trouble from early morning till late at night; if you would only take me with you and release me, I should be so happy."

Then the knight lifted the little maiden on his horse and rode home with her to his father's castle. There she was given beautiful clothes to wear and as much to eat and drink as she wished, and as she grew up, the young knight loved her so dearly that they were married with great rejoicings.

Now, when the two sisters saw little Two Eyes carried away by the handsome young knight, they were overjoyed at their good fortune. "The wonderful tree belongs to us now," they said; "even if we cannot break off a branch, everybody who passes will stop to admire it and make acquaintance with us, and who knows? We may get husbands after all."

But when they rose the following day, lo! the tree had vanished, and with it all their hopes. And on this very morning, when little Two Eyes looked out of her chamber window of the castle, she saw, to her great joy, that the tree had followed her.

Little Two Eyes lived for a long time in great happiness, but she heard nothing of her sisters till one day, two poor women came to the castle to beg for alms. Little Two Eyes saw them, and, looking earnestly in their faces, she recognized her two sisters, who had become so poor that they were obliged to beg their bread from door to door.

But the excellent sister received them most kindly and promised to take care of them and give them all they wanted. And then they did indeed repent and feel sorry for having mistreated her in their youthful days.

The Fair One With the Golden Locks

by Comtesse d'Aulnoy

There was once a most beautiful and amiable princess called "The Fair One with Locks of Gold," for her hair shone brighter than gold and flowed in curls down to her feet, a wreath of beautiful flowers always encircled her head, and pearls and diamonds.

A handsome, wealthy, young prince whose territories joined hers was deeply in love with the reports he heard of her and sent to demand her in marriage. The ambassador sent with proposals was most sumptuously attired and surrounded by lackeys on beautiful horses and charged with every kind of compliment from the anxious prince. The latter hoped he would bring the princess back with him. Still, I don't know whether she was not that day in good humour or did not like the speeches made by the ambassador, I don't know, but she returned thanks to his master for the honour he intended for her and said she did not incline to marry. When the ambassador arrived at the king's chief city, where he was expected with great impatience, the people were highly afflicted to see him return without the Fair One with the Locks of Gold; and the king wept like a child. There was a youth at court whose beauty outshone the sun, the gracefulness of whose person was not to be equaled, and for his gracefulness and wit, he was called Avenant: the king loved him, and indeed everybody except the envious. Avenant being one day in company with some persons, inconsiderately said, "If the king had sent me to the Fair One with Locks of Gold, I dare say I could have prevailed on her to return with me." These enviers of Avenant's prosperity immediately ran open-mouthed to the king, saying, "Sir sir, what does your majesty think

Avenant says? He boasts that if you had sent him to the Fair One with the Golden Hair, he could have brought her with him; which shows he is so vain as to think himself more handsome than your majesty and that her love for him would have made her follow him wherever he went." This put the king into a violent rage. "What!" said he, "does this youngster make a jest at my misfortune and pretend to set himself above me? Go and put him immediately in my great tower, and there let him starve." The king's guards went and seized Avenant, who thought no more of what he had said, dragged him to prison, and used him most cruelly.

One day when he was almost entirely spent, he said to himself, fetching a deep sigh, "Wherein can I have offended the king? He is not a more faithful subject than myself, nor have I done anything to displease him." The king happened at that time to pass by the tower; and stopped to hear him, notwithstanding the persuasions of those with him; "Hold your peace," replied the king, "and let me hear him out." Having done and being incredibly moved by his sufferings, he opened the tower door and called him by his name. Upon which, Avenant came forth in a sad condition and, throwing himself at the king's feet, "What have I done, sir," said he, "that your majesty should use me thus severely?" "Thou hast ridiculed my ambassador and me," replied the king, "and hast said that if I had sent thee to the Fair One with Locks of Gold, thou couldst have brought her with thee." "It is true, sir," replied Avenant, "for I would have so thoroughly convinced her of your transcending qualities that it should not have been in her power to have denied me, and this, surely, I said in the name of your majesty." The king found, in reality, he had done no injury, so he took him away with him, repenting heartily of the wrong he had done him. After giving him an excellent supper, the king sent him into his cabinet. "Avenant," said he, "I still love the Fair One with Locks of Gold; I have a mind to send thee to her, to try whether thou canst succeed," Avenant replied. He was ready to obey his majesty in everything and would depart the following day. "Hold," said the king, "I will provide the first with a most sumptuous equipage." "There is no necessity for that," answered Avenant; "I need only a good horse and your letters of credence." Upon this, the king embraced him, delighted to see him so soon ready.

On a Monday morning, he took leave of the king and his friends. Being on his journey by break of day and entering into a spacious meadow, a good thought came into his head; he alighted immediately and seated himself by the bank of a little stream that watered one side of the meadow and wrote the sentiment down in his pocketbook. After he had done writing, he looked about him every way, being charmed with the beauties of the place, and suddenly perceived a large gilded carp, which stirred a little, and that was all it could do, for having attempted to catch some little flies, it had leaped so far out of the water, as to throw itself upon the grass, where it was almost dead, not being able to recover its natural element. Avenant took pity on the poor creature and thought it was a fish day. He might have carried it away for his dinner. Still, he took it up and gently put it again into the river, where the carp, feeling the refreshing coolness of the water, began to rejoice and sunk to the bottom; but soon rose again, brisk and gay, to the side of the river; "Avenant," said the carp, "I thank you for the kindness you have done me; had it not been for you, I had died, but you have saved my life, and I will reward you." After this short compliment, the carp darted itself to the bottom of the water, leaving Avenant not a little surprised at its wit and great civility.

Another day, as he was pursuing his journey, he saw a crow in great distress: being followed by a giant eagle, he took his bow, which he always carried abroad with him, and aiming at the eagle, let fly an arrow, which pierced him through the body, so that he fell dead; which the crow seeing, came in an ecstasy of joy, and perched upon a tree. "Avenant," said the crow, "you have been extremely generous to succor me, who am but a poor wretched crow, but I am not ungrateful and will do you as good a turn." Avenant admired the wit of the crow and continued his journey, and he entered into the wood so early one morning that he could scarcely see his way, where he heard an owl crying out like an owl in despair. So looking about everywhere, he finally came to a place where certain fowlers had spread their nets in the nighttime to catch little birds. "What pity 'tis," he said, "men are only made to torment one another or to persecute poor animals who never do them any harm!" So saying, he drew his knife, cut the cords, and set the owl at liberty; who, before he took wing, said, "Avenant, the fowlers are coming; I should have been taken, and must have died, without your assistance: I have a grateful heart, and will remember it."

These were the three most remarkable adventures that befell Avenant in his journey. When he arrived at the end of it, he washed, combed, and powdered his hair and put on a suit of cloth of gold: which, having done, he put a rich embroidered scarf about his neck, with a small basket, wherein was a little dog which he was very fond of. And Avenant was so amiable and did everything with so good a grace that when he presented himself at the palace gate, all the guards paid him great respect. Everyone strove who should first give notice to the Fair One with Locks of Gold that Avenant, the neighbouring king's ambassador, demanded an audience. The princess, on hearing the name of Avenant, said, "It has a pleasing sound, and I dare say he is agreeable and pleases every body; and she said to her maids of honour, go fetch me my rich embroidered gown of blue satin, dress my hair, and bring my wreaths of fresh flowers: let me have my high shoes, and my fan, and let my audience chamber and throne be clean, and richly adorned; for I would have him everywhere with truth say, that I am the Fair One with Locks of Gold." Thus all her women were employed to dress her as a queen should be. At length, she went to her great gallery of looking glasses to see if anything was wanting, after which she ascended her throne of gold, ivory, and ebony, the fragrant smell superior to the choicest balm. She also commanded her maids of honour to take their instruments and play to their singing so sweetly that none should be disgusted.

Avenant was conducted into an audience chamber, where he stood so transported with admiration that, as he afterward said, he had scarcely power to open his lips. At length, however, he took courage and made his speech wonderfully well, wherein he prayed to the princess not to let him be so unfortunate as to return without her. "Gentle Avenant," said she, "all the reasons you have laid before me are excellent, and I assure you, I would rather favour you than any other; but you must know, about a month since I went to take the air by the side of a river, with my maids of honour; as I was pulling off my glove, I pulled a ring from my finger, which by accident fell into the river. This ring I valued more than my whole kingdom, whence you may judge how much the loss of it afflicts me. And I have made a vow never to listen to any marriage proposals unless the ambassador who makes them shall also bring my ring. This is the present you have to make me; otherwise, you may talk your heart out, for months and even years shall never change my resolution." When he returned to his lodgings, he went to bed supperless; and his little dog, who was called Cabriole, made a fasting night of it too and went and lay down by his master; who did nothing all night but sigh and lament, saying, "How can I find a ring that fell into a great river a month ago? It would be folly to attempt it. The princess enjoined me this task, merely because she knew it was impossible," he continued, greatly afflicted; which Cabriole observing, said, "My dear master, pray do not despair of your good fortune; for you are too good to be unhappy. Therefore, let us go to the riverside when it is the day." Avenant made no answer but gave his dog two little cuffs with his hand and, being overwhelmed with grief, fell asleep.

But when Cabriole perceived it was broad day, he fell a barking so loud that he woke his master. "Rise, sir," said he, "put on your clothes, and let us go and try our fortune." Avenant took his little dog's advice; got up, dressed, went down into the garden, and out of the garden, he walked insensibly to the riverside, with his hat over his eyes and his arms across, thinking of nothing but taking his leave; when all on a sudden he heard a voice call, "Avenant, Avenant!" upon which he looked around him, but seeing nothing, he concluded it was an illusion and was proceeding in his walk; but he presently heard himself called again. "Who calls me?" said he; Cabriole, who was very little and looked closely into the water, cried out, "Never believe me if it is not a gilded carp." Immediately the carp appeared and, with an audible voice, said, "Avenant, you saved my life in the poplar meadow, where I must have died without your assistance; and now I am come to requite your kindness. My dear Avenant, here is the ring which the Fair One with Locks of Gold dropped into the river." He stooped and took it out of the carp's mouth, to whom he returned a thousand thanks. And now, instead of returning home, he went directly to the palace with little Cabriole, who skipped about, and wagged his tail for joy, that he had persuaded his master to walk by the side of the river.

The princess was told that Avenant desired an audience: "Alas," said she, "the poor youth has come to take his leave of me! He has considered what I urged impossible and is returning to his master." But Avenant, being admitted, presented her the ring, saying, "Madam, behold I have executed your command; and now, I hope, you will receive my master for your royal consort." When she saw her ring, which was noways injured, she was so amazed that she could hardly believe her eyes. "Surely, courteous Avenant," said she, "you must be favoured by some fairy, for naturally, this is impossible." "Madam," said he, "I am acquainted with no fairy; but I was willing to obey your command." "Well, seeing you have so good a will," she continued, "you must do me another piece of service, without which I will never marry. There is a certain prince who lives not far from hence, whose name is Galifron, and whom nothing would serve but that he must need to marry me. He declared his mind to me, with most terrible menaces, that if I denied him, he would enter my kingdom with fire and sword; but you shall judge whether I would accept his proposal: he is a giant, as high as a steeple; he devours men as an ape eats chestnuts; when he goes into the country, he carries cannons in his pocket, to use instead of pistols; and when he speaks aloud he deafens the ears of those that stand near him. I answered him that I did not choose to marry and desired him to excuse me. Nevertheless, he has not ceased to persecute me and has put an infinite number of my subjects to the sword: before all other things, you must fight him and bring me his head."

Avenant was somewhat startled by this proposal, but having considered it awhile, "Well, madam," said he, "I will fight this Galifron; I believe I shall be vanquished, but I will die like a man of courage." The princess was astonished at his courage and said a thousand things to dissuade him from it, but all in vain. At length, he arrived at Galifron's castle, the roads all the way being strewed with the bones and carcasses of men that the giant had devoured or cut in pieces. It was not long before Avenant saw the monster approach, and he immediately challenged him. Still, there was no occasion for this, for he lifted his iron mace, and had certainly beat out the gentle Avenant's brains at the first blow, had not a crow perched upon the giant's head at that instant, and with his bill pecked out both his eyes. The blood trickled down his face, to which he grew desperate, and laid about him on every side; but Avenant took care to avoid his blows and gave him many significant wounds with his sword, which he pushed up to the very hilt; so that the giant fainted, and fell with loss of blood. Avenant immediately cut off his head; and while he was in an ecstasy of joy for his success, the crow perched upon a tree and said, "Avenant, I did not forget the kindnesses I received at your hands when you killed the eagle that pursued me; I promised to make you amends, and now I have been as good as my word." "I acknowledge your kindness, Mr. Crow," replied Avenant; "I am still your debtor and your servant." So saying, he mounted his course and rode away with the giant's horrid head. When he arrived at the city, everybody crowded after him, crying out, "Long live the valiant Avenant, who has slain the cruel monster!" so that the princess, who heard the noise and trembling for fear she should have heard of Avenant's death, durst not inquire what the matter was. But presently after, she saw Avenant enter with the giant's head; at the sight of which she trembled, though there was nothing to fear. "Madam," said he, "behold, your enemy is dead, and now, I hope, you will no longer refuse the king, my master." "Alas!" replied the Fair One with Locks of Gold, "I must still refuse him unless you can find means to bring me some of the water of the gloomy cave. Not far from hence," continued she, "there is a bottomless cave, about six leagues in compass; the entrance into which is guarded by two dragons. The dragons' dart fire from their mouths and eyes, and when you have got into this cave, you will meet with a bottomless hole, into which you must go down, and you will find it full of toads, adders, and serpents. At the bottom of this hole is a kind of cellar that runs the fountain of beauty and health. This is the water I must have; its virtues are wonderful; for the fair, by washing in it, preserve their beauty; and the deformed it renders beautiful; if they are young, it preserves them always youthful; and if old, it makes them young again. Now judge you, Avenant, whether I will ever leave my kingdom without carrying some of this water along with me." "Madam," said he, "you are so beautiful that this water will be of no use to you; but I am an unfortunate ambassador whose death you seek. However, I will go in search of what you desire, though I am certain never to return."

At length, he arrived at the top of a mountain, where he sat down to rest, giving his horse liberty to feed and Cabriole to run after the flies. He knew that the gloomy cave was not far off and looked about to see whether he could discover it; and at length, he perceived a horrid rock as black as ink, whence issued a thick smoke; and immediately after, he spied one of the dragons casting forth fire from his jaws and eyes; his skin all over yellow and green, with prodigious claws and a long tail, rolled up in a hundred folds. Avenant, with a resolution to die in the attempt, drew his sword, and with the phial which the Fair One with Locks of Gold had given him to fill with the water of beauty, went towards the cave, saying to his little dog, "Cabriole, here is an end of me; I never shall be able to get this water, it is so well guarded by the dragons; therefore when I am dead, fill this phial with my blood, and carry it to my princess, that she may see what her severity has cost me: then go to the king my master and give him an account of my misfortunes." While he was saying this, he heard a voice call, "Avenant, Avenant!" "Who calls me?" said he; presently, he espied an owl in the hole of an old hollow tree, who, calling him again, said, "You rescued me from the fowler's net, where I had been assuredly taken, had you not delivered me. I promised to make you amends, and now the time has come; give me your phial; I am acquainted with all the secret inlets into the gloomy cave and will go and fetch you the water of beauty." Avenant most gladly gave the phial, and the owl, entering without any impediment into the cave, filled it and, in less than a quarter of an hour, returned with it well stopped. Avenant was overjoyed at his good fortune, gave the owl a thousand thanks, and replaced with a merry heart to the city. Having arrived at the palace, he presented the phial to the Fair One with Locks of Gold, who had nothing further to say. She returned Avenant's thanks and gave orders for everything requisite for her departure: after which she set forward with him. The Fair One with Locks of Gold thought Avenant very amiable and said to him sometimes upon the road, "If you had been willing, I could have made you a king; and then we need not have left my kingdom." But Avenant replied, "I would not have been guilty of such a piece of treachery to my master for all the kingdoms of the earth, though I must acknowledge your beauties are more resplendent than the sun."

At length, they arrived at the king's chief city, which understood that the Fair One with Locks of Gold had come. He met her and made her the wealthiest present in the world. The nuptials were solemnized with such demonstrations of joy that nothing else was discoursed of. But the Fair One with Locks of Gold, who loved

Avenant in her heart, was never pleased but when she was in his company and would always be speaking in his praise: "I had never come hither," said she to the king, "had it not been for Avenant, who, to serve me, has conquered impossibilities; you are infinitely obliged to him; he procured me the water of beauty and health; by which I shall never grow old, and shall always preserve my health and beauty." The enviers of Avenant's happiness, who heard the queen's words, said to the king, "Were your majesty inclined to be jealous, you have reason enough to be so, for the queen is desperately in love with Avenant." "Indeed," said the king, "I am sensible of the truth of what you tell me; let him be put in the great tower, with fetters upon his feet and hands." Avenant was immediately seized. However, his little dog Cabriole never forsook him but cheered him the best he could and brought him all the court news. When the Fair One with Locks of Gold was informed of his misfortunes, she threw herself at the king's feet and, all in tears, brought him to release Avenant from prison. But the more she besought him, the more he was incensed, believing her affection made her so zealous a suppliant on his behalf. Finding she could not prevail, she said no more to him but grew pensive and melancholy.

The king took it into his head that she did not think him handsome enough, so he resolved to wash his face with the water of beauty, hoping the queen would then conceive a greater affection for him than she had. This water stood in a phial upon a table in the queen's chamber, where she had put it, that it might not be out of her sight. But one of the chambermaids going to kill a spider with her besom, by accident threw down the phial, and broke it so that the water was lost. She dried it up with all the speed she could, not knowing what to do. She thought she had seen a phial of clear water in the king's cabinet as she had broken. Therefore, without any more ado, she fetched that phial and set it on the table in place of the other. This water which was in the king's cabinet, was sure water that he made use of to poison the great lords and princes of his court when they were convicted of any great crime; to which purpose, instead of cutting off their heads or hanging them, he caused their faces to be rubbed with this water, which cast them into so profound a sleep that they never waked again. One evening, the king took this phial and rubbed his face well with the water, after which he fell asleep and died. Cabriole was one of the first to know of this accident and immediately ran to inform Avenant of it, who bid him go to the Fair One with Locks of Gold and reminded her of the poor prisoner. Cabriole slipped unperceived through the crowd, for there was a great noise and hurry at court upon the king's death, and getting to the queen, "Madam," said he, "remember poor Avenant." She called to mind the afflictions he had suffered for her sake and his fidelity. Without speaking a word, she went directly to the great tower and took off the fetters from Avenant's feet and hands herself; after which, putting the crown upon his head and the royal mantle about his shoulders, "Amiable Avenant," said she, "I will make you a sovereign prince, and take you for my consort." Avenant threw himself at her feet and returned her thanks in terms of the most passionate and respectful. Everybody was delighted to have him for their king: the weddings were the most splendid in the world, and the Fair One. with Locks of Gold, lived a long time with her beloved Avenant, both happy and contented in the enjoyment of each other.

The Hedley Kow

by Joseph Jacobs

Once, an old woman earned a poor living by going errands and such like for the farmers' wives roundabout the village where she lived. It wasn't much she earned by it, but with a plate of meat at one house and a cup of tea at another, she shifted to get on and always looked as cheerful as if she hadn't wanted in the world.

Well, one summer evening, as she was trotting away homeward, she came upon a big black pot lying at the side of the road.

"Now that," said she, stopping to look at it, "would be just the very thing for me if I had anything to put into it! But who can have left it here?" and she looked round about as if the person it belonged to must be not far off. But she could see no one.

"Maybe it'll have a hole in it," she said thoughtfully: —

"Ay, that'll be how they've left it lying, hinny. But then it'd be fine to put a flower in for the window; I think I'll take it home, anyway." And she bent her stiff old back and lifted the lid to look inside.

"Mercy me!" she cried and jumped back to the other side of the road; "if it is fit brim full o' gold PIECES!!"

For a while, she could do nothing but walk round and round her treasure, admiring the yellow gold and wondering at her good luck and saying to herself about every two minutes, "Well, I do be feeling rich and grand!" But presently, she began to think how she could best take it home with her; and she couldn't see any other way than by fastening one end of her shawl to it and dragging it after her along the road.

"It'll certainly be soon dark," she said to herself, "and folk'll not see what I'm bringing home with me, and so I'll have all the night to myself to think what I'll do with it. I could buy a grand house and all, and live like the Queen herself, and not do a stroke of work all day, but sit by the fire with a cup of tea, or maybe I'll give it to the priest to keep for me and get a piece as I'm wanting; or maybe I'll bury it in a hole at the garden-foot, and put a bit on the chimney, between the chiney teapot and the spoons—for ornament like. Ah! I feel so grand, and I don't know myself rightly!"

And by this time, already rather tired of dragging such a heavyweight after her, she stopped to rest for a minute, turning to ensure her treasure was safe.

But when she looked at it, it wasn't a pot of gold but a great lump of shining silver!

She stared at it, rubbed her eyes, and stared at it again, but she couldn't make it look like anything but a great lump of silver. "I'd have sworn it was a pot of gold," she said, "but I reckon I must have been dreaming. Now, that's a change for the better; it'll be far less trouble to look after, and none so easy stolen; yon gold pieces would have been a sight of bothering to keep them safe. Ay, I'm well quit of them; and with my bonny lump, I'm as rich—!"

And she set off homewards again, cheerfully planning all the great things she would do with her money. However, it wasn't very long before she got tired again and stopped once more to rest for a minute or two.

Again she turned to look at her treasure, and as soon as she set eyes on it, she cried out in astonishment. "Oh, my!" said she; "now it's a lump o' iron! Well, that beats all; and it's just really convenient! I can sell it as easily and get a lot of penny pieces. Ay, hinny, and it's much handier than a lot o' yer gold and silver as having kept me from sleeping o' nights thinking the neighbours were robbing me—and it's a real good thing to have by you in a house, ye never can tell what ye mightn't use it for, and it'll sell—ay, for a real lot. Rich? I'll be just rolling!"

And on she trotted again, chuckling to herself on her good luck, till presently she glanced over her shoulder, "just to make sure it was there still," as she said to herself.

"Eh, my!" she cried as soon as she saw it; "if it hasn't gone and turned itself into a great stone this time! How could it have known I was terrible, wanting something to hold my door open with? Ay, if that isn't a good change! Hinny, it's a fine thing to have such good luck."

And, all in a hurry to see how the stone would look in its corner by her door, she trotted off down the hill and stopped at the foot beside her little gate.

When she had unlatched it, she turned to unfasten her shawl from the stone, which this time seemed to lie unchanged and peaceably on the path beside her, There was still plenty of light, and she could see the stone quite plainly as she bent her stiff back over it, to untie the shawl end; when, all of a sudden, it seemed to give a jump and a squeal, and grew in a moment as big as a great horse. It threw down four skinny legs, shook out two long ears, flourished a tail, and went off kicking its feet into the and laughing like a naughty mocking boy.

The old woman stared after it till it was fairly out of sight.

"WELL!" she said at last, "I do be the luckiest body hereabouts! Fancy me seeing the Hedley Kow all to myself and making so free with it too! I can tell you, and I do feel that GRAND—"

And she went into her cottage and sat by the fire to think about her good luck.

The Fiddler in the Fairy Ring

by Juliana Horatia Ewing

Generations ago, a farmer's son once lived with no great harm and no tremendous good. He always meant well, but he had a poor spirit and was too fond of idle company. One day his father sent him to market with some sheep for sale, and when business was over for the day, the rest of the country folk made ready to go home, and more than one of them offered the lad a lift in his cart.

"Thank you kindly, all the same," said he, "but I am going back across the downs with Limping Tim."

Then a steady old farmer spoke and bade the lad go

home with the rest and by the main road. For Limping, Tim was an idle, graceless kind of fellow, who fiddled for his livelihood, but what else he did to earn the money he squandered, no one knew. And as to the sheep path over the downs, it stands to reason that the highway is better traveling after sunset, for the other is no such concise cut; and has a big fairy ring so near it that a butter-woman might brush it with the edge of her market cloak, as she turned the brow of the hill.

But the farmer's son would go his own way, with Limping Tim and across the downs.

So they started, and the fiddler had his fiddle in his hand and a bundle of marketings under his arm, and he sang snatches of strange songs, the like of which the lad had never heard before. And the moon drew out their shadows over the short grass till they were as long as the great stones of Stonehenge.

At last, they turned the hill, and the fairy ring looked dark under the moon, and the farmer's son blessed himself that they were passing it quietly when Limping Tim suddenly pulled his cloak from his back and, handing it to his companion, cried, "Hold this for a moment, will you? I'm wanted. They're calling for me."

"I hear nothing," said the farmer's son. But before he had got the words out of his mouth, the fiddler had disappeared entirely. He shouted aloud, but in vain, and had begun to think of proceeding on his way when the fiddler's voice cried, "Catch!" and there came, flying at him from the direction of the fairy ring, the bundle of marketings which the fiddler had been carrying.

"It's in my way," he then heard the fiddler cry. "Ah, this is dancing! Come in, my lad, come in!"

But the farmer's son was not totally without prudence, and he took good care to keep at a safe distance from the fairy ring.

"Come back, Tim! Come back!" he shouted, and, receiving no answer, he adjured his friend to break the bonds that withheld him and return to the right way, as wisely as one man can counsel another.

After talking for some time to no purpose, he again heard his friend's voice, crying, "Take care of it for me! The money dances out of my pocket." And in addition to that, the fiddler's purse was hurled to his feet, where it fell with a heavy chinking of gold within.

He picked it up and renewed his warnings and requests, but in vain, and after waiting for a long time, he made the best of his way home alone, hoping that the fiddler would follow and come to reclaim his property.

The fiddler never came. And when there was a fuss about his disappearance, the farmer's son, who had but a poor spirit, began to be afraid, to tell the truth of the matter. "Who knows, but they may accuse me of theft?" said he. So he hid the cloak, bundle, and money bag in the garden.

But when three months passed, and still the fiddler did not return, it was whispered that the farmer's son had been his last companion, and the place was searched, and they found the cloak, the bundle, and the money bag, and the lad was taken to prison.

When it was too late, he plucked up a spirit and told the truth; but no one believed him, and it was said that he had murdered the fiddler for his money and goods. And he was taken before the judge, found guilty, and sentenced to death.

Fortunately, his old mother was a Wise Woman. And when she heard that he was condemned, she said, "Only follow my directions, and we may save you yet, for I guess how it is."

So she went to the judge and begged for her son three favours before his death.

"I will grant them," said the judge, "if you do not ask for his life."

"The first," said the old woman, "is that he may choose the place where the gallows shall be erected; the second, that he may fix the hour of his execution; and the third favour is that you will not fail to be present."

"I grant all three," said the judge. But when he learned that the criminal had chosen a particular hill on the downs for the place of execution, and an hour before midnight for the time, he sent to beg the sheriff to bear him company on this important occasion.

The sheriff placed himself at the judge's disposal, but he commanded the attendance of the Gaoler as some protection; and the Gaoler, for his part, implored his reverence for the chaplain to be of the party, as the hill was not in good spiritual repute. So, when the time came, the four started together, and the hangman and the farmer's son went before them to the foot of the gallows.

Just as the rope was being prepared, the farmer's son called to the judge and said, "If your Honour walks twenty paces down the hill, to where you will see a bit of paper, you will learn the fate of the fiddler."

"That is, no doubt, a copy of the poor man's last confession," thought the judge.

"Murder will out, Mr. Sheriff," said he, and he hastened to pick up the paper in the interests of truth and justice.

But the farmer's son had dropped it as he came along, by his mother's direction, in such a place that the judge could not pick it up without putting his foot on the edge of the fairy ring. No sooner had he done so than he perceived an innumerable company of little people dressed in green cloaks and hoods dancing around in a circle as wide as the ring.

They were about two feet high and had aged faces, brown and withered, like the knots on gnarled trees in hedge bottoms, and they squinted horribly; but, despite their seeming age, they flew round and round like children.

"Mr. Sheriff! Mr. Sheriff!" cried the judge, "come and see the dancing. And hear the music, too, which is so lively that it makes the soles of my feet tickle."

"There is no music, my Lord Judge," said the sheriff, running down the hill. "It is the wind whistling over the grass that your lordship hears."

But when the sheriff had put his foot by the judge's foot, he saw and heard the same, and he cried out, "Quick, Gaoler, and come down! I should like you to be a witness to this matter. And you may take my arm, Gaoler, for the music makes me feel unsteady."

"There is no music, sir," said the Gaoler, "but your worship doubtless hears the creaking of the gallows."

But no sooner had the Gaoler's feet touched the fairy ring than he saw and heard like the rest, and he called lustily to the chaplain to come and stop the unhallowed measure.

"It is a delusion of the Evil One," said the parson; "there is not a sound in the air but the distant croaking of some frogs." But when he, too, touched the ring, he perceived his mistake.

At this moment, the moon shone out, and in the middle of the ring, they saw Limping Tim the fiddler, playing till significant drops stood out on his forehead and dancing as madly as he played.

"Ah, you rascal!" cried the judge. "Is this where you've been all the time and a better man than you as good as hanged for you? But you shall come home now."

Saying which, he ran in and seized the fiddler by the arm. Still, Limping Tim resisted so stoutly that the sheriff had to go to the judge's assistance, and even then, the fairies so pinched and hindered them that the sheriff was obliged to call upon the Gaoler to put his arms about his waist, who persuaded the chaplain to add his strength to the string. But as ill luck would have it, just as they were getting off, one of the fairies picked up Limping Tim's fiddle, which had fallen in the scuffle, and began to play. And as he began to play, everyone began to dance—the fiddler, the judge, the sheriff, the Gaoler, and even the chaplain.

"Hangman! hangman!" screamed the judge, lifting first one leg and then the other to the tune, "come down, and catch hold of his reverence the chaplain. The prisoner is pardoned, and he can lay hold too."

The hangman knew the judge's voice and ran towards it, but as they were now entirely within the ring, he could see nothing, either of him or his companions.

The farmer's son followed, warning the hangman not to touch the ring. He directed him to stretch his hands forwards in hopes of catching hold of someone. The wind blew the chaplain's cassock against the hangman's fingers in a few minutes, and he caught the parson around the waist. The farmer's son then seized him in like fashion, and each holding firmly by the other, the fiddler, the judge, the sheriff, the Gaoler, the parson, the hangman, and the farmer's son all got safely out of the charmed circle.

"Oh, you scoundrel!" cried the judge to the fiddler; "I

have an excellent mind to hang you up on the gallows without further ado."

But the fiddler only looked like one possessed and upbraided the farmer's son for not having the patience to wait three minutes for him.

"Three minutes!" cried he; "why you've been here three months and a day."

This the fiddler would not believe, and as he seemed in every way beside himself, they led him home, still upbraiding his companion, and crying continually for his fiddle.

His neighbors watched him closely, but one day he escaped from their care, wandered away over the hills to seek his fiddle, and came back no more.

His dead body was found upon the downs, face downwards, with the fiddle in his arms. Some said he had seen the fiddle where he had left it, had been lost in a mist, and died of exposure. But others held that he had perished differently and laid his death at the door of the fairy dancers.

As to the farmer's son, it is said that he went home from the market by the high road, spoke the truth straight out, and was more careful of his company.

Midsummer-Night

by Mrs. W. K. Clifford

The children were very much puzzled about what to do, for it was Midsummer night, and they knew that there was a dream belonging to it, but how to come across it, they could not tell. They knew that the dream had something to do with fairies, a queen, and all lovely things, but that was all. At first, they thought they would sit up with the doors and windows open and the dog on the steps, ready to bark if he saw anything unusual. Then they felt sure they could not dream while wide awake, so three of them went to bed, and one dozed in the corner of the porch with her clothes on. Presently the dog barked, two children in their nightgowns ran out to see, and one took off her nightcap and looked out of the window, but it was only old Nurse coming back from a long gossip with the village blacksmith's wife and mother-in-law. So the dog looked foolish, and Nurse was angry and put them all to bed without any more ado.

"Oh," they cried, "but the fairies, the queen, and the flowers! What shall we do to see them?"

"Go to sleep," said Nurse, "and the dream may come to you;—you can't go to a dream," she added, for you see, she was just a peasant woman and had never traveled far, or into any land but her own.

So the children shut their eyes tightly and went to sleep, and I think that they saw something, for their eyes were very bright the following day, and one of them whispered to me softly, "The queen wore a wreath of flowers last night, dear mother, and, oh, she was gorgeous."

The Willow-Wren and the Bear

By Brothers Grimm

Once in summer-time, the Bear and the wolf were walking in the forest, and the Bear heard a bird singing so beautifully that he said:

'Brother wolf, what bird is it that sings so well?' 'That is the King of birds,' said the wolf, 'before whom we must bow down.' In reality, the bird was the willow wren. 'IF that's the case,' said the Bear, 'I should very much like to see his royal palace; come, take me thither.' 'That is not done quite as you seem to think,' said the wolf; 'you must wait until the Queen comes,' Soon afterward, the Queen arrived with some food in her beak, and the lord King came too, and they began to feed their young ones. The Bear would have liked to go at once, but the wolf held him back by the sleeve and said: 'No, you must wait until the lord and lady Queen have gone away again.' So they took stock of the nest's hole and trotted away. The Bear, however, could not rest until he had seen the royal palace and, when a short time had passed, went to it again. The King and Queen had just flown out, so he peeped in and saw five or six young ones lying there. 'Is that the royal palace?' cried the Bear; 'it is a wretched palace, and you are not King's children. You are disreputable children!' When the young wrens heard that, they were furious and screamed: 'No, we are not! Our parents are honest people! Bear, you will have to pay for that!'

The Bear and the wolf grew uneasy, turned back, and went into their holes. The young willow wrens, however, continued to cry and scream. When their parents again brought food, they said: 'We will not so much as touch one fly's leg, no, not if we were dying of hunger, until you have settled whether we are respectable children or not; the bear has been here and has insulted us!' Then the old King said: 'Be easy, he shall be punished,' and he at once flew with the Queen to the Bear's cave and called in: 'Old Growler, why have you insulted my children? You shall suffer for it—we will punish you by a bloody war.' Thus war was announced to the Bear, and all four-footed animals were summoned to take part in it, oxen, asses, cows, deer, and every other animal the earth contained. And the willow-wren gathered everything which flew in the air; not only birds, large and small, but midges, hornets, bees, and flies had to come.

When the time came for the war to begin, the willow-wren sent out spies to discover who was the enemy's commander-in-chief. The most crafty gnat flew into the forest where the enemy was assembled and hid beneath a tree leaf where the password was to be announced. There stood the Bear, and he called the fox before him and said: 'Fox, you are the most cunning of all animals. You shall be general and lead us.' 'Good,' said the fox, 'but what signal shall we agree upon?' No one knew that, so the fox said: 'I have a fine long bushy tail, which almost looks like a plume of red feathers. When I lift my tail quite high, all is going well, and you must charge; but if I let it hang down, run away as fast as you can.' When the gnat had heard that, she flew away again and revealed everything, down to the minutest detail, to the willow-wren. When day broke and the battle was to begin, all the four-footed animals came running up with such a noise that the earth trembled. The willow wren with his army also came flying through the air with such a humming, whirring, and swarming that everyone was uneasy and afraid, and on both sides, they advanced against each other. But the willow-wren sent down the hornet with orders to settle beneath the fox's tail and sting with all his might. When the fox felt the first string, he started so that he lifted one leg from pain, but he bore it and still kept his tail high in the air; at the second sting, he was forced to put it down for a moment; at the third, he could hold out no longer, screamed, and put his tail between his legs. When the animals saw that, they thought all was lost and began to flee, each into his hole, and the birds had won the battle.

Then the King and Queen flew home to their children and cried: 'Children, rejoice, eat and drink to your heart's content. We have won the battle!' But the young wrens said: 'We will not eat yet. The Bear must come to the nest and beg for pardon and say that we are honourable children before we do that.' Then the willow-wren flew to the Bear's hole and cried: 'Growler, you are to come to the nest to my children and beg their pardon, or else every rib of your body shall be broken.' So the Bear crept thither in the greatest fear and begged their pardon. And now, at last, the young wrens were satisfied, sat down together, ate and drank, and made merry till quite late into the night.

Three Feathers

by Joseph Jacobs

Once upon a time, there was a girl married to a husband she never saw. And this was because he was only at home at night and would never have any light in the house. The girl thought that was funny, and all her friends told her there must be something wrong with her husband, some significant deformity that made him want not to be seen.

Well, one night, when he came home, she suddenly

lit a candle and saw him. He was handsome enough to make all the women of the world fall in love with him. But scarcely had she noticed him when he began to change into a bird, and then he said: "Now you have seen me, you shall see me no more unless you are willing to serve seven years and a day for me, so that I may become a man once more." Then he told her to take three feathers from under his side, and whatever she wished through them would come to pass. Then he left her at a great house to be a laundry-maid for seven years and a day.

And the girl used to take the feathers and say:

"By virtue of my three feathers, may the copper be lit and the clothes washed, mangled, folded, and put away to the missus's satisfaction."

And then she had no more care about it. The feathers did the rest, and the lady set great store by her for a better laundress she had never had. Well, one day, the butler, who had a notion of having the pretty laundry maid for his wife, said to her he should have spoken before, but he did not want to vex her. "Why should it when I am but a fellow servant?" the girl said. And then he felt free to go on and explain he had £70 laid by with the master and how she would like him for a husband.

And the girl told him to fetch her the money, and he asked his master for it and brought it to her. But as they went upstairs, she cried, "O John, I must go back, sure I've left my shutters undone, and they'll be slashing and banging all night."

The butler said, "Never you trouble, I'll put them right." and he ran back while she took her feathers and said: "By virtue of my three feathers may the shutters slash and bang till morning, and John not be able to fasten them nor yet to get his fingers free from them."

And so it was. Try as he might, the butler could not leave hold nor yet keep the shutters from blowing open as he closed them. And he was angry but could not help himself, and he did not care to tell of it and get the laugh on him, so no one knew.

Then after a bit, the coachman began to notice her, and she found he had some £40 with the master, and he said she might have it if she would take him with it.

So after the laundry maid had his money in her apron as they went merrily along, she stopped, exclaiming: "My clothes are left outside. I must run back and bring them in." "Stop for me while I go; it is a frost night," said William, "you'd be catching your death." So the girl waited long enough to take her feathers out and say, "By virtue of my three feathers may the clothes slash and blow about till morning, and may William not be able to take his hand from them nor yet to gather them up." And then she was away to bed and to sleep.

The coachman did not want to be everyone's jest and said nothing. So after a bit, the footman came to her and said: "I have been with my master for years and have saved up a good bit, and you have been here three years and must have saved up as well. Let us put it together and make us home, or stay at service as pleases you." Well, she got him to bring the savings to her as the others had, and then she pretended she was faint and said to him: "James, I feel so queer, run-down cellar for me, that's a dear, and fetch me up a drop of brandy." Now no sooner had he started than she said: "By virtue of my three feathers may there be slashing and spilling, and James not be able to pour the brandy straight nor yet to take his hand from it until morning."

And so it was. Try as he might, James could not get his glass filled, and there was slashing and spilling, and right on it all, down came the master to know what it meant!

So James told him he could not make it out, but he could not get the drop of brandy the laundry maid had asked for, and his hand would shake and spill everything, yet come away, he could not.

When he returned to his wife, this got him in for a regular scrape, and the master said: "What has come over the men? They were all right until that laundry maid of yours came. Something is up now, though. They have all drawn out their pay, yet they don't leave, and what can it be anyway?"

But his wife said she could not hear the laundry maid being blamed, for she was the best servant she had and worth all the rest.

So it continued until one day, as the girl stood in the hall door, the coachman said to the footman: "Do you know how that girl served me, James?" And then

William told me about the clothes. The butler said, "That was nothing to what she served me," He spoke of the shutters clapping all night.

The master came through the hall, and the girl said: "By virtue of my three feathers, may there be slashing and striving between master and men, and may all get splashed in the pond."

And so it was, the men fell to disputing which had suffered the most by her, and when the master came up, all would be heard at once, and none listened to him, and it came to blows all round, and the first they knew they had shoved one another into the pond.

When the girl thought they had had enough, she took the spell off, and the master asked her what had begun the row, for he had not heard in confusion.

And the girl said: "They were ready to fall on anyone; they'd have beat me if you had not come by."

So it blew over for that time, and she made the best laundress ever known through her feathers. But to make a long story short, when the seven years and a day were up, the bird-husband, who had known her doings all along, came after her, restored to his shape again. And he told her mistress he had come to take her from being a servant and that she should have servants under her. But he did not speak of the feathers.

And then he bade her give the men back their savings.

"That was a rare game you had with them," said he,

"but now you are going where there is plenty. Leave them to each their own." So she did, and they drove off to their castle, where they lived happily ever after.

The Pied Piper

by Joseph Jacobs

Newtown, or Franchville, as it was called of old, is a sleepy little town, as you all may know, upon the Solent shore. Exhausted now, it was once noisy enough, and rats made the noise. The place was so infested with them as to be scarce and worth living in. There wasn't a barn, corn rick, storeroom, or cupboard, but they ate their way into it.

Not cheese, but they gnawed it hollow, not a sugar puncheon, but cleared out. Why was the very mead and beer in the barrels not safe from them? They'd gnaw a hole in the top of the tun, and down would go one master rat's tail, and when he brought it up round, would crowd all the friends and cousins, and each would have sucked at the tail.

Had they stopped here, it might have been borne. But the squeaking and shrieking, the hurrying and scurrying, so that you could neither hear yourself speak nor get a wink of good honest sleep the live-long night! Not to mention that Mamma must sit up and watch over baby's cradle, or there'd have been a giant ugly rat running across the poor little fellow's face and doing mischief.

Why didn't the good people of the town have cats? Well, they did, and there was a fair stand-up fight, but in the end, the rats were too many, and the pussies were regularly driven from the field. Poison, I hear you say? Why they poisoned so many that it fairly bred a plague. Ratcatchers! Why wasn't a ratcatcher from John o' Groat's house to the Land's End that hadn't tried his luck? But do what they might, cats or poison, terrier or traps, there seemed to be more rats than ever, and every day a fresh rat was cocking his tail or pricking his whiskers.

The Mayor and the town council were at their wits' end. As they sat one day in the town hall racking their poor brains and lamenting their hard fate, who should run in but the town beadle? "Please, your Honour," says he, "here is a very queer fellow come to town. I don't rightly know what to make of him." "Show him in," said the Mayor, and in he stepped. A queer fellow, indeed. For there wasn't a colour of the rainbow, but you might find it in some corner of his dress, and he was tall and thin and had keen, piercing eyes.

"I'm called the Pied Piper," he began. "And pray what might you be willing to pay me if I rid you of every rat in Franchville?"

Well, much as they feared the rats, they feared parting with their money more, and fain would say they have higgled and haggled. But the PiperPiper was not a man to stand nonsense, and the upshot was that fifty pounds were promised him (and it meant a lot of money in those old days) as soon as not a rat was left to squeak or scurry in Franchville.

Out of the hall stepped the PiperPiper, and as he stepped, he laid his pipe to his lips, and a shrill keen tune sounded through street and house. And as each note pierced the air, you might have seen a strange sight. For out of every hole, the rats came tumbling. There were none too old and none too young, none too big and none too little to crowd at the Piper'sPiper's heels and with eager feet and upturned noses to patter after him as he paced the streets. Nor was the PiperPiper unmindful of the little toddling ones. For every fifty yards, he'd stop and give an extra flourish on his pipe to give them time to keep up with the older and more potent of the band.

Up Silver Street he went, and down Gold Street, and at the end of Gold Street is the harbour and the broad Solent beyond. And as he paced along, slowly and gravely, the townsfolk flocked to door and window, and many a blessing they called down upon his head.

As for getting near him, there were too many rats. And now that he was at the water's edge, he stepped into a boat, and not a rat, as he shoved off into deep water, piping shrilly all the while, but followed him, plashing, paddling and wagging their tails with delight. He played until the tide went down, and each master rat sank deeper and deeper in the slimy ooze of the harbour until every mother's son was dead and smothered.

The tide rose again, and the PiperPiper stepped on shore, but never a rat followed. You may fancy the townsfolk had been throwing up their caps, hurrahing, stopping up rat holes, and setting the church bells a-ringing. But when the PiperPiper stepped ashore and not so much as a single squeak was to be heard, the Mayor and the Council, and the townsfolk generally, began to hum and to ha and to shake their heads.

For the town money chest had been sadly emptied of late, where would the fifty pounds come from? Such an easy job, too! Just getting into a boat and playing a pipe! Why the Mayor himself could have done that if only he had thought of it.

So he hummed and ha'ad and at last, "Come, my good man," said he, "you see what poor folk we are;

how can we manage to pay you fifty pounds? Will you not take twenty? 't will be good pay for your trouble."

"Fifty pounds was what I bargained for," said the PiperPiper shortly, "If I were you, I'd pay it quickly. I can pipe many tunes, as folk sometimes find to their cost."

"Would you threaten us, you were strolling vagabond?" shrieked the Mayor, and at the same time, he winked to the Council; "the rats are all dead and drowned," muttered he; and so "You may do your worst, my good man," and with that, he turned short upon his heel.

"Very well," said the PiperPiper, and he smiled quietly. With that, he laid his pipe to his lips afresh, but now there came forth no shrill notes, as it were, of scraping and gnawing, and squeaking and scurrying, but the tune was joyous and resonant, full of happy laughter and merry play. And as he paced down the streets, the elders mocked, but from school-room and play-room, nursery and workshop, not a child ran out with eager glee and shouted following gaily at the Piper'sPiper's call. Dancing, laughing, joining hands, and tripping feet, the bright throng moved along Gold Street and Silver Street, and beyond Silver Street lay the cool green forest full of old oaks and wide-spreading beeches. You might catch glimpses of the Piper'sPiper's many-colored coat in and out among the oak trees. You might hear the children's laughter break and fade and die away as more profound into the lone green wood the stranger went, and the children followed.

All the while, the elders watched and waited. They mocked no longer now. And watch and stay as they might, never did they set their eyes again upon the PiperPiper in his particolored coat. Never were their hearts gladdened by the song and dance of the children issuing forth from amongst the ancient oaks of the forest.

The Golden Ball

By Joseph Jacobs

There were two lasses, daughters of one mother, and as they came from the fair, they saw a right bonny young man stand at the house door before them. They never saw such a bonny man before. He had gold on his cap, gold on his finger, gold on his neck, a red gold watch chain—eh! But he had brass. He had a golden ball in each hand. He gave a ball to each lass, and she was to keep it; if she lost it, she was to be hanged. One of the lasses, 't was the youngest, lost her ball. I'll tell thee how. She was by a park-paling, and she was tossing her ball, and it went up, and up, and up, till it went fair over the paling; and when she climbed up to look, the ball ran along the green grass, and it went right forward to the door of the house, and the ball went in, and she saw it no more.

So she was taken away to be hanged by the neck till she was dead because she'd lost her ball.

But she had a sweetheart, and he said he would go and get the ball. So he went to the park gate, but it was shut; so he climbed the hedge, and when he got to the top of the hedge, an old woman rose out of the dyke before him and asked if he wanted to get the ball, he must sleep three nights in the house. He said he would.

Then he went into the house and looked for the ball, but could not find it. Night came on, and he heard bogles move in the courtyard, so he looked out o' the window, and the yard was full of them.

Presently he heard steps coming upstairs. He hid behind the door and was as still as a mouse. Then in came a big giant five times as tall as he, and the giant looked round but did not see the lad, so he went to the window and bowed to look out. As he bent on his elbows to see the bogles in the yard, the lad stepped behind him, and with one blow of his sword, he cut him in twain so that the top part of him fell in the yard, the bottom part stood looking out of the window.

There was a great cry from the bogles when they saw half the giant come tumbling down to them, and they called out, "There comes half our master; give us the other half."

So the lad said, "It's no use of thee, thou pair of legs, standing alone at the window, as thou hast no eye to see with, so go join thy brother;" He cast the giant's lower part after the top position. Now when the bogles had gotten all the giant, they were quiet.

Next night the lad was at the house again, and now a second giant came in at the door, and as he came in, the lad cut him in twain, but the legs walked onto the chimney and went up them. "Go, get thee after thy legs," said the lad to the head, and he cast the head up the chimney too.

The third night the lad got into bed, and he heard the bogles striving under the bed, and they had the ball there, and they were casting it to and fro.

Now one of them has his leg thrust out from under the bed, so the lad brings his sword down and cuts it off. Then another thrusts his arm out at another side of the bed, and the lad cuts that off. So, at last, he had maimed them all, and they all went crying and wailing off and forgot the ball, but he took it from under the bed and went to seek his true love.

The lass was taken to York to be hanged; she was brought out on the scaffold, and the hangman said, "Now, lass, thou must hang by the neck till thou be dead." But she cried out:

"Stop, stop; I think I see my mother coming!

O, mother, hast brought my golden ball

And come to set me free?"

"I've neither brought thy golden ball

Nor come to set thee free,

But I have come to see thee hung

Upon this gallows tree."

Then the hangman said, "Now, lass, say thy prayers, for thou must die." But she said:

"Stop, stop; I think I see my father coming!

O, father, hast brought my golden ball

And come to set me free?"

"I've neither brought thy golden ball

Nor come to set thee free,

But I have come to see thee hung

Upon this gallows tree."

Then the hangman said, "Hast thee done thy prayers? Now, lass, put thy head into the noose."

But she answered, "Stop, stop; I think I see my brother coming!" And again she sang, and then she thought she saw her sister coming, then her uncle, then her aunt, then her cousin; but after this, the hangman said, "I will stop no longer, thou 'rt making the game of me. Thou must be hung at once."

But now she saw her sweetheart coming through the crowd, and he held over his head in the air her golden ball; so she said:

"Stop, stop; I see my sweetheart coming!

Sweetheart, I hast brought my golden ball.

And come to set me free?"

"Aye, I have brought thy golden ball

And come to set thee free,

I have not come to see thee hung

Upon this gallows tree."

And he took her home, and they lived happily ever after.

The Duck Pond

By Mrs. W. K. Clifford

So little Bridget took the baby on her right arm and a jug in her left hand and went to the farm to get the milk. On her way, she went by the garden gate of a large house that stood close to the farm, and she told the baby a story:—

"Last summer," she said, "a little girl, bigger than you, for she was just able to walk, came to stay in that house—she and her father and mother. All about the road just here, the ducks and the chickens from the farm, and an old turkey, used to walk about all day long, but the poor little ducks were very unhappy, for they had no pond to swim about in, only that narrow ditch through which the streamlet is flowing. When the little girl's father saw this, he took a spade and worked and worked very hard, and out of the ditch and the streamlet, he made a little pond for the ducks, and they swam about and were very happy all through the summer days. Every morning I used to stand and watch, and presently the garden gate would open, the father would come out, leading the little girl by the hand, and the mother brought a large plateful of bits of broken bread. The little girl used to throw the bread to the ducks, and they ran after it and ate it up quickly while she laughed out with glee, and the father and the mother laughed too just as merrily. Baby, the father had blue eyes and a voice you seemed to hear with your heart.

"The little girl used to feed the chickens too, and the foolish old turkey that was so fond of her would run after her until she screamed and was afraid. The dear father and the little girl came out every morning while the black pigs looked through the bars of the farmyard gate and grunted at them as if they were glad. I think the ducks knew that the father had made the pond, for they swam round and round it proudly while he watched them, but when he went away, they seemed tired and sad.

"The pond is not there now, baby, for a man came by one day and made it into a ditch again, and the chickens and the ducks from the farm are kept in another place.

"The little girl is far away in her own home, which the father made for her, and the dear father lives in his own home too—in the hearts of those he loved."

That was the story that Bridget told the baby.

"Once Upon A Time: Timeless Tales for Young Hearts" is a cherished collection that invites families to step into a magical world together. These enchanting stories have the power to ignite young imaginations, foster a love of reading, and create lasting memories.

We believe that every child deserves the gift of storytelling. By sharing these timeless tales, we hope to inspire a generation of curious, compassionate, and courageous individuals.

Prepare to be enchanted once more! The second book in the *Once Upon A Time* series is on its way. Filled with new adventures and timeless lessons, it promises to be another magical journey for young readers and their families.

Thank you for choosing *Once Upon A Time*. We hope these stories bring joy, wonder, and inspiration to your family.

kidsbooksnook.com